To Colin & Anne

with l

T

26/4/80

HAYSEED

In preparation for the series by the same author

Gleanings

To be a Farmer's Girl

The Last Mophrey

HAYSEED

L.G.J.Layberry

MIDAS BOOKS

First published in 1980 by
Midas Books
12 Dene Way, Speldhurst
Tunbridge Wells, Kent TN3 0NX

ISBN 0 85936 240 X

Designed and produced by
Chambers Green Ltd
Tunbridge Wells

Printed and bound
in Great Britain by
Redwood Burn Limited
Trowbridge & Esher

THIS STORY IS DEDICATED TO
TWO CHARMING FRIENDS.
EDITH GRAY
WHO INSPIRED IT
AND
SHIRLEY HINKLY
WHO ADMIRED IT.

Acknowledgements

The author's grateful acknowledgements are due to Julia Tompkins, who designed Meg's outfit for the Hunt Ball; Uncle Jack, for details of pre-1914 farming, and Lloyds Bank, Edenbridge for information on interest rates in 1911.

Chapter One

Robert pedalled laboriously along the rough farm drive. His canvas bags, suspended one each side of the rear wheel, were still half full of newspapers, and made his machine bump heavily into the pot-holes. The gate at the end of the drive was closed. At this time of the morning the yard beyond would be full of cows; all visitors had to walk through them to reach the farm house. He leant his cycle in the hedge, took out a *Daily Mail* and *Farmer & Stockbreeder*, lifted the wooden latch and slipped through.

Picking his way carefully to avoid the paddled mud and dung, he lifted his eyes from time to time to look at the cows. They were of varied colours, mostly red, but some were roans, a few red-and-white and one entirely white. There was a bull in the yard with them, but Robert knew that as long as the cows were present to attract the bull's interest, it was quite safe to walk through the herd. The huge animal turned his crested neck to stare at the paperboy, lowered his head, breathed heavily into the ground for a moment, then reverted to inspecting his female companions.

Robert called out a word of greeting to the two cowmen. He wished he could pause and chat with them, but knew that this would make him unpopular with Mr Wyndham, the farmer. He sighed. He would not mind being a cowman–though their work did seem to be hard, dirty and smelly. At least it was more interesting than delivering newspapers.

He climbed the stone steps up into the dairy and approached the back door. The maid was washing the churns and cooling equipment with a great clanging and splashing. The girl nodded to Robert as he edged past. He stepped into the huge kitchen and placed the papers on the scrubbed deal table. Mrs Wyndham suddenly appeared, a big jolly woman, with thick brown hair framing a beaming red face.

'Hello, Bob! Like a cup of cocoa?'

'Yes, please!'

He sat down in the windsor chair just inside the door and looked enviously round the kitchen as he had done many times before. So different from the cramped living quarters in the shop which was Robert's home. The grandfather clock standing against the wall opposite offered a welcome to visitors. Its loud and perpetual tick underlined the steadfast permanence of the farm. The huge black cooking range on Robert's right kept the room pleasantly warm. Saucepans and two steaming kettles were always at the ready as if a big meal were about to be prepared. It was all so different from his mother's greasy gas stove. Farming was the life, he decided.

He emptied his mug, and left hurriedly as Mr Wyndham came through the door. There were more papers to deliver in Elstree, and then half-an-hour's ride back home to Mill Hill. He never seemed to be home early enough to please his father.

As he propped his machine against the kerb outside his home he looked with distaste at the flaking paint of the single-fronted shop. 'John Felton, Newsagent, Tobacconist and General Stores. Papers delivered free.' The proprietor had taken over the business at the time of his marriage twenty years before and had the smart signboard prepared and erected, and the whole shop front painted to match. It had not been touched since. The business had never quite come up to expectations. His growing family had absorbed the profits as fast as he made them.

'Where the devil have you been all the morning?' he asked as his son dawdled in. 'Wasting time on those Elstree farms, I suppose. You'd be more good to me if you put your back into my business. It'll be a good thing when Billy leaves school. Then he can do the rounds and you can stay here in the shop where I can keep an eye on you. Your mother's got the dinner ready, so take over while I go and have mine. Don't fall asleep!'

Robert did not answer; he was used to his father's acidity. He slouched round the counter to sit down on the hard chair, where he was screened from the view of passers-by.

A spare copy of the *Farmer & Stockbreeder* lay on the counter. He was about to reach for it when the shop door opened and Billy, Betty and Jack tumbled in for dinner.

When the communicating door slammed behind his brothers and sister, he reached again for the paper. The urgency of getting away was growing on him; he scanned the magazine purposefully, he would have plenty of time to read it if he was not interrupted.

The crammed layout and the diversified pictures of the farming journal were full of information. A rectangular panel at the top contained the comprehensive title *The Farmer & Stockbreeder and Chamber of Agriculture Journal – Est. 1843* superimposed on a background of wheat, oats and barley heads and a few wild flowers. Between this design and the main panel of illustrations was the boldly printed line reading: 'London, Monday Evening, February 18, 1911. One Penny Weekly'.

1911 was coronation year; Robert wondered if he would be able to go down to London and see the celebrations. He continued his examination of the paper. Something of everything on the front page, he thought as he idly turned it over. Inside there were columns of advertisements for cod liver oil, hay, farmers' suits, steam ploughing engines and rat poison. Then a couple of pages of breeders' announcements describing pedigree studs, herds and flocks from all parts of England and Wales. They read like a school geography lesson, but were in Robert's eyes considerably more glamorous. He came to the section headed 'Farms and Estates' and glanced down the columns of farms for sale and to let. The rents were in the region of £1 per acre or less (Robert assumed that this meant annually) and the highest priced farms for sale rarely exceeded £20 per acre.

The next section was 'Situations Vacant'.

The first column was headed with an announcement describing assisted passages to Australia. He could travel to Western Australia for £5, and to Victoria or New South Wales for £6.

He read right through the vacancies. Some of the advertisers seemed very fussy. 'Wanted, Cowman, of good address, married or single, over 28 preferred. Experience with cattle, pigs and milk retailing.'

'Wanted, Cowman, experienced for Dairy Shorthorns. (Single preferred) Character strictly investigated. 22s. per week, with cottage.'

One caught his eye. 'Wanted, a smart youth about 17 to work on farm; milk, Comfortable home; small premium. Lincs. S.L. c/o Robinson's, Spilsby, Lincoln.'

Small premium! He discarded Lincoln and read on.

'Wanted, a respectable Youth, 15-20, able to drive milk to station and make himself generally useful. Total Abstainer; Live in as family.—Ratcliffe, Oakleigh Farm, Hartnall, Derby.

This was what he had been looking for. He seemed to meet all the qualifications. His age was right. He was sure that he could drive milk to the station. Every day of his life he saw lads younger than he driving milk carts. He picked up a label from the floor, snatched a new pencil from the tray behind the counter and scribbled the name and address, returning the magazine to its place just as his father opened the door.

'Go and get your dinner, Bob,' he said shortly, 'before the three youngsters eat it all. Afterwards you can go to the station and pick up the magazines off the afternoon train.'

Robert slipped into the kitchen and sat down to a huge plateful of warm beef stew with plenty of vegetables. He ate pensively, paying no heed to the chatter of his brothers and sister.

His mother came in from the scullery and hustled the three younger children to school. She served Robert with a liberal helping of 'Spotted dog'. 'You can help me with the washing-up, Rob, before you go to the station.'

He did so without remark.

'You're quiet today, boy.'

'Been thinking a lot, Mum.'

'What about? Not the shop, I'll bet.'

'What I'd do if I had lots of money.'

'Ha! But you can't have lots of money without working—and in something different to newspapers and cigarettes.'

He flung the damp tea-cloth over the line, and touched his mother on the shoulder as he turned to leave the kitchen.

'Bye, Mum!'

She looked surpised. 'Goodbye, lad. But you're only going to the station, you know. Not to Margate for a week's holiday.'

From behind the counter, Mr Felton brought his son back to earth. 'Better pump that back tyre up, right hard. You've a big load to bring back.'

Robert did his father's bidding, mounted his machine and rode away. He did not turn down Hammers Lane, which was his nearest route to the station, but continued up the High Street to the post office. With some trepidation he went in and filled in a form to withdraw £1 on demand. To his surprise, it was given to him without question. He pocketed the book and the golden sovereign and hurried on to the station. The porter on duty welcomed him. 'Hello Bob! You're early today! Train's not due for twenty minutes.'

Robert knew that, but wanted to have a surreptitious look at the time-tables. He did not want to ask the booking-clerk about changes and connections. He found that the train which brought the magazines was a stopping train to St Albans where he could board a fast train to Derby. When the train was signalled he rushed to the hatch and blurted out 'Single to St Albans, please.'

'Are you going on a visit then, Bob?' asked the clerk. He regarded the sovereign with surprise, and counted out the change with great deliberation. Robert scooped the money up hastily and ran up the steps and over the bridge. He saw the guard fling out his father's two bundles of papers as the train came to a halt. Nothing to do with him now! He jumped into an empty third-class carriage and in less than a minute the train moved on, the little engine belching out great clouds of black smoke as it gathered speed. Robert huddled into a corner and made himself as inconspicuous as he could.

'All change! All change!' called the porter at St Albans. The boy got out and hurried into the booking office. As he boldly bought his ticket he realised half his money had already gone. Platform two the man had said. Of course, that would be the afternoon express which shrieked through Mill Hill at ten to three.

He glued his face to the window, watched the changing scene

as the train sped on. He was absorbed by the glimpses of farming operations revealed from the railway line which slashed through the fields. Here Shorthorn cows grazed beside the railway fence, there a flock of sheep. Bare arable fields were neatly ploughed by pairs of straining horses. Sometimes the line cut so close to a farm that he could look straight down into the yard. It seemed vaguely indecent. As the February afternoon wore on, the scene gradually changed. There were no cows in the fields after four nor horses in the furrow. Twilight was slowly embracing the countryside.

By the time the train left Leicester twilight had become darkness. He could see only lights from scattered buildings. He was now thrown back upon his own thoughts, which were becoming doubts.

It dawned upon him how rash he had been to leave home and travel a hundred miles in answer to an advertisement. The farmer might already have engaged someone or might want to see several applicants before making a decision. Would the farmer necessarily think Robert was the lad for the job? Of course, he still had sufficient money to get him home; but the thought of returning and facing his father's cutting tongue daunted him.

Finally the train drew in to the long platforms of Derby. Robert alighted in a deafening hiss of escaping steam. An unpleasant thought struck him. He had assumed from the address in the journal that the farm was within easy reach of Derby. His heart was in his boots as he asked an ageing ticket collector.

'Hartnall? Hartnall?' said the man wrinkling his brows in perplexity and scratching his greying head. 'Oo—ah! That'll be seven or eight miles out—Repton way. There's no station there, though. You'll have to get off at Willington—on the Burton line. Train leaves platform five at six forty-eight.'

Robert felt relieved. He had twenty minutes to wait and would have liked to buy some refreshment from the tea-room; but he was loath to spend any more money.

An ancient train clanked into platform five. Robert jumped thankfully aboard with a handful of late shoppers and a few clerical workers returning home. As he listened to the conversation in his carriage, he quite failed to understand the slow, deliberate speech. The train stopped once and then bustled on through the dark fields. As it stopped with a jerk, Robert read 'Repton and Willington' in the light of an oil lamp. He alighted with a thumping heart, waited while the other passengers departed, and then accosted the porter-cum-ticket collector.

'Master Ratcliffe, Oakleigh Farm, Hartnall,' repeated the man. 'Ee, that's three or fower marls away. You've just missed their milk cart–left a quarter o' an hour agoo. That'd a' bin just reight. Ah don't know how to tell thi to get theer, lad. Ba Gum, Ah do, though. Here's Master Johnson's milk just comin' in. He goes past Oakleigh and'll give you a lift, Ah daresay.'

A lean horse swung in at the station gate. The man backed his two-wheeled float up to the milk-platform and heaved up a churn.

'Edgar! There's a young lad here wants to go to Ratcliffes of Oakleigh. Ah towd him you'd mebbe give him a ride theer.'

The man peered across. 'Ah coom on lad. You meight as well gie me a lift wi' these churns and earn your ride.'

Robert ran across at once, climbed into the float, seized the handle of the nearest churn and together they raised the huge seventeen gallon container on to the milk-stage. He was strong for his age but the effort required was almost beyond him. The job completed, they set off into the unknown. The horse apparently knew that the urgency had departed for he ambled gently. They turned away from the village and were soon driving over a long bridge which spanned a river. Even in the semi-darkness its brisk flow was discernible.

'What river is this?' the boy asked.

'Ay? What didst say? What river is it? Ba gum, lad wheer's thi bin all thi life? It's the Trent, lad.'

Robert blushed. He was glad Edgar could not see him clearly in the dim light of the candle-lamps. He recalled some lines from Scott which he had learnt at school.

'Many a banner shall be torn,
And many a knight to earth be born,
And many a sheaf of arrows spent,
Ere Scotland's king shall cross the Trent!'

'It's a funny tarm o' night to be going to Oakleigh.'

Robert looked across at Edgar. 'I'm going there for a job.'

'Are you, by gum? Where's your box? You must have some working clo'es! You're not going to work in them Sunday togs art?'

'As a matter of fact, I haven't got the job yet. I'm just going to apply for it.'

'Ee, You're a reight 'un. You've come a long way–ah can tell that by your talk–to try for a job at eight o'clock at neight at a place wheer you've niver bin. Well, I don't know!'

There was silence for a few minutes, broken only by the clop-clop of the horse's hooves and the grinding of the steel-rimmed wheels on the stony road.

'Wheer didst start from, lad?'

'I came from Mill Hill, just this side of London.'

'London? Well, I don't know!'

Edgar tried again. 'Bin wi' cows or osses, mainly?

'Er, neither really. I've never worked on a farm before.'

'Aye? A big lad like thee niver bin on a farm? Well, I don't know!

Robert began to feel foolish.

'Ah should think Master Ratcliffe 'ud be a good man to work for. Very nice family. Sam's the owdest son and works on the farm—does the 'osses mainly. Then there's the girl, Meg, about your age; helps her mother in th' ouse; and a younger lad at school. There's another man as lives i' the rickyard cottage—Ernie Wagstaff; sort o' cowman-labourer. You could get on well there, Ah daresay.'

Bob thought so too.

They jog-trotted through the lamp-lit streets of Repton.

'She's taking her own tarm,' said Edgar. 'Ah niver push her on the way 'ome. 'Er does all her fast runnin' on the way t' station. Th' milk train dunt wait for onybody!'

Fifteen minutes later they came to a cross-roads where Edgar pulled the mare to a reluctant halt.

'Here's where we part comp'ny, lad. Ah goo straight on, you turn left. Walk up th' lane for about a quarter o' a mile and you come to a big gate on the right that opens into a farm drive. Oakleigh farm's three fields from the road. Mind you shut all th' gates. Good luck lad. Come on, mare, Tchk!'

The milk-cart rattled away into the night. Robert watched it until the red spot at the back of each lamp disappeared from view. Then he set off along the dark road frightened, homesick, and very hungry.

Chapter Two

Robert's feet moved quickly, but his thoughts lagged behind. At least the shop, with its gas lighting, was brighter than this dark lane with its high hedges. It was all strange and eerie, and he began to feel jumpy. Suddenly the moon appeared from behind a cloud and this cheered him up until he realised that the shadows were nearly as frightening as the total darkness.

In five minutes–it seemed much longer–he arrived at the gate described by Edgar. It was a heavy oak gate and swung easily when he lifted the big wooden latch. But Robert was feeling more unsure of himself with every passing minute and walked slowly up the drive.

He passed through another gate. There were sheep grazing in this field, a few lying comfortably in the ruts of the drive. Startled, they jumped up abruptly and darted away across the field. Swishing and the faint thudding of many small hooves indicated that they had spread their alarm, and the whole flock was on the move. As Robert breasted a slight rise he came within sight of the farm buildings. He approached the gate with his heart beating fast. The house was square and high with a strong stack of chimneys at each end. Light shone from the window facing the farmyard–obviously the living-room. On his right as he entered the gate was the great square of the farm buildings, with the manure pit in the middle. The farmyard tang was not unpleasant to him and the faint clinking of cow chains from within the sheds seemed to add a touch of homeliness.

He walked past the kitchen window and saw a family within. He moved on round the house, gingerly mounted two steps and found himself in a lean-to over the back door. The moon had appeared once more and in its diffused light he recognised the milk cooling equipment suspended from its brackets, with the milk churns beside it and several upturned milk buckets on a shelf nearby. A window from the scullery looked out to the cooling shed and showed a reflection of light from the kitchen. He stood there a moment breathing hard, trying to overcome the sinking feeling in his stomach. He desperately wanted to turn and run. Then he caught the murmuring voices and became rational again. Afer all, he was only applying for a job. He raised his fist, and rapped firmly on the heavy door.

The conversation stopped at once.

'Who the devil's that?'

Immediately the door was pulled open with a jerk, to reveal

the tall figure of a young man. He wore a collarless flannel shirt with sleeves rolled up to expose muscular forearms. An old tweed waistcoat, hardly large enough to button up, showed his bulging chest. His soiled cord breeches and thick woollen stockings gave the impression that his lower limbs did not lack strength either.

'Well?' he said uncompromisingly, 'What dost want?'

Robert's spirits sank lower. Once more he felt like bolting away into the darkness.

'Er–I've come about the job,' he blurted out.

'The devil you have.' He called over his shoulder, 'Dad, here's a lad says he's come after th' job!'

'Well, ask him in,' said a deep, slightly irritable voice from inside. 'Don't stand theer with th' door open, leeting the draught in. Bring him in and let's have a look at him.'

Robert stepped inside and followed the farmer's son through the scullery into the huge kitchen. The soft light from the hanging oil-lamp was sufficient to make his eyes blink after being so long in the dark. The size of the room almost overpowered the town boy. Black oak dressers seemed to line every wall except where the long casement looked out on to the farm yard. The wall adjoining the scullery was almost wholly taken up by a black-leaded kitchen range, the fire in the centre glowing and faintly roaring. On the vast hob, three polished copper kettles whispered to each other. Although the room was so large the fire made it pleasantly warm.

There was a semi-circle of five windsor chairs round the fireplace. As Robert walked in he passed behind the master of the house, who motioned him to take up a position where all could see him. Opposite the master sat the mistress, who appeared to be looking at the same *Farmer & Stockbreeder* which had sent him off on this escapade. A son of about twelve–the resemblance was quite striking–sat reading a book next to his mother. A fine girl of about Robert's own age, with a mass of yellow hair tied behind the neck sat knitting. The older son moved his chair nearer to his sister to allow Robert to stand in the vacant space.

The farmer scrutinised the boy with the same interest he would have shown in a horse offered for sale. 'So you've come about the job, have you? Been on a farm before?'

'I've never *worked* on a farm before,' answered Robert nervously, conscious that the whole family, although they pretended not to take notice, was listening to every word.

'What work have you been doing?'

'Er, delivering papers. My father keeps a paper shop and I did the round. I used to call at several farms and I read the *Farmer & Stockbreeder* whenever I got the chance. That's how I saw your advert and decided to try for the job.'

'You haven't wasted much time, have you? Th' paper only came out to-day. But you see, lad, when a farmer advertises in a weekly that circulates all over the country, he expects to get a letter or two and take a bit o' time over his decision. I s'pose you thought the early bird stood more chance of catching the worm?'

'Yes, something like that', said Robert, beginning to feel slightly less nervous.

'Meg, get him a chair. He keeps standing on one leg like a stork and it puts me off.'

Everyone smiled dutifully at this quip but the girl coloured slightly as she put down her knitting on the table. She brought another chair.

'By the way, what's your name?'

'Robert Felton.'

'It'll be Bob if you work for me. No fancy names on this place.'

The boy felt a thrill of encouragement.

'Well, where is your father's business?'

'Mill Hill.'

'And where the devil might that be?'

'Just this side of London. On the main Midland line,' he added vaguely, hoping that this made it sound not quite so far away.

'Bloody hell!' shouted the farmer, sitting bolt upright in his chair with astonishment. 'D'ye mean to tell me you've come all the way up from London to a place you don't know, on the off-chance. You must be daft, lad or your father must be to let you do it. Whatever was he thinking of?'

'Well—er—he doesn't know. I mean, I didn't tell him.' He reddened as the whole family gazed at him.

'You mean you've run away from home?' asked Mr Ratcliffe, sternly.

Robert's uneasiness increased as the group focussed attention on him.

'I just went to the station with the trade-bike for the afternoon parcels. Left the bike there and caught the train. On the spur of the moment, I s'pose.'

'What, without leaving any message for your family?'

The boy nodded miserably.

'Well, Ah think that was downright irresponsible, reckless and selfish. To leave your job in th' middle of the day, and your bike where it might be pinched and your father waiting for the papers for his trade and wondering where you'd got to! By gum, that sort o' behaviour wunna do, lad. Wunna do at all. It shows you're keen, but that's all that can be said in favour. But why did you run off? Were you treated badly at home?

'Not really.' His voice broke a little and he was on the verge of tears.

The farmer pressed his point.

'We couldn't have such irresponsibility on a farm. You must understand that. How do I know you won't run away from me in th' middle of a job, leaving the calves and pigs not fed and the milk-hoss at the station while you took a ticket to Timbuctoo or somewhere? By gum, the very thought of it makes me go hot and cold.'

'Oh, no! I wouldn't do a thing like that, Mr Ratcliffe. I'm fond of animals. I promise I wouldn't leave without notice. But I'm sure I'd like it here too much to want to leave at all.'

'I shouldn't be too sure o' that, lad. I like a full day's work from everybody–and unless you're fond o' work you won't feel like stopping here.'

He paused and sat back in his chair. The silence was broken only by the ticking of the grandfather clock. The boy sat still, scarcely daring to breathe. After what seemed like an hour to Robert, the farmer took a deep breath and delivered his verdict.

'Well, young feller, I'll give you the job for a while. You've shown keenness in coming here off your own bat. It's only fair you should have a chance to see it through. Then you'll be able to judge whether you like farmin' well enough to carry on wi' it. You left home early i' the afternoon, you say? You've had nothing to eat since, I take it?'

'Fry up those cold potatoes, Meg,' said his wife. 'He can have the rest of the meat pie with 'em. There's enough of the apple-pie left for at least one helping. Put that in the oven. Cold meat pie is all right, but cold apple-pie is a mite too chilly. And put enough milk on for all us cocoas. It's getting near time.'

She snatched a cloth from a dresser drawer and bustled about laying the table. Robert, almost fainting with hunger felt his mouth water at this talk of food. But the farmer was speaking to him about clothes.

'Them togs you're wearing are no good for farm work. They look like Sunday clothes, or at least Saturday-night duds. Maggie, is there a pair o' Sam's trousers for him? And he can wear my owd boots.' He addressed Bob again. 'On Friday Mrs Ratcliffe goes with me into Derby and she'll get you some breeches, socks, boots and a shirt or two and maybe a second-hand jacket. By the way, how old are you?'

'Sixteen last month.'

'Ah–just Meg's age. Well, Ah'll pay you four bob a week to start wi'. But you'll get nowt until you've paid for the clothes.'

Robert hastily pointed out that he had a Post Office bank-book, and could withdraw money to pay for anything he needed.

'If you've got money in the bank, let it stay there. It's the best place for it. And remember you're living in our house. You'll take notice of us just as if we were your parents. You understand that?'

'Yes, Mr Ratcliffe.'

'Right. Now set yourself at the table and get some o' that grub into you. They've got it about ready.'

Robert attacked with gusto the huge plateful of fried potatoes and steak-and-kidney pie which Meg placed in front of him. Mrs Ratcliffe looked across:

'And after you've had your supper, my lad, you're going to write a letter to your mother and father telling them where you are. They must be worried sick. I know I would be if it were one o' mine.'

'I haven't got any paper.'

'That's a difficulty that can soon be got over,' intervened Mr Ratcliffe. 'We've plenty, and a penny stamp too, I daresay. You'll write the letter, as Mrs Ratcliffe says, and Arthur'll post it when he goes to school in the morning.'

Mrs Ratcliffe seized an armful of bed-linen from a cupboard near the fire-place and disappeared up stairs with it. When she returned, she produced a pad of lined paper, an envelope, pen and ink and silently placed them beside his plate, where he could not possibly ignore them. Then, while the Ratcliffe family drank cocoa from huge mugs, and dipped frequently into a tin of plain biscuits, Robert wrote a short and apologetic note to his parents.

'If you've finished your letter Bob, you'd better go to bed,' said the farmer's wife. 'You must be tired after coming such a long journey—all the way from London! We're all going to bed as soon as we've finished us cocoa. There's an extra candlestick on the dresser.'

In the unfamiliar house and with strangers, Robert felt homesick and lonely. He would be glad to get to bed so that he could be alone with his thoughts.

'I'll show you the way,' said Arthur, lighting another candle and leading the way up a flight of wide stairs, and then up a second flight, slightly narrower and fitted with older carpet. 'You'll have this floor to yourself for a bit, but there are four bedrooms up here, and I'm going to have one of them for myself soon. I'm sharing a room with Sam now. But now I'm eleven I think I should have a room of my own, only I didn't want to come up here on my own. Mum promised that when another lad came, I could sleep up here in the next room. By the way, I shouldn't come upstairs in your boots again. Mum'll put her foot down about that!'

Robert was touched by the younger boy's friendliness, but on the verge of tears he said good-night rather abruptly and closed the door. There was a small bedside table behind the door, beyond that a single iron bedstead and in one corner a solid chest of drawers. He stepped to the square window and looked out into the moonlight. He found that he was looking down the drive along which he had walked so hesitantly, ninety minutes before. He could dimly see the ewes spaced widely over the field, lying in comfortable positions. Everything seemed open and limitless, quite different from the close-packed houses and gardens which comprised the view from the window of his little shared bedroom in Mill Hill. He undressed quickly. The lino was icy to his bare feet and he was glad of the home-made rug beside his bed. Shivering, he climbed into the high bed. He missed the bouncing company of his two younger brothers. They had slept together every night for as long as he could remember. Perhaps Billy and Jack were missing him too. But at least they were in the old familiar house, not sleeping under someone else's roof for the first time in their lives.

Although he felt so tired sleep would not come. What would his mother be thinking now? She had never shown him much affection—she was too busy maybe. He wished now that he had left a note for her.

He fell asleep at last, but slept fitfully, accompanied by strange nightmares. He was travelling on the train, which would not move fast because the fireman was stoking it with bales of newspapers. He looked out of the window and saw his father pursuing the train on a tradesman's bicycle, waving a copy of the *Farmer & Stockbreeder*. His mother was on the track too, ladling stew and dumplings into a paper-bag, and holding it out to him as the train sped away. Then his carriage was full of travellers, who spoke loudly together about the wicked young man who had failed to deliver their paper. He turned his back and looked out of the carriage window. Sam was there, ploughing a grass field and keeping pace with the train. Mr Ratcliffe and the rest of his family were trying to drive cows out of the way of the ploughman. Mrs Ratcliffe appeared carrying a meat-pie in one hand and an apple-pie in the other. Arthur holding a letter, dragged a red pillar-box behind him. 'Bob, Bob, where's my letter?' his mother cried. 'Bob, Bob I'll shake you if—' he woke with a start to see Mr Ratcliffe looming over him, shaking his shoulder vigorously.

'Bob, Bob, wake up, lad. By gum, you're a heavy sleeper. I've been shaking you for a couple o' minutes. Get up and come down. It's quarter to six and I like everybody at work by six o'clock. There'll be a cup o' tea in the kitchen.'

He lit Bob's candle from his own and walked quickly away downstairs in his stockinged feet.

The boy sat up with a stifled groan and dragged himself out of bed, almost stupefied by lack of rest. He pulled on his socks and the worn corduroy trousers Mrs Ratcliffe had given him the night before, and jogged unwillingly downstairs. The kitchen looked cold and dreary. Sam and his father were sitting at the big table sipping tea. A third mug was there, already filled.

'When you've drunk your tea, put on them owd boots o' mine by the fireplace. They'll do until we get you some more at the end o' th' wik. And tie a bit o' string round your ankles so your trousers don't dangle in the muck. Sam, you and Ernie can start milking. Ah'll show Bob how to do a bit o' feeding.'

He picked up a hurricane lamp, Sam took another, and together they left the kitchen. The son gathered some buckets and entered the cowshed with a tremendous clanging. Bob followed Mr Ratcliffe down the yard to the big double doors half-way down.

'Shut the door, Bob' said the farmer, 'Must keep the draught out at milking time. Th' cows' bags're nesh while they're letting the milk down, and they could easy catch cowd. Now, this is the mixing shed, and up above is the chop-loft. Every day we shovel what we want for mixing down through that trap-door.'

He lit a stub of candle, which even with the hurricane lamp provided only a feeble illumination and indicated a small pile in the centre of the floor.

'This is a mixture of oat-straw chop, mangolds and wet grains which we feed the cows on, plus a bit of hay and a pound or so of cake, to the best milkers. I want you to start feeding 'em with this now. Fill that truck, push it along the feeding passage, and give each cow two buckets. Start at the other end o' shed 'cos that's where we start milking. Take care to keep the truck on the rails, mind. It's easier that way.'

A narrow-gauge railway line started from the middle of the milking place and ran the length of the feeding passage. A box-like truck on four flanged wheels was used for transporting the bulky feed. Bob seized a wide shovel and filled the truck energetically, threw an empty bucket on top and rumbled his load along to the far end of the shed where Mr Ratcliffe, Sam and a middle-aged man in a blue neckerchief, were preparing to start milking in the flickering candle-light. He hurriedly fed the three cows at the end and as the milkers seized their stools and squatted down under their respective cows, Bob trundled his little wagon back along the passage and fed the other cows one by one. They rattled their chains and tossed their heads eagerly as he prepared to feed them, although some started back at the sight of a stranger—wariness which they overcame when the appetising mixture tumbled into the manger under their noses. There were forty cows in all—twenty each side of the mixing-place. He filled the truck three times and fed them quickly. Then the farmer called him.

'Bob, come with me and watch me set the cooler going.'

He hurried round to the front of the cowshed, where Mr Ratcliffe picked up two brimming buckets of milk. 'Bring that other bucket, lad,' he said and led the way to the cooling-shed outside the back door of the farmhouse.

'We put the receiving can on its bracket—so,' he explained. 'Lodge the upper sieve—or sye as we call it round here—inside it; then you can pour the milk in. If you can't reach to put the milk up, then use the stone steps at the back.' He showed Bob how to screw the water-pipe on to the threaded pipe at the bottom of the cooler. 'Th' water trickles along inside these corrugations, and the milk trickles down outside. Th' water comes out warm and the milk is cowd when it reaches th' bottom. Put the churn underneath with another sye in the top of it, and set the milk running. Remember, the churn 'owds seventeen gallons, so you only want about five buckets up i' the can to fill th' churn. You'll soon learn the time it takes for a churn to fill. There's three buckets gone in now. Bring two more up and then change the churn. Now, we've just finished milking in the top shed, so you can feed 'em round again with two buckets of chop apiece. Then there are two fold yards out at the back behind the dutch barn. Put as much as you can carry in a bag and take three lots like that to each yard. It's light enough now to see over there.'

Bob thought cows' appetites insatiable. He attended to the cooling too, leaving the feeding from time to time to collect buckets of milk from the milkers, and stagger with them to the cooler. But he also took note of what the others were doing. He observed his employer take a skipful of cattle-cake from a bag and give a few handfuls to certain cows. Bob tried to memorise these cows but gave up as they looked so nearly alike to him. After milking his last cow, Sam disappeared into the stable to attend to the horses, and Ernie took the long-bladed hay-knife, sharpened it with a coarse whetstone and cut great squares of hay from the stack in the dutch barn. These he carried on his head and deposited at various points along the feeding-passage.

The milk cooling completed, and the churns measured up and rolled aside, Ernie made off to his cottage at the end of the rickyard. Sam wheeled a barrowful of manure from the stable, tipped it into the manure pit, and then joined his father and Bob in the scullery where they all washed at the rain-water pump over the shallow sink. Bob, having been busy for fully two hours, was absolutely famished, he could hardly control his eagerness to get to the meal-table when he saw the plates of porridge standing ready.

The master and mistress sat opposite each other near the kitchen range—now glowing and cracking merrily. Arthur and Meg sat in the middle and at the other end Bob sat opposite the massive Sam. Porridge was followed by bacon, eggs and fried bread, and there was a loaf on the table with butter, jam and marmalade to round off the meal.

'That's right, eat as much as you can, Bob,' said the farmer, 'There's nowt like getting plenty o' packin'. The more you eat, the more work you'll be able to do. I want you to be as big as Sam theer, in a couple o' years.'

His mouth full, the boy nodded without replying, but felt a glow of warmth at the implication that he was already a member of the family.

'Did you sleep well, Bob?' asked the mistress.

Bob's mouth was still full, so the farmer answered for him.

'Sleep well? I should think he did. I shook him so hard and so long that I tho't the legs o' the bed 'ud wear holes i' the floor. By gum, if he works as hard as he sleeps, he'll be able to do all the work o' the place before long and the rest of us'll have an easy time.' He turned to more important matters. 'Sam, you'd better start ploughing Squarelands today. We've left it late, but I didn't want it turned over until the sheep 'ud cleaned up the turnip-tops.'

'But there's piles o' hedge brushings along that top hedge, Dad. They're going to get in my way!'

'Then tell Ernie to go up there and get 'em burnt. He can do that before he goes on with ditching in the river meadows.'

Arthur sat listening to this farming talk until his mother glanced at the clock.

'Arthur, you'll miss your train if you don't get off. It's quarter-past eight already, and the train goes at twenty-five to. Four miles on a bike takes a bit o' doing. And don't forget Bob's letter.'

The youngster seized his satchel from the dresser, sauntered out of the kitchen, and half-a-minute later they saw him cycle past the window.

'I don't think Arthur is that keen on grammar school,' said Meg, 'Nother cup of tea, Bob?' She refilled his cup without waiting for a reply.

'You're right, Meg, and I think it's just as well,' said Sam. 'I left school when I was thirteen to work on the farm, and I reckon Arthur'd be happier doing the same. The three R's is all that's necessary in farming. If a lad can read, write and calculate, he'll do well enough. When did you leave school, Bob?'

'I left at thirteen too,' Bob admitted. He sensed the subject was a bone of contention in the household, and he was not sufficiently sure of himself to take sides. 'Dad needed my help in the shop.'

'That's neither here nor there,' said Mr Ratcliffe. 'I want Arthur to stay at school until he's sixteen at least, so I can put him to a firm of auctioneers. They seem to make a lot more out o' farming than the farmers themselves, so we might as well get one member of the family in on it.'

'Then I suppose I'd better marry an auctioneer, then we'd have two in the family,' suggested Meg.

'That's enough of that, Miss,' said her father, 'Time enough to think of that a few years on.'

He turned away and Meg pulled a wry face. Bob realised it was for his benefit and coloured slightly.

'All this wrangling at the breakfast table,' Mrs Ratcliffe said, in mock dismay. 'What must Bob think of us? If you men can sit around all day talking, we women can't. Get started on the milk things, Meg. Mrs Wagstaff will soon be here to get going in the kitchen, and she allus pulls a long face if we're not ready for her.'

Bob thought this broad hint was aimed at him. He tried to gulp down the remains of his giant cup of tea.

'Yes, come on, Bob,' said the master. 'Don't choke yourself with that cup of tea, either—at least not before you've done the day's work! We'd better get cracking outside. Th' women want us out o' the way, and the cows need us in the yard. You can help me with the cows all day, and free Ernie for a full day i' the fields. After a day or two, you'll be able to do most o' the yard work yourself—there's allus somebody i' the house if owt goes wrong.'

'Will Bob take the milk tonight, Dad?' asked Sam as they walked through the cooling-shed, where Meg was already sorting out the equipment.

'No, Sam! We don't even know if the lad can drive a hoss. Ah know Bluebird's quiet, but she's fast and needs close watching. He'll go with you for a night or two, and you'll teach him to drive. Mebbe by the end of the week he can do it on his own.'

Chapter Three

Mr Ratcliffe had never before employed a lad who was completely new to farming, and he tried to keep this in the forefront of his mind as he explained each operation in the cowshed routine.

'If you're going to help me look after these cows, you've to start at the beginning and learn a few basic facts. Cows—in fact all farm animals—are creatures of habit. Any sudden change in the food, or in the order of operations, might put 'em off their milk yield for a day or two. So they must be fed, watered, milked, cleaned out and bedded down at the same time every day. What we're going to do next is water 'em and clean the sheds out. Milking cows drink plenty o' water as you can imagine, because they eat a lot of dryish food; and of couse, milk is nearly nine-tenths water. Some of the best milkers drink ten or fifteen gallons a day, so we turn 'em out to drink at the pond in the field twice a day.'

Bob knew all about this from his daily calls to Wyndham's and other farmers at home but thought it wiser to say nothing.

'And as we don't want the cows spreading all over the paddock, we keep the pond fenced off from the grass. Now we'll untie the cows, half at a time, and while they're out you can clear the muck out o' the grip and wheel it to the muck-hole. I'll feed the hay into the mangers and scatter fresh bedding along the back end of the cow-standings—we call them heel-stones. The bull comes out of his box and mixes with the cows while they're in the yard. If any are on heat he'll attend to them. That's a good bull, Bob. I gave eighty guineas for him at Brum last March. I like to try and improve my herd by getting the best bull I can afford. Sam's just gone out with his hosses so we can shut the gate and start letting the cows out.'

Bob was a little nervous about walking between two large cows, finding the hook in the chain and freeing it. He was afraid they would swing their heads round violently and strike him. But he found that they were adept at avoiding contact. As they were freed from the chain, they stepped straight back with an eager stride before turning. The boy hurried from cow to cow unhooking the chains rapidly and allowing them to drop in a heap in the manger.

'Don't be in such a tear, lad. There's a reight way and a wrong way to untie cows. Don't drop the chain in the manger, or when the cow comes in again you'll have to bend down to pick it up, and your head'll be mighty close to hers. If she moved suddenly her horns might cut your face open. If you look, there's a place to hang the chain up.'

Robert attacked the work with vigour filling the barrow many times in order to clear the manure which filled the gutter —'grip' Mr Ratcliffe called it. He was dubious at first about wheeling the loaded barrow up a rising plank, along the muck-hole wall and tipping off his load; but once he had got the balance of the muck-encrusted barrow he managed it quite well.

The farmer showed him how much rich-scented hay to put into the mangers, against the cows' return to their standings.

'These Trent-side meadows produce some grand hay. I like to make it as good as I can. There's nowt like high-quality hay for milk. You'd better take a good armful round to the young calves. I'll show you where they are.'

He led the way past the cooling-shed to the back of the house. Inside a small brick building, with doors tightly closed and windows covered with sacking to exclude draughts, were three little pens, each holding two very clean calves, bright-eyed, frisky and inquisitive.

'These are the youngest, Bob. We feed 'em on milk-substitute for three months, but Meg or Mrs Ratcliffe does that part—messing about with warm water and such-like, nowt to do wi' us. We give 'em their hay and bed 'em up. Put a batten o' straw into each pen. I like 'em to have a good bed—keeps 'em clean and healthy. But be careful to pick out the string when you cut the batten open. If a calf gets a bit inside, it'll die for sure. Break Meg's heart and wreck my bank-balance.'

'Why are they in these small places? Why not put them all into one larger pen. It'd save time.'

'Well, because they're fed on liquid food from buckets twice a day—they're always eager for it. Try going in among six calves with six buckets on your arm and setting 'em down one at a time! When they're weaned and on dry food they can go together. I'll show you the older ones.' He led the way into a larger building at right-angles to the nursery. It held larger calves with shining roan coats and abundant energy. When the door was opened suddenly and they sensed the presence of a stranger, they burst into a frightened gallop round their pen, tails outstretched, noses pointing and nostrils flared. After two circuits they realised that the stranger had no designs on them, and came to a sudden halt. They stood in a tight bunch, breathing hard and still looking apprehensively towards the two figures at the door.

'Stupid beasts; they'll soon get used to you. But they're a grand lot aren't they? I'm quite proud o' them. There's eighteen in here, and with the six youngsters next door make our quota for the year. I like to rear two dozen every winter, half heifers and half bullocks. The heifers are needed to maintain the milking herd o' course, and the bullocks bring in useful extra cash. They fatten easily on these meadows by the end of their second summer.'

They went into dinner when Meg called them at twelve-thirty. Bob was pleased with his morning's achievements, and the farmer secretly delighted with such an apt pupil. Sam had come in from the field a few minutes previously, and throughout the meal kept up a conversation with his father on farming matters, most of which was well above Bob's head. Mrs Ratcliffe and Meg were occupied with serving the meal and addressed each other in monosyllables. Bob was not included in either conversation. His uneasiness must have communicated itself to Meg, for in a lull in her father's discussion, she asked:

'How did you get on with the cows, Bob?'

'Pretty well,' hoping his employer would not disagree.

'You'll have to be careful when you start milking. It's a messy job. The cows'll flick their dirty tails across your face, tread on your toes, put a foot in the bucket, and sometimes kick you in the grip, muck and all!'

'If you don't shut up, Meg,' reprimanded her father, 'I'll have you out there milking. Bob'll do well enough I daresay, when he's learnt a bit more.'

'Pull her hair, Bob,' advised Sam. 'Th' little madam's trying to take the rise out of you. I'd smack her behind if she were a year or two younger.'

Bob laughed at the first suggestion; Meg coloured at the second. Before he went out, Bob tried to catch Meg's eye to reassure her of his friendliness but she avoided his glance.

Mr Ratcliffe took him into the stable just as Sam was leaving with his ploughing team. 'Major's our hoss today, Bob. I'll show you how to put him in the cart.' Sam called out 'Careful with that hoss, mind. I'll want him ploughing tomorrow.'

His father chuckled.

'Sam should worry! Now, Bob. We've got three good farm hosses, the two Shire mares, Violet and Flower, and this leggy gelding, Major. Sam needs two every day for field-work, and we need one for the odd carting jobs; so to keep 'em all in reg'lar work, Sam leaves a different one in the stable every day. Major's what we call a half-legged hoss, that is heavy enough for field-work and light enough to trot if necessary. We take the milk with him sometimes, but I don't like trotting these heavy hosses too much—it jars their cannon bones. Have you ever harnessed a hoss?'

'No.'

'Well, you'll never start any younger, so you can have a go now. As you can see, a hoss's collar is big at the bottom and narrow at the top, and it's got to go over the hoss's head, which is wide at the top and tapers towards his nose. So what do we do?'

'Put it on upside down, I s'pose.'

'Right you are! Well—here's the collar and there's the hoss. Remember, a hoss holds his head high when his collar's being put on, so be prepared to reach up.'

Bob approached the great black horse with some fear, especially nervous walking by the muscular legs and the steel-shod hooves and only a little less scared by the towering black-and-white head which seemed almost out of reach.

'Take his head-stall off first,' reminded his employer. It was easier than he had thought. As the leather collar was passing over the horse's eyes, Major pushed co-operatively. The boy swivelled the collar round at the narrowest part of the horse's neck, and then let it slide down to fit snugly over the shoulders. The saddle followed, then the bridle, and Bob was surprised when Major obligingly opened his mouth to have the snaffle bit put in. Finally Bob backed the horse out of his stall and led him round to the cart-hovel where Mr Ratcliffe showed him how to hook up to one of the carts inside the shed, in shafts pointing skywards.

'We're going to get a load of mangolds from the clamp and tip 'em outside the mixing-place. I'll show you how to start the oil-engine and put them through the pulper. Then you can go up to the loft and push down a fair bit o' chop; you'll soon learn how much, throw some wet grains out o' the pit, and mix the lot together for feeding tonight and tomorrow morning. By the time we've done that, it'll be time to water the cows again.

Bob loved the work, and felt he was doing something worthwhile. He forked mangolds into the pulper, shovelled pulp, chop and grains into a great heap with tremendous enthusiasm, and then turned the whole heap over twice with an energy that pleased Mr Ratcliffe.

When they went in to the evening meal at six o'clock, Bob was hungry and tired, but happy. He felt he had already earned his right to be there. After the meal the milk had to be taken to the station. He was so keen to get started that he bolted his scrambled egg, bread and cheese, and a huge slice of home-made cake at breakneck speed.

Mrs Ratcliffe watched with amusement.

'I like to see a lad eat well, then I know there's nothing much wrong with him.'

'Can I go with them to the station, Dad?' asked Arthur during the meal.

'No you can't. I daresay you've got some homework to do. If you haven't you should have. In any case Bluebell's got enough to pull without your weight.'

'You used to let me go.'

'That was in the summer, Arthur,' Meg pointed out. 'And before you started at the grammar school. Now you've got homework to do, there'll be no more rides in the milk-cart for you. I wouldn't mind going myself. It'd be a change from being cooped up in this blessed house every day of the week bar Sunday!'

'Now, Meg,' said her father. 'I was talking to Arthur. Bob's never driven a hoss before, and Sam's going with him to show him how to handle the mare. When he does the milk run on his own, there's no reason why Arthur shouldn't go with him sometimes—though why he should want to beats me.'

'It's something new, Arnold,' his wife expostulated. 'You were a boy yourself once.'

'Maybe. Anyway, Arthur, you've got homework to do, and if you're going with Bob you must do that first. Set into it as soon as you come home from school. I'm paying good money for you to go to the grammar, and I intend to see it's not wasted.'

'Give over, Father,' said Mrs Ratcliffe. 'Must Arthur's school come into every discussion?'

Sam pushed his chair noisily under the table.

'Come on, Bob, let's get out o' this. Put th' labels on th' churns, Meg, we'll be up here for 'em in five minutes.'

'Bossy!' muttered his sister, as Sam and Bob disappeared through the kitchen door.

'You know which is the milk hoss?'

'Yes, that dark grey-looking mare,' Bob replied, hoping to sound knowledgeable.

'Dark-grey be damned! That's what we call a blue-roan, lad. There aren't many about that colour. That's why she's called Bluebell. 'Er's a reight good little mare, fast and all. But sometimes I wish we'd a hoss a shade heavier for the milk-run and the other odd jobs. Dad uses Bluebell for market and similar trips, which means we have to use Major for the milk—and I don't care for that. I'd rather have another lightish hoss—for the farm, and leave Bluebell for the house. I've got two empty stalls here.'

He covered the animal with a few swift strokes from a dandy brush while he was talking. 'Now put the tackle on her, Bob. There it is, straight behind you.'

Bluebell was quickly harnessed, hitched into the varnished

milk-float and driven round to the cooling-shed door.

'I'll drive till we get on the road,' said Sam. 'I don't want any varnish scraped off by the gateposts. Ask Meg for some matches to light the lamps. We'd better take another couple o' candles, too. These might burn out before we get back.'

Between them they hoisted the seventeen-gallon railway churns on to the low floor of the float, fastened up the back-board, and fixed the seat in position. This was merely a strong plank spanning the width of the vehicle and held in position by metal pegs.

Bob opened and shut the three gates crossing the drive, jumping in and out of the float as if his life depended on it. Once on the public highway, Bluebell set off into the darkness at a spanking pace. Sam handed the reins to Bob, who took them rather nervously.

'Is it all right to go as fast as this in the dark, Sam?'

'Yes, sure. The mare doesn't need a light to see where she's going. The candles in the lamps aren't for the hoss, but for other people to see us. You don't really need to drive a hoss along an open road; just keep the reins from getting slack and the hoss'll pick its own way. And you only hold the reins in your left hand. Leave your right hand free for holding a whip or giving signals. As you twist your hand, move one rein or the other. When you're driving a pair on land it's different. You hold one line in each hand then, because they're wider apart, and there's a good deal of movement in turning a pair o' hosses straight round on the headland of a field. But you're doing well enough, Bob. Keep her going.'

After his first nervousness, Bob found he was enjoying the experience. The sense of being in command was thrilling. He discovered that he had to be careful not to move the reins unnecessarily. So sensitive was Bluebell's mouth, that the slightest jerk would cause her to deviate. She carried on tirelessly at her swinging trot. The spring-loaded float bounced easily over the rough country lane, the iron-shod wheels occasionally grinding up spots of grit.

Bob felt quite an established driver as the mare swung into the station. It was with a shock that he realised it was only twenty-four hours ago when he had first arrived.

'Anything for us tonight, Jack?' Sam asked the porter as he handed in the consignment note.

'Ah've seen nowt, Sam.'

'Allus ask if there's owt for us, Bob,' explained Sam. 'There's bits and pieces coming all the time—a spare part, a can o' grease, a bag o' seeds and the like.'

The journey home seemed faster and noisier, the empty

churns rattling more than the full ones. They stopped halfway to change one of the candles, Bluebell fidgeting restlessly at this unscheduled stop in her homeward dash. She was still full of energy when she returned to her stall and shook herself thankfully as the harness was whipped off.

'Just wipe a cloth over her, Bob, to smooth over the saddle and collar marks. Then give her a double-handful of oats in half a skip of chop, fill her rack with hay, shake back her bedding, and she'll do until I come out at half-past nine.'

'Now and again,' continued Sam as he led the way back to the kitchen, 'you can put a bit o' neatsfoot oil on the leather part o' the tackling. A bit o' metal polish on the buckles is not a bad idea. You can do that sort o' thing in the evening, when the weather gets a bit warmer.'

They entered the kitchen and joined the others in front of the fire. Bob felt part of the group now, and liked the feeling. It gave him assurance he had never known at home. He intended to listen intently to everything that was said and store it up in his mind.

'Good thing the milk's keeping up,' said the farmer. 'No money from owt else at this time o' the year. And there won't be either till we get some fat lambs away in July and a few fat beast in August and September. How's the ploughing going in Squarelands?'

'Just reight. That field lays high and dry, and I'll have no trouble ploughing it in a fortnight.'

'Good! We'll be able to drill the oats practically right away after just a couple o' harrowings. Now we've got Bob here to help in the yard, we ought to be able to keep Major at full work on the farm. There's plenty of jobs Ernie can do with him.'

'Ernie's too old, Dad, to keep up wi' that fast hoss. T'ud be a better idea to let Bob take him, and keep Ernie in for the yard work.'

'In time maybe. But I want Bob to learn the cowman's job thoroughly first. He can't take everything in all at once.'

'All this farming talk,' complained Meg. 'Can't we talk about something else round the fireside?'

'Such as?' queried her father.

'Well—why not the Coronation celebrations?'

'The Coronation celebrations—you've got something there, Meg. It'll be a rare treat for the young folk, and there's going to be a bonfire late in the evening. The vicar mentioned on Sunday that they've got the spot marked out, so we can start getting the stuff down, even if it's still a few months away. We've got lots of hedge-brushings. Ernie can start picking 'em up tomorrow and cart 'em down to the village. We've no grains to fetch this week, so we can spare tomorrow. But on Friday Ernie'll have to help Bob with the cows, 'cause I'll be at Derby. I'll need Bluebell too, so Major'll have to do the milk run in the evening.'

'Yes, I was telling Bob that we need another milk hoss, heavier than Bluebell, so she can be left for the house jobs.'

Meg looked across at her mother in exasperation. Mrs Ratcliffe smiled indulgently at her daughter and in a motherly way at Robert too. He wished he could join in the conversation, but non-farming topics did not hold the stage for long in this household. He realised it would not have been considered respectful to talk with anyone else while Mr Ratcliffe or Sam was speaking. Anyway, Arthur was engrossed in a Henty novel from the school library, Meg was busy knitting and Mrs Ratcliffe sat restfully re-reading the weekly papers, *The Derbyshire Advertiser, Burton Chronicle* and the *Farmer & Stockbreeder*.

The heat of the fire, the conversation of Sam and his father, added to sheer physical weariness made it impossible for Bob to keep awake. He dozed off and did not wake until Meg nudged him and told him that the cocoa was on the table. He emptied his mug and staggered sleepily up to bed. He suffered no nightmares on his second night.

'Think he'll do, Maggie?' the farmer said to his wife when the rest of the family had gone upstairs.

'He seems a pleasant enough lad, I must say, and I'm beginning to like him. But it's too soon to judge. He's only been here a day yet. Still, Arthur seems to be taking to him, and I think Meg's inclined that way too. Sam's only too glad to have a lad about him to instruct in his own way. So who are we to disagree?'

Mr Ratcliffe chuckled.

'I'd disagree soon enough if he wasn't suitable, I can assure you. But I'm beginning to take a fancy to him too. He works hard, he's anxious to learn, thinks what he's doing, and he's quick. He's cheerful too, and—yes he's gentle, I believe. He's the type we want to have living in the house, with Meg and Arthur at home. But he might get homesick yet for his own people and his paper round. We'll just have to keep our fingers crossed. I don't want to be continually changing the lad i' the house.'

Friday morning was a time of great bustle at Oakleigh Farm. Mr Ratcliffe, who invariably shaved overnight, had a morning shave in addition. Meg supervised the breakfast while her parents got ready for their weekly outing. The farmer put on his fully-cut breeches and polished brown boots and leggings. Mrs Ratcliffe was resplendent in her fur-collared brown coat and muff. The best harness was put on Bluebell, shining from the vigorous grooming which Bob had applied before breakfast.

The high spring cart was pulled out of the shed behind the calf-pens. It was varnished dark green, with its owner's name and address in neat one-inch letters in the offside front corner—'A. S. A. Ratcliffe, Oakleigh Farm, Hatnall, Derby'. Finally the farmer and his wife came out of the kitchen. When Mr Ratcliffe climbed up into the cart his fourteen stones caused the springs to flatten. Mrs Ratcliffe joined him from the other side, snuggling into the depths of her winter clothes, for the February wind was very keen. Meg placed a basket of eggs in the back of the cart, Bob stepped aside and the handsome mare broke into a proud trot. She moved briskly away in such a style as to make it appear that she considered this more important than hauling the milk to the station.

Bob carried on with his yard-work helped by the uncommunicative Ernie. Meg was in charge of the housework, and cooked a meal of stew and dumplings, followed by the unchangeable apple pie. Bob felt at a disadvantage during the meal, which was eaten to the accompaniment of much friendly wrangling and cross-chat between Meg and Sam. Bob sensed that Meg was putting on an act for his benefit. He ate quickly and then hurried outside to continue with his mixing and watering single-handed, as Ernie had returned to his field-work.

'See what you've done now, Meg,' said Sam. 'You've driven Bob out twenty minutes early with your chuntering, and I'm sure that wasn't on your mind.'

'You get back to those blooming horses, Sam Ratcliffe and let me get on with my work. If I want to talk to Bob I'll go out to the yard to do it.'

'Don't you dare hinder the lad,' replied Sam, serious and authoritative. 'We don't want him to get into bad habits. He came here to work, not to be a chatting companion for thee.' He strode out to the stable. Meg did not put her suggestion into effect, which was fortunate, for Bob was still shy of her. He was absorbed in the afternoon's work when he heard a shout from the house, and saw Bluebell and the smart spring-cart standing there, and Mr and Mrs Ratcliffe and Meg unloading baskets, boxes and parcels. Bob wondered excitedly if his new clothes were among the luggage. He hurried across the yard, put away the cart, and then led the mare to the stable, where he stripped off the damp harness and rubbed her down briskly.

He gave her half-a-bucket of water to drink—he had learnt that a thirsty, sweating horse must only have a limited quantity—and some rolled oats mixed with hay chop. He patted her as he stepped back, well pleased with his work.

'Have a good rest and feed, Bluebell old girl. I shall want you in about two hours for the station trip.'

'You'd better take Major, tonight, Bob,' said Mr Ratcliffe, who had been scrutinising the efforts of his new hand with approval. 'Bluebell's done sixteen miles pretty fast today and she doesn't want any more tonight. As you're taking the big hoss for the first time, Sam'll go with you once more, but after that you'll do the milk job on your own. Think you'll manage it?'

'I'm sure I will, Mr Ratcliffe.'

'Aye, I think you will, lad. Onyway, get started watering the cows now, or we'll be late finishing. By gum, here's Sam with his hosses already!'

Bob hurried in after milking, but found he had to eat fried fish and chips, prepared by Meg, while her mother described her adventures in the county town. Mr Ratcliffe noted Bob's expectancy with amusement.

'Better show Bob his outfit before he goes to Willington, Maggie, otherwise he'll push Major to the limit in a hurry to get home.'

'Oh, all right! Here they are, Bob.' She swept up an armful of parcels from the big dresser and spilled them on to the table.

'There you are, Bob—a good pair of heavy boots, eight-and-six. Stiff leggings, two shillings, and two pairs o' grey socks at one-and-six. There are two flannel shirts at half-a-crown each, and a smart pair of cord breeches, but they cost ten-and-six. That's all the new stuff, but I got you a serviceable coat and waist-coat from a stall in the Morledge for three-and-six the two. There's a lot of wear in 'em yet. When you get them on you'll look like a real farm chap. Oh, and I got you a second-hand railwayman's topcoat for five shillings. Just the thing for driving in wet weather—the nap'll keep a whole day's rain out. Don't put 'em on to drive to the station tonight. They all want airing, and I'll do that for you this evening.'

Major's long, powerful legs covered the miles quickly but Bob was delighted to find that he was as easy to control as the little blue mare. He felt on top of the world that night. But he was very self-conscious when he came down stairs the next morning in his new breeches. When he heard his hob-nailed boots ring on the stone floor he was embarrassed, imagining everybody was looking at him. He seemed to get through his work in less time, and was hungrier than ever when he went in to breakfast. The postman arrived during the meal and Meg went to the door to collect the letters. One was for Bob; he instantly recognised the cheap standard envelope from his father's shop. All the Ratcliffe family took an interest in his letter, and conversation ceased as he opened it and read it through.

'Dear Robert,' he read,

'We received your letter on Thursday morning and I must say it was a relief to your mother who had worried a lot about you. For my part, I think you have acted in an ungrateful, wicked way. You were always treated well at home, and had no reason to run off in such a deceitful way. You had a good chance here to be my right-hand man, and you've thrown it away. Keeping a shop such as ours is an honest worth-while occupation, and one that a man can be proud of. If you prefer to be a hayseed sort of chap, that's your funeral.

'I have had to take Billy away from school to do the round, and I must say he does it quicker than you. I hope you have got sufficient suitable clothes. I found you had taken your bank-book which would have been empty but for my insistence. It is no use sending your other clothes on. Your Sunday suit is too small for you and will come in for Billy, and that applies to your other things. You have cut yourself away from us, and will have to make the best of it.

'I am not sure that I approve of the farmer you are living with. If he takes on a boy who turns up without credentials he must be a doubtful character. I hope you make a better job of farming than you did of the papers. Although you have treated us so badly I still wish you well. This is still your home, and if you can find time to get away from the farm, which is unlikely, we shall still accept you here and give you a bed and a meal. You are such a long way away that I don't suppose Mill Hill will see you again. I will close now, without any ill-feeling from me or your mother, although you have behaved so badly towards us.

'Your affect. Father,
John Felton

'P.S. Your mother sends her love.'

Chapter Four

Robert was disheartened by his father's letter, and particularly by its scornful references to farming. He felt uncomfortable at the slur on Mr Ratcliffe, for whom he had developed respect. If he read out that sentence it would seem he agreed with it. But the family all looked expectant as he folded the letter and returned it to its envelope, so he said. 'Dad wishes me well in my new life. He says he would like to see me if I ever get time to leave the farm. My mother seems to miss me most. I wish she had written and not dad!'

Mr and Mrs Ratcliffe instantly recognised that a hidden depth of misery lay behind those few sentences, and the three younger members of the family took their cue from their parents, and did not press Bob for information. Mr Ratcliffe decided that it would be in the best interests of the farm if Bob quickly forgot his melancholy. Unwittingly he underlined Mr Felton's hope.

'Well, Bob, I certainly think you'll make a better farmer than a newsagent. You look the part now, anyway. But breakfast's over now and the farm work must go on. It's Saturday today, and I like the work finished half-an-hour earlier, so those who want can catch a train to town in reasonable time. On Sundays, too–we're not exactly heathens in this house. I like the milk chap to be back from the station in time to go to church if he wants to. We all go to church sometimes–it's expected of us, and makes for a friendly village life. I'd like you to fit in like a member of the family.'

Bob brightened up and hurried outside to his work. Somewhat to his dismay, he found himself saddled with Arthur's help. But he soon found that the youngster's help brought quite a saving in time. Arthur could do most of the jobs more efficiently than he could himself. The boy was so keen to help his new companion, that he rushed around at a speed which left even the energetic Bob breathless. He bounced mangolds into the cart with a skill Bob lacked, started the oil engine with ease, and pulped the roots, while Bob pushed down the chop and shovelled out the brewers grains.

'We're coming to the end of the grains,' Bob said.

'That's all right, there'll be a truck in on Tuesday, I daresay. We have a big truck load every fortnight and Sam fetches it from the station–six cart loads with the high boards on the carts.'

'Wonder if I'll be sent with him.'

'Shouldn't think so. Sam generally takes two carts himself one hoss tied behind the other cart. You see, Bob, on a long trip like that, more time is spent walking than loading, and my dad thinks it's wasteful to have two men walking with two hosses and carts when one can do it and not take much longer.'

Bob was impressed by Arthur's knowledge of his father's methods. Mr Ratcliffe entered the mixing-place.

'Arthur, if you're going to help—don't talk so much. You've talked Bob into a stupor already, seemingly. Your mother's got a note for Mrs Bagnall, so bike down to the vicarage with it will you? The boy seems to have hooked on to you Bob,' the farmer continued, as they watched Arthur scamper up the yard to the house. 'It'll probably go on for a week or two. Well, that's all right. You've certainly got round everything a lot earlier today. If I'd known he was going to help that much, I'd 'a got you to clean out the bull's pen while the cows were drinking; but you can do it next Saturday afternoon, if he's helping. See he keeps at it, though, so there's no time wasted. I'd rather he did that instead of staying at school footballing and such-like.'

Bob was surprised and slightly mortified when in the evening Arthur, unknown to his father, demonstrated he knew how to milk a cow. Bob could not bring himself to ask a boy so much younger than himself for advice. But this was forgotten in the pride he felt in taking the milk on his own for the first time. He had assumed that he would be alone, but at the last moment Arthur demanded to be allowed to go with him, claiming that he had finished his homework. The mare was fidgety to be away, and the youngster proved his worth by standing at her head while Meg completed the consignment note. Arthur was also useful in opening the three drive gates while Bob drove through in splendour. But for the town boy, the real thrill was when they set off at full-speed along the lane. The night was clear with a touch of frost, and Bluebell made the most of it. Bob considered himself an expert driver by now, and was thrilled to have a sprightly horse under his control. To be carried along at fifteen miles per hour was another thrill.

'Let me drive, Bob!'

'No, Arthur!'

'Why not? I can drive as well as you.'

'Yes, I daresay. Perhaps better. But I'm in charge of this mare, and unless your Dad says I'm to let you drive, I'm not going to. Besides, I like driving, and this is an important job!'

'Everybody does, as far as I know. But why is the job so important?'

'Well Arthur, we're taking away the whole of one day's produce of the farm!'

'That's a funny way of putting it; but I suppose you're right.'
Bluebell hurried on.

'Do you like your new school, Arthur?'

'Oh, it's not so bad. I can do the work all right. But it's the thought of having to stay at school so long that I don't like. I'm not twelve yet and I'd still be at school if I'd stayed at the new village school. But now I'm at the grammar school, my dad's going to insist that I stay there until I'm sixteen. I'd rather be on the farm.'

'But it won't be too bad, surely. You'll be able to work on the farm at week-ends.'

'It's not the same. And I don't want to sit in an office working out the sale-price of other people's stock. Going out for farm sales, squatting behind an old table in a shed filling in delivery slips for my father's friends. I shan't like it, I'll feel a proper fool.'

'But that's only the first year or two, I should think. As you get older you'll become a fully-fledged auctioneer and be one of the bosses.'

'Perhaps, when I'm about twenty-five or thirty. But I'll have to pass exams first. That part doesn't bother me, but I'll be an old man before I have a farm of my own.'

'You might make a lot of money at auctioneering and be able to buy a bigger farm!'

'I expect that's what dad thinks. He knows all the auctioneers in Burton, Lichfield and Derby. They're well off and own property, but I don't know if any of 'em has a farm. Dad probably thinks that Oakleigh Farm won't be much to divide between the three of us.'

'Will he divide it up into three smaller farms, do you think?'

'No, he can't do that. We're only the tenants. It doesn't belong to us. Belongs to the squire, Colonel Ratcliffe at the Hall. Same name as us but no relation. Owns most o' the land round here and farms the Home Farm, nearer in to Repton. His milk comes in to the station, same as ours, with a smart turn-out too, cleaned and polished and all that; but no better than ours really. Their hoss is grand to look at, too, but not as fast as Bluebell, nowt near. There's not a milk hoss coming in to Willington as good as our Bluebell!'

They delivered the milk, struggling to lift the heavy churns from the float up to the milk stage. Bob realised he would have to devise an alternative way of unloading when he was alone. They searched, loaded the four empties and collected from the parcels-office a keg of blood-salts for the horses.

Bluebell set off at her usual rapid pace on the homeward run. Occasionally Bob leaned forward and made coaxing noises with his lips, as he had seen Sam do, to urge her to greater efforts. She responded enthusiastically at first. But before they reached Repton she flagged, and reduced her speed to about half. Her rhythmic steps became broken and uneven, and the milk float seemed to move in jerks, causing the empty churns to rock and jangle their tops together.

'Come on, Bluebell, come on! You're never like this, girl. We want to get home.'

Arthur stood up and peered ahead.

'Whoa, Bob, whoa! I think she's lame. She's nodding her head up and down as if she's afraid to put her nearside front foot to the ground. Pull into the side and let's have a look!'

Bob did so, feeling alarmed.

'See how she's sweating,' said Arthur knowledgeably, 'She must be in pain.'

'Well, what are we going to do?'

'We might have to leave the float here, walk her home slowly on the grass at the side o' the road, and then come back with Major for the float. But let's have a look first. I'll stand by her head while you lift her foot up—the front one this side.'

This was quite new to Bob, but he did not want to appear ignorant to his young companion. He bent down gingerly and lifted Bluebell's fetlock by the convenient tuft of hair. To his surprise, the foot came up easily. He put his other hand under the toe and inverted the sole. The moon appeared from behind a cloud just long enough for him to see the cause of the trouble.

'Well, I'm jiggered. Look here, Arthur! There's a sharp stone wedged in between the shoe and this triangular piece in the middle . . .'

'The frog?' asked Arthur, leaving the mare's head and coming round to inspect.

'Eh?'

'That piece is called the frog. No wonder she couldn't run! The stone is cutting into the frog and it's big enough to stop her putting her foot down level. It's like a pebble in our boots. Can you get it out?'

Bob tore feverishly at the obstruction with his fingers. After breaking his nails, he proclaimed it immovable without a chisel.

Arthur dug his hand into his trouser pocket and produced a huge pocket-knife bristling with gadgets.

'Ever seen one o' these? Called a jack-knife, and this spiky thing's for getting stones out of horses' hooves. Never had a chance to try it before. Let's see if it works.'

In turn they prised and poked, levered and jabbed at the offending stone. At length it edged out and fell to the ground. Bob let the foot drop down and patted the mare affectionately.

Bluebell tossed her head and brought it round sharply towards him as if in gratitude. Finding her foot no longer painful, she set off at an even greater pace as if to make up for lost time.

Mr Ratcliffe was sitting comfortably in his usual chair reading the *Derbyshire Advertiser* when they entered the kitchen. Arthur settled down at once with his library book, Bob took his chair between Meg and Sam, coughed uneasily and then blurted out, 'Bluebell picked up a stone in her foot, Mr Ratcliffe.'

'Not unusual on a stony road,' grunted the master without looking up. 'There was nowt wrong with her foot when you brought her in along th' drive. I thought she was sprouting wings to help her along.'

Sam jumped to his feet.

'I'd better go down to stable and look at her. Ah wouldn't like anything to happen to the little mare!'

'Leave her, Sam, you go down last thing. You can trust the lads to take a stone out surely? She couldn't 'a come in at that pace if she'd been hurt, could she?'

Sam grunted and resumed his slow perusal of the *Farmer & Stockbreeder*. Bob felt elated at the casual way Mr Ratcliffe took his competence for granted. Of course, Arthur was the real hero of the evening, and Bob waited for him to give his version. But the younger boy was absorbed in his book. A stone in the foot, if it did no serious damage, was not worth talking about.

The work went ahead rapidly on Sunday morning. At breakfast time Mrs Ratcliffe enquired if Bob wanted to go to church.

'Come with us if you like, but we're not forcing you. Meg and I always go in the morning, and Arthur, because he's in the choir. Dad and Sam usually go in the evening. They're in the choir too, and sometimes in the mornings their voices are missed, I can tell you. But we can't all go at the same time, as the farm can't be left to look after itself entirely.'

'That's just a habit we've got into,' commented her husband. 'I don't suppose anybody'd run away wi' the place in the hour-and-a-half we were at church. Might be better if we went together in the evening. But it'd be a bit of a rush for the milk chap to do it in time.'

'Thank you, I'd like to go,' Bob said. He had attended Sunday School as a small child for several years, but since he started to deliver papers he had never been to morning service. 'But I don't know the way to get there. I s'pose I can make a bee-line for the steeple.'

'No need for that, my lad. We'll all go together. Now you men clear out and get on with your yard work, and Meg and I'll get the dinner ready. We leave here at twenty-to-eleven, although if we go across the fields, as we do when it's dry, we can do it in ten minutes.'

As he was a choir-boy, Arthur set off before the others. Bob wore the clothes in which he had arrived at Oakleigh, and felt shabby beside Meg and her mother in their Sunday best.

They left the farmyard by the main gate and struck off across the short winter grass, cropped close by ewes, who grazed without concern at the trio of humans.

As they passed over the brow of the field they came in sight of the church two fields below them. The Norman spire towered above the countryside. The bell-ringers now started, the clamour of the bells bursting out from the louvres and shattering the silence. Bob had never particularly noticed church bells before. They sounded so pleasant here as he sauntered across this Derbyshire pasture on a February morning, so bright and open as to hint of spring.

'Don't they sound grand?'

'They call this peal Kent Treble Bob Major,' said Mrs Ratcliffe. 'Though the Lord knows why. But Sunday morning wouldn't be Sunday morning without the bells. There's something about them takes you back to all the milestones of your life. I don't like to be too close to them, though. They can be too noisy!'

As they neared the low, grey wall of the church-yard, Bob noticed a group approaching the church from the right; a tall military-looking man accompanied by a well-dressed woman and others at a respectful distance.

'What would that party be?' he enquired.

'That's Squire Ratcliffe and the Hall servants,' said Meg. 'They always turn up in strength. The servants have to. Those who stay behind this week have to come next Sunday, and so on. That's Colonel Ratcliffe and his wife in front. They've a son, Mortimer, but he's at Cambridge, studying. The Hall is a lovely place. There's a private drive, leading from the Hall across the Park, by the fishpond, and through the rhododendron shrubbery right up to the church wall. There are gas lamps along there, too, just like in the roads in the village. They light them on Sunday evenings in the dark months. At the church end of the drive there are special gates to let them in, and a direct path to the side-door of the church, where they occupy a separate aisle. We call it the Ratcliffe aisle. There's lots of Ratcliffe tombs in there, as well as in the church-yard. Not our family, you understand. Dad's people came from the other side of Derby. It's a well-known Derbyshire name.'

They climbed a stile over the stone wall and followed a path among the gravestones. The tumbling tones of the peal were replaced by a single warning bell. They joined the group pressing through the Gothic doorway and filed into one of the front pews in the central aisle.

Bob was astonished to see that the church was three-quarters filled. He whispered his surprise to Meg. 'It's a fine morning. Church is always fuller in good weather.' Her mother nudged her sharply. 'Don't talk in church!'

Bob was impressed with the scene. A wintry sun shone through the coloured windows and bathed the interior in an aura of light. Headed by the priest, the choir paced round from the vestry to their appointed places each side of the chancel to the music of the opening psalm. The organ thundered out its rolling notes. Every member of the congregation appeared to be singing heartily. Bob found it uplifting, and joined in with enthusiasm. Meg, who took it all for granted, was amused by his intentness, but Mrs Ratcliffe noticed his fervour with approval.

When they streamed out of the church after the blessing, Mrs Ratcliffe introduced him to the vicar. 'Glad to see you, young man,' he said and turned aside to greet someone else.

Although Mrs Ratcliffe was anxious to get home to her cooking, she could not avoid chatting to some of her special friends and Meg was drawn into a group of girls of her own age. Arthur was still in the vestry, so Bob was left on his own, and, too shy to talk to strangers, he sauntered down the little path to the stile which gave access to Mr Ratcliffe's field.

He paused and waited for his companions to catch up. He had hoped to chat to Meg on the way home, but Arthur monopolised him all the way across the fields, while Mrs Ratcliffe talked to her daughter. Mr Ratcliffe and Sam were in the ewes' pasture inspecting the sheep. They joined the church group and entered the farm gate together.

The leisurely Sunday dinner was a luxury in the Ratcliffe household. They sat down at one o'clock to consume an unhurried meal of roast beef, potatoes, brussels sprouts and Yorkshire pudding, followed by an extra large helping of apple-pie, flooded with custard. As the yard-work did not re-start until three-thirty, the men were encouraged to retire into the drawing-room and sleep off the heavy meal. Much to the surprise of everyone, Bob offered to stay in the kitchen and help with the washing-up. Sam put his chair away noisily to show his disapproval and marched purposefully into the sitting-room. Meg put her tongue out at him as his broad shoulders turned away. Mrs Ratcliffe said, 'Well Bob, if you insist on helping with the washing-up, *I'm* going into the other room for a lie down.'

Arthur, who had switched his allegiance from Henty to one of Nat Gould's racing novels, was contemptuous of a male who condescended to help with women's chores.

'Thanks, Bob,' said Meg as they attacked the huge stacks of dirty dishes. 'Nice of you to give up your afternoon rest to help me.'

'Why shouldn't I? I'm not tired.'

'You'll get sleepy, though. Every male in this house has a nap on Sunday afternoon until milking-time. You'll get as bad as the rest.'

'I don't know. I think I'd rather talk. This seems about the only chance I'll have. Your dad's conversation is a bit above my head.'

'You'll pick it up. Then you'll be as keen as they are. Nothing but farm, farm, farm. The women don't get a look-in while the men are in the house. How are you settling down—on the farm I mean? Do you like it here, Bob?'

'Not half!' His enthusiasm made her laugh. It was the first time he had seen her so relaxed.

'I say, Meg, do we have to join 'em in the sitting-room now we've finished the washing-up.'

'No, let's stay out here—it's warmer anyway, with the stove. You have dad's chair, and I'll take mum's. Why do you like it so much here? It seems pretty ordinary to me.'

'I like the whole feel of the place, and I like your family. Your father's a fair man to work for, and he makes it interesting. Sam's the same too—he will have things done exactly as he says, though. For his age, Arthur knows an awful lot about farming. Your mother's lovely, thoughtful and all that. And you . . .' he paused.

'Well, what about me?'

'You . . . oh well, you're just you, Meg,' and then added lamely, 'When you're older you'll be just as beautiful and nice as your mother.'

'Huh! That's fairly safe to say, Bob Felton. A girl *is* more likely to resemble her mother than anyone else. You're right, though, about Mum. She's kind and has a knack of making you think your opinions matter. She can be stubborn, though. You can't allus get round her. If she puts her foot down it stays down. Even dad realises that.

'I'm fond of dad too, you know. He's always been good to us. He's one of the best. A bit short-tempered sometimes and blows off steam but then he's the boss, and no one takes too much notice of his explosions. Sam thinks he ought to be on the same footing. He's far too bossy, as if the farm were his already. I get very cross when he orders me about. Of course, we all love Arthur. He's the baby of the family. Dad and mum have their work cut out to stop spoiling him.'

Bob could not help thinking that she was also a strong candidate for spoiling, not only by her parents but by her elder brother, in spite of his masterful ways. It was all so different from his own crowded childhood, as he tried to explain to Meg.

'The living quarters were so small. The whole front of the house was taken up by the shop, so we had to live in the kitchen and scullery–all six of us. The shop was always open, so you couldn't settle down to anything–somebody would always be getting up to attend to a customer. My mother worked hard, but what with the large family and the shop, she never seemed to catch up. My father was always complaining–nobody seemed able to do enough for him. Just the way he'd got into, I s'pose. The business took all his time. He was always making grand plans to expand, but never carried them out. Us kids were on top of each other all the time, so there was a lot of squabbling. That's why I notice the peace here. Our kids at home'll be glad of the extra room now that the biggest bird has flown. I don't think that I ever want to go back to Mill Hill. I'd like to think of this as my home now.'

'Farm lads do change their jobs sometimes,' warned Meg, feeling that for his own sake she ought not to let him think that he was an absolute permanency.

'I won't change mine unless I have to. This is a grand place and I like it here!'

'I like it, but then I was born here, in this very house, and I don't suppose I'll leave until I get married. Dad and mum came here when they were newly-married–straight from the church, mum told me–and I expect they'll stay here the rest of their lives. It suits us–it's a good farm, a decent landlord, and we know everyone in the village. Not that anything very exciting ever happens in Hartnall–only the Sunday School treat, the Squire's garden party and the school concert, the Hunt ball and the Point-to-Point. This year we'll have the Coronation fete as well.'

'Won't it interfere with haymaking?'

'Bob Felton, you're as bad as dad and Sam. Haymaking can take a back seat for one day.'

'It must be grand to actually take part in making the hay. I've never done any you know.'

'You can get fed up with haymaking, the same as anything else. Especially when we have a wet day or two, just when it's fit for carrying. Plenty of bad tempers about then, I can tell you. Dad sometimes keeps one or two at haymaking right through the evening, and the others have to do the milking on their own.'

'Oh, yes, milking. I say, Meg, do you think you could tell me how to milk, so that I could surprise your father and Sam. I feel such a fool not being able to do anything without being shown how.'

'*Tell* you how to milk? I never heard of anybody being *told*! It's a job you have to learn by practice. Once you've learnt, you never forget though. I suppose there are some points about it could be explained. Nobody ever explained it to me, though. I had to work it out for myself.'

'Have you done much milking, Meg?'

'Enough to milk a cow fairly quickly. When I was about eleven, Dad broke his leg, and it was an awful long time getting better. We hadn't anybody living in the house then, and Ernie was ill at the same time–jaundice or something. So Sam tried to keep up with the field-work and mum and I did the milking with a bit of help from the neighbours. It was very difficult. I didn't miss much school either. But at the end of the three months I was a fair milker.'

'Can you tell me something that would help?'

'I don't see why not. Most people, when they start make the mistake of squeezing the whole teat. I did, and so will you.'

'Is that wrong, then?'

'Yes, of course. A cow's teat is like a hollow tube with a hole at each end but at one end the hole is bigger. Now what would happen if you squeezed a tube full of liquid?'

'The liquid would spurt out at both ends!'

'Yes, but most would come out of the biggest hole. In a cow's teat, the biggest hole is where the teat joins the bag. So if you just squeeze the teat you simply send the milk back up into the bag. Can you understand that?'

'Yes, I suppose so.'

'What you've got to do, then, is trap the milk in the teat and hold it there before you try to force it out at the smallest end. You do this by pinching the top of the teat with the thumb and fore-fingers. Then squeeze the rest of the teat with your other fingers, work downwards, and milk is bound to come out. Give me your finger and I'll show you. I squeeze the bottom of your finger tightly with my first finger and thumb to cut off the circulation, and then squeeze the rest of the finger with my middle, third and little finger. You get into the habit of doing it quickly and no one can tell by looking that you are doing it that way. And the cow doesn't "let her milk down" straight away. It takes her half-a-minute or so to realise that you are going to relieve her of her load, so no one can draw a strong squirt of milk at once, unless the cow's running it. Some do that because they've got weak valves or something.'

'And is that all there is to it?'

'There's a lot more really. Sitting at the cow, for instance. You've got to set your stool so that your body's at the right angle. Men, when they're milking, stick their heads into the cow's flank. The pressure stops the cow from kicking. When she lifts her foot to kick, and she nearly always does so the side you're milking, the weight of your head in her flank will push her off balance. When she feels herself going she'll put her foot down again quickly to steady herself. Also if the cow tenses her muscles to kick, you can sense it within your head and neck. This gives you time to get your forearm down to stop her putting her foot in the bucket. It's easier for men than women, because they have short hair. They can put on an old cap and push into the cow's flank, muck and all, as hard as they like. But women don't like to do that, not even if we wear a bonnet, because your hair soon begins to smell cowy. All the soap in the world won't take that cowy smell away at one washing.

'Course, there are some cows you can't stop from kicking. They'll kick with temper and fright, and knock you sprawling into the grip. But you're not likely to be milking a cow as rough as that for a long time.

'First-calf heifers can be troublesome when they first come into the shed. They're not used to handling, you see, and have to be trained to it. I say, don't go to sleep, Bob, when I'm talking to you. Just like a boy. As soon as he's got the knowledge he wants, he just nods off, leaving me talking to an empty room. He might as well have gone to sleep in the other room with dad and Sam. Wake up, Bob you little sleepy-head! Oh . . .'

Her exasperation petered out in a sigh when she realised that he was too deeply asleep to hear or care.

At half-past three Mr Ratcliffe opened his eyes, got up from his armchair and stretched luxuriously, then walked out into the kitchen in his stockinged feet, Sam following. He stopped and stared in amused surprise.

'Well, I'm damned, look at this, Sam—Bob and Meg sound asleep each side o' kitchen fire. I suppose the front room wasn't good enough for 'em. Hanged if they don't look like the babes in the wood, curled over in those wooden chairs.'

'Don't look much like babes to me,' said Sam, 'I never heard a babe snore like Bob. Come on, Bob, wake up and get these cows fed. Let Meg sleep on, dad. She'll be mad when she wakes up and finds us all gone.'

Bob heard as he struggled sleepily to his feet. He dallied over putting on his boots, and when the other two had gone, walked over to the sleeping girl. He tenderly straightened the flaxen head from its drooping position, gently shook the shoulder, let his hand rest a moment on the soft upper-arm, then hurried out as the girl stirred.

Chapter Five

As the raw dampness of February gave way to the blustering winds of March, work took on a new urgency at the farm. The winter routine was hard and laborious but now, with the spring cultivations in addition, it seemed a feverish race against time. Sam did not help with the milking these busy days, but went out at seven o'clock with his two horses to make the most of the dry weather.

Bob learned to drive Major as he hauled the fertiliser-distributor applying phosphates before drilling. Major was a fast horse, and the farmer felt that the sixteen-year-old had a better chance of keeping up than middle-aged Ernie, who was content to take over the yard-work. He helped Bob load the twelve-stone bags on to the dray, and then the youth walked behind the wide distributor, driving Major with a pair of Sam's old plough-lines, and watching the grey dust fall out from underneath the long box. He stumbled as he was dragged at a brisk walking pace over the cloddy fields. His feet ached and burned by milking-time, but he still enjoyed the work. Sam, who was usually in the same field, kept a watchful eye on him, and noted with approval the energy and keenness of his young helper. On the coldest days, Meg would arrive in the field at about eleven o'clock carrying a steaming can of cocoa or tea, and sometimes a slice of her own home-made cake. She always stayed while they paused for refreshment, tolerating both the teasing of her brother and Bob's silent admiration. It was an example of the family team-work cleverly fostered by the farmer. On chilly days, and even with the cutting wind, Bob managed to keep warm while he was striding after the energetic Major; but when he drove Bluebell to the station after tea he was glad of the railwayman's overcoat which Mrs Ratcliffe had brought him from Derby.

Sam confided to his father that he was very pleased with Bob's work on the land, and frequently returned to the subject nearest his heart.

'I tell you, dad,' he would say as they sat round the glowing range after tea, 'We need another little hoss—light enough so that he could run the milk in quick time, but heavy enough to make a pair with Major, at a pinch. Bob could use 'em, sometimes harrowing a field in front of the drill or behind it. It'd give me more time for the heavier jobs.'

'That's all very well, Sam, but I'm not sure we've got enough work for another hoss—certainly not in the winter, when they lie in, and that's when the stable work is. Doesn't matter so much in the summer when they're at grass–we can always use another hoss then for the hay and corn harvest. And what will Bluebell do to earn her keep if we get another lightish hoss for the milk? We don't need a trap hoss regularly–once a week to Derby and less often to Burton.'

'Mum and I could use her for shopping or to go visiting in the village,' suggested Meg brightly.

'Oh, very nice, Miss! I'm likely to buy a new hoss so as you two can go gallivanting with the old 'un. And who's to drive Bluebell on such jaunts? I wouldn't trust her with either of you!'

'Thank you very much, Farmer Ratcliffe,' said his wife tartly. 'I can remember the time when you were only too pleased for me to drive the milk to the station. And us not long married! For a few days you insisted I went with you to the station, because you couldn't bear to let me out of your sight . . .'

'Nonsense, Maggie! Why, I never heard of such an idea!'

'Oh yes, you did! But when you found that I could drive old Nobby as well as you, you let me take the milk myself quite a few times while you were busy with the spring drilling. We used to fill the churns three-parts full so they weren't so heavy for me. And that artful, jibbing old Nobby was harder to drive than Bluebell.'

'I don't recall it at all,' said Mr Ratcliffe untruthfully. At that moment the milk float with its load of empty churns rattled by the kitchen window, and he had an excuse to change the subject. 'Here's Bob and Arthur back now. I wonder if they've brought that bag o' grass seed.' Ten minutes later the lads came in, Bob carrying a small sack which he left in the scullery, and Arthur clutching a square box which he gave to his mother. 'Here's your tea, Mum.'

'Ah, I have been waiting for that. One-and-eight a pound for a fourteen-pound box from Garston's o' Glasgow is better than paying one-and-ten a pound in Derby–and better tea, too.'

'Never mind about the tea. What about this extra hoss?' asked Mr Ratcliffe, much to everyone's surprise.

'Another hoss? That's the stuff,' said Arthur enthusiastically. 'Can I have it? I could do a lot at week-ends!'

He was ignored. Bob sat down thankfully by the fire–he was tired and chilled. He looked across at his employer with a forced interest.

'Come on, Bob, you're in this,' said Mr Ratcliffe. 'Sam's trying to persuade me to buy another hoss to do the milk run instead of Bluebell–and other work, of course.'

'What–not use Bluebell for the station work? I shouldn't like that. I love driving her. What do we want another milk hoss for?'

'Shut up, Bob,' said Sam. 'You're not helping at all. Here's me trying to persuade the gaffer to buy another tit for the farm, and you're not backing me up.'

'It's not that I'm against it,' Bob said hastily. 'But I didn't want to stop using Bluebell.'

He realised that an extra horse would be an advantage for the field-work. He longed to drive a pair, and thought it unlikely that he would ever achieve this unless there were four field-horses, as Sam was jealous of his rights.

'I daresay we could use another horse at this time of the year. Don't know about the winter, though. We seemed to be able to manage with three then. I suppose you could get one now, see how things go, and if it's not wanted, sell it again in the autumn.'

'Never mind about selling it again . . .' protested Sam, but his father interrupted.

'I think that's a good idea to work from. I daresay I can just about afford another hoss. Where's that *Farmer & Stock-breeder*?'

He found that he was sitting on it and dragged it out from beneath him, slightly dish-shaped.

'Ha, here it is. Well, I'm blowed! The sales are this week! Today's Wednesday, isn't it? They start today and carry on tomorrow and Friday. Well, I'm not going at such short notice, and that's it!'

'There's another sale in a fortnight,' Sam pointed out. 'Not so big, but there'll be a good few there—and cheaper maybe, as it's not such a big sale.'

'Trust you to 'a spotted that,' his father grunted. 'All right! I'll go to Crewe on Friday the twenty-sixth and buy a lightish vanner, God willing—and providing we're well up with the work.'

It was an important decision and excited all the members of the household. Sam was pleased because he had unexpectedly achieved what he had been pressing for. Bob could not help being interested because it seemed that the new horse would be mainly for his use. Arthur was thrilled, because he assumed that the more horses there were on the farm, the greater would be his chance of driving one of them. Mrs Ratcliffe felt that anything which kept her menfolk happy must be a good idea while Meg was of the private opinion that another horse on the place would add to their standing in the village.

But their hopes were set back the next morning when Ernie did not turn up for milking. Bob was feeding the first shed when Mrs Wagstaff hurried in. He heard her tell the farmer that her husband had suffered awful stomach pains in the night and was worn out. Could Arthur take a letter to the doctor on his way to school?

'Well, that's a blow. But you can't help it, Mrs Wagstaff. Thanks for coming over. Yes, Arthur'll take a message to the doctor, and it'll have to be a letter, because he can't wait to speak to Dr Warburton. Let us know how Ernie gets on.' As the woman hurried away he added to Sam, 'If Ernie's going to be away, Arthur'll have to get up an hour earlier and milk a cow or two before he goes to school. Can't afford to get too far behind at this time of the year. Bob. . .' he raised his voice so that it could be heard all down the long cowshed. 'Get that first feeding done quickly and then come round here and start milking; Ernie's not comin'. It's about time you started, anyway.'

The boy needed no second bidding. He practically ran up and down the feeding-passages with the trucks of chop, his hobnailed boots striking sparks from the concrete floor as he slithered about. When he carried up the first load of milk and set the cooler running Meg came out of the scullery, and he told her the great news.

'If you're going to start milking you'll need to wear a slop, or you'll get milk all over your knees and reek for evermore like the other farm lads. There's an old one of Sam's in the cellar. I'll get it for you.'

She brought him an old buff coat, rather ragged and without buttons. He donned it with a doubtful pride, tied it round his waist with string, and hurried back into the top shed.

'Don't forget what I told you,' Meg called after him.

Mr Ratcliffe had just sat down to the last cow and Sam was about to leave for the lower shed. 'Get Ernie's stool and come with me, Bob, or you can use one o' the spare stools over the beam, there.'

'Let him have a go at old Darby first, Sam,' called out the master as they departed. 'She's about the easiest thing down there.'

'Sit down and get stuck in Bob,' Sam said as they stood behind an old red cow. 'Turn your cap back to front first, or the peak'll stop you from putting your full weight into her flank. That helps to keep her still, and you to keep your position. You've se'n us do it enough times.'

Bob did as he was told, putting his ankles together, lodging the base of the bucket on them, and gripping the top with his knees. He pushed his head into the cow's flank, turning it sideways to face the cow's rear as he had seen the others do. Then another thought occurred to him, he swivelled his stool to swing the open bucket from beneath the cow, and lightly massaged her udder to remove the straw and dust which would otherwise have dropped into the milk.

'Been keeping your eyes open, I see,' Sam said with grudging approval.

Bob drew his hand gently two or three times down each teat, and suddenly felt them swell with milk. The cow was letting her milk down exactly as described by Meg. Concentrating on her instructions, he gripped the upper end of the teat tightly with thumb and forefinger, his left hand on the nearer front teat, his right on the further. Then he squeezed firmly with his other three fingers in quick succession. A great stream of hot milk issued from each of the two teats in turn, striking the bottom of the bucket with a resounding, long-drawn-out ring.

Sam stared wide-eyed, with his head pushed slightly forward.

'Dad! Bob's been having us on. He nigh knocked the bottom out o' the bucket with his first stream!'

Bob managed to finish milking his first cow with a respectable amount of froth on the surface—in itself an achievement, he was told. But he could not at once master the rhythmn of continuous rapid milking; the strain on his fingers and wrists sometimes seemed too great. And he was not confident of his vulnerable position under the cow's flank. Even when he began to feel he could control the mobility of the cow he was milking, he remained nervous of her stall-mate looming large behind him. She might step across suddenly and send him sprawling.

For the rest of the week Arthur got up with the other three and milked a few cows before preparing for school. Bob milked his own three—Darby, Cocky and Spot—in between feeding the cows, and Meg took over the cooling of the milk.

Sam was worried that Ernie's absence would prevent the visit of his father to Crewe. But to his relief Ernie returned to work the following Monday.

Bob continued to milk a few cows in the morning to allow Sam to get out earlier with his horses. Mr Ratcliffe and Ernie concentrated on the yard-work, which now included lambing, while Bob spent his days driving Major on the dusty arable fields. This strenuous use of his limbs gave him an enormous appetite, and although he ate a huge breakfast he still looked forward to Meg's appearance at eleven with a hot drink and snack. But during lambing Meg was often called on to assist with the ewes, and was sometimes unable to visit the horse-men. Bob was depressed on such days and Sam short-tempered, but of course they did not complain, for help to the ewes was more important than trips to the field for their well-being.

The last two fields were successfully drilled in dry conditions—'perfect' according to Sam—before the rain set in. Seeing the clouds thickening, Sam and Bob worked late in the evening to finish sowing the Sevenacres. Mr Ratcliffe and Ernie had been left to do the afternoon milking on their own, so the evening meal was very late, and Bob had to hustle Bluebell to catch the milk train. He returned very weary—his limbs aching and his feet tingling. Major had seemed in an exceptional hurry that day. Bob nodded off as soon as he sat down, but Mr Ratcliffe, who had been studying time-tables since tea, broke into the boy's slumber.

'If you're as tired as that, Bob, you'd better get off to bed. I shall want you up at half-past four in the morning!'

'What?'

'Yes, you'd certainly better go to bed now. I want to leave here at five o'clock tomorrow morning to catch a train from Burton at five-fifty. You'll come with me and bring Bluebell back. It's a slow journey to Crewe from here—change at Utoxeter and Stoke apparently—that's why I must start early. I'll call you, so don't try and keep awake, or you'll only have a broken night and be fit for nowt tomorrow.'

Not much fear of a broken night, thought Bob as he dragged his weary body upstairs, threw off his clothes, and slumped into bed. He was asleep as soon as his head touched the pillow, and woke to find his master standing over him with a candle in the otherwise pitch dark March morning.

'Get up, now, Bob. Slip down and give Bluebell half a feed then come back for tea and sandwiches. When you've had a snack, harness up the mare and have her here with the trap, while I get washed and shaved.'

When Bob returned after a hurried visit to the stable he found Meg in the kitchen wearing her heavy boots and a thick coat.

'What on earth are you doing up at this hour?'

'Well, I'm not letting you go to Burton on an empty stomach. It might be nearly seven when you get back, and with dad away the milking will be late finishing. It could be nine before you get your breakfast. Knowing your appetite, I doubt if you'd survive until then. If there are any sandwiches left over when dad's had his, take 'em with you.

'Secondly, there are three or four more ewes to lamb. I'm just going out to look at them, so I'll borrow that lantern if you don't mind.'

'Will you be all right out there alone in the dark? I'll come out with you if you like!'

'Don't you be so silly, Bob Felton! Look after your own work. You get Bluebell and the trap up here as soon as you can. If dad misses that train, your life won't be worth living for a day or two—nor ours!'

Bob took the hint; he cooled the tea by swamping it with

milk, swallowed it as quickly as he could, bolted a couple of sandwiches, and took a third with him as he hurried down to the stable. He harnessed the mare, put her in to the trap, and halted her by the kitchen door just as his employer emerged, looking smart and affluent, in his heavy coat, pork-pie hat and walking-stick.

'Get your coat, Bob, it's just starting to rain. Otherwise you'll be wet through when you get back. Take the cart lamps in with you and light 'em at the same time.'

Mr Ratcliffe took the reins and with Bob beside him drove off into the gloomy darkness. The boy admired the master's driving skill. He appeared to make no movement with his hands, but the mare trotted on swiftly under complete control.

'I really don't know why I'm going all this way to buy a blooming hoss, Bob. Three or four hours each way in a slow train! It's hardly wuth it. We've managed well enough so far, and it'll be another mouth to feed. But Sam wants it and he's a good lad. When you've got keen chaps, it's worth doing it their way sometimes. In fact this new hoss won't be for Sam's use, but for yours. It'll be your hoss more than his. What do you think about that?'

'I don't know, Mr Ratcliffe. I hope you're not buying it entirely on my account. Sam knows what he wants, but I don't know that I do. This time next year, I might know perhaps.'

'That's all right, Bob, I was just trying you out. An extra hoss is not a bad thing. One o' the others might get lame or spring a sore shoulder. A spare hoss comes in handy at such times.'

'If you get one, will he come home today?'

'Not quite sure about that, lad. *If* I can get a hoss-box straight away, and they can hook it on my train, then I'll come home with it. I hope that can be arranged. It'll be getting late o' course—there'll be a lot of hosses leaving Crewe by train to-night. I'm not likely to be at Willington before the milk train comes in. Ask the porter if a hoss-box has been notified, and the time of arrival. If there is one, it'll be mine and I'll be in it. So wait for me, and the new hoss can trot home behind the milk float. I don't know, though! Better bring Sam with you, and the riding saddle and bridle. He can ride the hoss back home. That'll please him! If I can't get the hoss on a train today, or if I don't buy one, I'll send a telegram saying what time I'll arrive at Willington. In that case bring the milk as early as you can to save me waiting over-long. Come to think of it, I might send a telegram either way. It'll only cost sixpence.'

Streaks of grey were showing through the darkness as they neared the village of Newton Solney. They could just see the winding course of the Trent gleaming far below them on their right. On reaching the outskirts of the town they turned right and crossed the long narrow bridge over the river. Bob was struck by the cloying, heavy smell of the town. The tang of hops and of roasting malt seemed to be everywhere. There was little traffic to be seen other than an early tram-car as Mr Ratcliffe swung the mare left-ward into the High Street. Bluebell's footsteps sounded strangely subdued as they thudded on the surface of wooden blocks. The trap gave a sharp lurch every time they moved, in or out of the tramway, as the lines could only be crossed safely at a fairly sharp angle. They turned into Station Street and Bluebell trotted gaily up the incline to the station.

There were several cabs there, and Bob noted with satisfaction that no horse was as lively as Bluebell, in spite of her seven-mile run at top speed.

Mr Ratcliffe handed him the reins and climbed heavily down.

'Here you are, Bob. I'm in plenty of time. Get off back right away. There's plenty of work waiting for you at Oakleigh. Don't push the mare, though. Let her take her own time. You can find the way back. Turn left at the High Street, right into Horninglow Street, over the bridge and then left into Newton. I'll see you at Willington later tonight.'

Driving Bluebell through the awakening streets of Burton in the best spring cart, aroused a lordly feeling in the youth. The solid rubber rims on the wheels were silent in comparison with the grinding noise of the iron-tyred milk-float. This is the life, he decided, as he bowled along the Newton road. It was by now almost full daylight. There was evidence of spring everywhere. The willow trees along the banks were breaking into pale-green buds, and some of the early catkins dangled their gold and green flowers. Hedge-row birds darted here and there for nest-building material. The damp spell had brought a warmer air, and even the grass seemed poised to start growing again.

Bob began to feel hungry and wished he had brought the remaining sandwiches. He was sure that Meg would have something to say about his leaving them. She was getting rather bossy, he decided, but he didn't really mind.

Meg was inspecting the ewes in the field by the farmyard entrance. She took her work as shepherd seriously. From the trap seat, Bob waved joyfully. She returned his greeting. Sam spotted this exchange from the stable. He commented on it, teasingly, at a belated breakfast.

Meg started to blush, then said quickly, 'I wasn't waving, I was shaking my fist!'

'Well, I don't know. Whatever for, girl?' asked her mother.

'He didn't take the sandwiches I put for him, and now he's

nearly starving. Serve him right!'

'They were reight good sandwiches, Meg,' said Sam. 'I cleared 'em up when I came down. Thought they were for me! Reckoned you'd decided to turn over a new leaf and look after your brother better!'

Bob was too busy satisfying his hunger to join in. Mrs Ratcliffe was secretly delighted at the pleasant camaraderie which existed in her household, although all she said was, 'Sometimes I wonder if you're ever going to grow up.'

There was great excitement during the afternoon milking when a telegraph boy turned up at the farmhouse on his red bicycle. Mrs Ratcliffe sent Meg down to the shed with the message.

'Here you are, lads, dad's order. "Arriving Willington seven ten with horse."'

'Good, I'm going,' said Arthur at once.

'Oh no you're not,' replied Sam. 'With Bob and me and the saddle in th' float, to say nowt about th' milk, there'll be no room for thee!'

While Bob and Sam were unloading the milk, the train drew into the station, the horse-box hitched behind the guard's van. Sam left Bob to collect the empty churns and hurried on to the platform. As Bob drove Bluebell round to the wicket gate which separated the platform from the station approach, Sam led the horse out of the dark vehicle. The new arrival looked magnificent. Glossy black, except for a dash of white between the eyes; half-a-hand taller than Bluebell, with proportionately stronger legs and heavier body, he was exactly what Sam had hoped for. The horse's eyes were bright, intelligent but restless; he seemed unwilling to stand still, trying to move on as Sam held him, and fidgeting when he was restrained.

Sam whistled. 'By gum, Dad, you've picked a reight 'un. This is about the showiest hoss I've seen. Hope he's as good as he looks.'

'That's what we've got to find out, Sam. But he cost a pretty penny—sixty guineas. Still, I liked the look of him and determined to have him. What do you think, Bob?'

But Sam was examining the horse's mouth.

'Why, Dad, he's only a three-year-old! What possessed you to get a hoss as young as that. He won't do for Bob to run the milk with for a while. He wunt stand unless Arthur goes with him every neight to hold his head.'

'We don't know that he won't stand, Sam.. He's only just broken in, mind. Perhaps he'll come to the work quicker than you think. You might have to use him on the farm for a bit until he gets quiet and safe. Anyway, a three-year-old'll grow into money for a year or two. He'll be wuth more at six than he cost me today. I didn't intend to buy such a young hoss, but once I'd seen this one I couldn't let him pass. Anyway, put the saddle on him and get him home. I'm going with Bob in the float. I shan't be sorry to get there, either. I've had a tiring day.'

He climbed into the float as Bob dragged out the saddle and threw it over the back of the black horse, then held his head while Sam adjusted the saddle to his liking.

'Come on, Bob, let's get off. Sam can follow at his own pace,' said the boss impatiently, and moved Bluebell on as Bob clambered over the backboard.

'Well, what do you think of him, Bob?' asked Mr Ratcliffe, when they were on their way.

'Er—he certainly looks grand, Mr Ratcliffe. He's so smart and so black that he'd be good enough for a top-class funeral.'

'Hell, that's a cheerful thought I must say. This hoss is supposed to be for you to work, and I wasn't aiming to set you up in the undertaking business. But what do you think we should call him?'

Bob thought hard for a few moments.

'I think perhaps we ought to wait until Meg and Mrs Ratcliffe have seen him. Perhaps they'll have some ideas on that, as well as Sam and Arthur.'

'You're a tactful lad, Bob. That's a good idea. Make it a family decision, eh? No harm in that, and it'll help to keep everybody sweet and interested. Sam's a fair way behind us now, I should think. He won't push that three-year-old at the same pace as Bluebell.'

At the farm, Bob quickly unloaded the churns, and had stripped Bluebell when Sam arrived and jumped down stiffly at the stable door. He led his mount into one of the empty stalls and removed the saddle, by which time the whole family were in the stable admiring the master's purchase.

'He's got plenty of energy,' was Sam's verdict. 'But he tends to like his own way too much.'

'He's just right for you, then Sam,' was Meg's instant rejoinder, 'You two'll make a good pair!'

Sam ignored this and walked from the horse's head, passing the palm of his hand over the horse's back as he did so. Bob stepped in close to examine the horse from behind. Meg pulled him back.

'Bob Felton, don't you know better than to stand close up to the heels of a strange horse? If he's a kicker, and you don't know he isn't, he'd send you across the stable and break all your bones!'

'That's it, Meg, tell him off,' said her father. 'By gum, lad, you said this hoss'd be reight for a funeral, but you don't want it to be your own, I reckon? Never stand close behind *any* hoss, strange or otherwise. Now, I'm pleased with what I bought today, but he's got to have a name. Anybody got ideas?'

After a moment or two of deep thought, Mrs Ratcliffe suggested 'Darkie'; Meg thought 'Black Beauty' would be ideal, and Arthur offered 'Captain' because, he said, he was to be a junior assistant to Major.

'What do you think Bob?' asked the farmer.

'Why not Diamond? That white patch on his face is shaped exactly like a diamond and his glossy coat shines like one, too.'

'It wun't shine like that for long when he gets to reg'lar work,' grunted Sam. 'And Diamond is about the most common name for a farm hoss there is. But it suits the hoss and it suits me.'

'Me too,' said his father. 'So Diamond it is.'

Meg tossed her head slightly, but made no comment.

It soon became clear that Diamond was not sufficiently reliable for float work. Unless someone stood with him all the time, he had a habit of wandering off whenever he felt like it. This would have been disastrous if he had decided to move just as the heavy milk churns were being lifted out. So to begin with he was used for a few carting jobs round the farm where there was always someone to hold his head. Mr Ratcliffe and Sam decided that some field work might quieten him down by sapping his energy, and Bob to his great delight used him as one of a pair with Major, first for chain-harrowing the hay fields, and then for rolling the cornfields with the heavy segmented Cambridge roll. Diamond was half-a-hand smaller than Major, and as a pair they were so unequal that Meg referred to them as 'Dot-and-carry-one'. Nevertheless Bob was proud to be entrusted with them, and as he plodded along behind the roller, he felt himself to be king of the field.

Diamond certainly began to learn restraint. He had to since he was attached to Major, and the larger better-trained horse declined to budge, preferring to conserve his energies for the rapid walk from one side of the field to the other, when Diamond had almost to trot to keep up.

Bob also used his rolling team to help work down the fourteen-acre field for the root crops, which included five acres of potatoes. Several times he rolled and harrowed the clods until the soil was fine enough for Sam to draw up the ridges, straight and true in the friable tilth. This took them till the middle of April, by which time the weather had become warm.

Chapter Six

During the damp weather earlier in the month, Bob and Ernie had mixed up the fertiliser for the potatoes. Bob was now sent to apply this to the potato ridges prior to planting. He thought potatoes could not fail to do well in such admirably-prepared soil, and mentioned this to Mr Ratcliffe the following morning at breakfast.

'You're right, Bob. Potatoes always pay well for good treatment. Glad to see you're taking an interest in 'em. But you might've had enough of 'em by the end of this week. Ever planted any field potatoes? No, of course you haven't! Now, I want you and Meg to set that five acres between you, starting today. You should do an acre a day between you, given good weather. Meg likes potato-setting. She's a dab hand at it and will show you how.'

'Yes, you'll be working for me this week, young Bob. So you'll jolly well have to pull your socks up!'

'Take a ton of seed with Major,' Mr Ratcliffe continued. 'That will plant an acre, which in that field is forty ridges, so your twenty bags should be set out accordingly. Meg'll show you. Sam'll be working in the same field getting the ground ready for the mangold and cabbage, and he'll come over and cover your potatoes every afternoon.'

Bob quickly harnessed Major, and loaded the potatoes from the Dutch barn. Meg met him at the gate, carrying two old buckets. She climbed tom-boyishly on top of the load, leaving Bob to lead Major and open up the three gates leading to the road, for the potato-field was one of the furthest from the farmstead.

'It'll take three buckets to plant a row this length,' she said knowledgeably, 'which means we'll have to fill up at each end and twice going across the field. So drop three bags at the top and bottom, seven bags about a third of the way down, and the other seven two-thirds of the way down. And don't laugh at me,' she added, as Bob chuckled at her precise instructions. He unloaded the potatoes, secured Major to a rail in the hedge, and presented himself to her.

'Now, Miss, what do we do next?'

She blushed slightly and glanced away.

'Well, the first thing is to fill the buckets with seed; but as I've already done that we can start. The spuds have to be placed in the bottom of the furrow a little bit over a foot apart. So drop each seed just in front of your front foot as you go along. And don't try to plant potatoes from a standing position—it takes longer, and they roll out of place. Get right down and put the potato in place. It can be back-aching, but your bucket gets lighter all the time. Hold your bucket in your left hand and plant with your right—like this.

She snatched a handful of seed potatoes from her bucket and darted forward in three little steps, depositing a potato with each bobbing movement. Bob followed suit, and found the job easy once he had fallen into a rhythm. The continuous bending caused some aching of the back muscles. At the end of the row Meg calmly sat on her bucket after refilling it, and motioned Bob to do the same.

'We don't have to bend double and stand on our heads all morning. We're entitled to a short rest at each end of the field. At least, I say we are, and I'm in charge of the job.'

Bob quickly became adept. He found he had two advantages over the girl. His breeches and leggings were less restricting for walking in the narrow ridges than Meg's ankle-length skirt. In addition, his hands were larger, so that he could grab five potatoes instead of three; the pauses while the hand was filled were fewer in his case. He forged ahead, not noticing he was leaving Meg yards behind.

'Bob Felton, you keep back here. What do you think you're doing right up ahead like that? I'm supposed to be teaching you to set potatoes not the other way about!'

'All right. But I'll plant a few in your row now and again to help.'

'You'll do no such thing. Sam'd be sure to notice, and I'd never hear the last of it. You put the brake on, and don't shoot ahead in that way. It's bad manners to turn your back on a lady! You keep back beside me and then I can talk to you if I want to.'

'Anything you say, Meg. What do you want to talk about?'

'All sorts of things—the Coronation mostly, though. It's only a few weeks away, and there's hardly anything ready except half the bonfire.'

'I don't suppose the King will notice!'

'It's not the King I'm thinking of, it's us! We want to have a real good time. We don't often have a chance in the country. I can hardly remember the last Coronation. I was only seven; same as you, I suppose. We're hoping to have coconut-shies, sports with prizes, and a meal for the children, perhaps a band in the evening for dancing before the bonfire is lit. Can you dance, Bob?'

'No! I never had a chance to learn. Will you teach me, Meg?'

'Of course I will, silly! Not by Coronation day, though, there won't be time for you to pick it up. But during the light evenings, if you can turn your thoughts away from the farm for an hour, I'll teach you the steps—probably on the concrete round the muck-hole.'

'That'll be nice. There'll be plenty of flies to keep us company. And in full view of the kitchen window, too!'

'Some people are never satisfied. But we'd better finish this row and get back for dinner. Sam's gone already.'

In the middle of the afternoon Sam brought the two mares and the ridge-plough to split the ridges behind the planters, to bury the newly-set potatoes.

'I was ready to scold you two for the time you've been sitting at the ends. But I see that you've still done more than I thought, so I'm saying nowt. But Bob, you'll just have to keep her at it. These wenches are rare 'uns for wasting time.'

'Sam Ratcliffe, will you please mind your own business and get these potatoes covered in. As a matter of fact, I'm supposed to be boss of this job!'

'Boss?' He reached out a long arm to ruffle her yellow hair. She side-stepped quickly to avoid contact, but stumbled against her bucket, lost her balance, and fell sprawling at Bob's feet. Sam guffawed and moved his team on up the row, while Bob smothered a smile.

'Bob, look what this bullying brother of mine has done. Don't stand grinning! Help me up!'

The weather remained fine and Bob and Meg enjoyed the job in each other's company. But on Friday Meg had to stay in the kitchen to prepare meals while her parents made their weekly trip to Derby. Bob reluctantly went to the potato-field alone.

She returned the following day, and with the unenthusiastic help of Arthur in the afternoon, all the potatoes were planted and covered in, which earned praise from Mr Ratcliffe, as the time taken was slightly less than the five days he had allowed.

'Meg's really taught Bob how to set "taters",' he confided to his wife. 'They certainly work well together as a team.'

'Yes, but I'm not too sure that it's a good thing to throw them together on their own too much. Meg's developing into a fine young woman, and Bob's growing fast too. So he should with the amount of food he eats!'

'Oh, come, Maggie there's no danger. They're only sixteen. More like brother and sister together, although come to think of it, the real brothers and sister in our family are not quite so gentle with each other. Seems to me they're always giving one another a sly dig—when they're not actually rowing. Anyway, Meg doesn't work on the farm often enough to make it a problem. We don't want her to be too much of an Amazon, although it is reassuring to know that she can turn her hand to most things at a pinch.'

The next important change in farm routine was turning the cattle out to grass. The warm weather in April had made the grass grow fast and in the first week in May Mr Ratcliffe said the time had come for the cows to lie out. There was still some hay left in the barn, and Bob asked the farmer why he did not keep the cows in until all this had been eaten, leaving the barn empty for the new crop.

'That'd never do, Lad. We must have a bit in hand for the hosses who need a bit cut into chop every day they're at work. And they mustn't have new hay, so we keep enough of the old crop back to last until Michaelmas at least. So the cows must go to grass as soon as there's enough there to keep 'em going, and I reckon that's now.'

The cows slouched to the gate leading to the pond enclosure which they had used twice every day for six months. Finding it closed, the foremost cows paused as if surprised, and waited patiently for it to be opened. Those following found no room to wait at the closed gate, and wandered to the right, up the concrete alley by the muck-hole towards the main yard entrance. To the left was another gate leading to West Pasture, closed all the winter. Finding it open, the leading cow stopped in astonishment, looked in both directions to see if anyone was watching, then stepped cautiously forward. She increased her pace, edged her front feet through the gate, stood still again for a moment, then jumped high into the air, kicked her hindlegs sideways and raced into the field, tail in the air. Other cows followed, slowly at first, then madly. They stampeded into the deep grass, bawling, snorting, and jumping in ecstasy. The cows still in the shed bawled frantically in reply, snatched at their chains, and jerked sharply backwards to free themselves, as if they thought they were to be left out of the picnic. Mrs Ratcliffe and Meg came out into the yard to watch for, as the mistress said, 'When grass-day comes, you know you've definitely left winter behind.'

'Yes, that's true,' said her husband 'And while you're out here, you can help steer these bullocks through the yard out on to the drive, so that we can take them to the first river meadow. Meg, you go down to the village road with Bob and guide 'em straight across. Look alive, or they'll be on your heels. Open the drive gates as you go.'

Bob and Meg trotted quickly through the three fields to the road, opened the gate opposite, and stood facing each other on either side of the entrance, to prevent the beasts from hurtling towards Hartnall or Repton. Soon the little crowd of yearlings came scampering down the drive in a cloud of dust and swishing tails. The foremost beasts skidded to a halt when they saw the highway crossing their path, then, pushed on by those at the rear, they trotted sedately across and through the gate opposite. When they felt their feet in the softer ground again, they stretched out their heads and tails and careered madly round the field twice before noticing a gate leading to a second field. They edged through this, gingerly at first, and galloped two more full circuits before bending their heads to sample the rich grass.

Bob and Meg leaned over the gate for a few minutes watching them. 'May's a lovely month,' Meg commented as they turned away. 'Plenty of grass, plenty of buttercups, and, by the river, plenty of May-blobs. In the woods the bluebells and other wild flowers are coming out–when I was little, we used to pick them after Sunday school. And the cows are all away from the buildings, except at milking time. It's going to be different for you from now on, Bob. No chop to mix, no truck-loads of mangolds to push round the mangers–just fetch the cows in from the field, tie 'em up and milk 'em. There'll be more milk, too–for a few weeks anyway. But we don't get paid quite so much for it. Golly, they're here with the heifers already–run down the road Bob and open the second gate on the left and turn 'em in there. I'll stay here and steer them in your direction.'

The heifers were quickly settled into another field by the river bank, and the five drovers walked slowly back to the farm together, Bob and Meg bringing up the rear.

'Going to turn my calves out today, Dad?' she called out to him as they entered the farmyard.

'Sure! Why not? Plenty of keep in the orchard for 'em.'

But Meg's calves refused to be evicted from their cosy little homes into the strange world beyond. Although the farm men pushed vigorously from behind, the calves dug in their little hooves, and would not budge.

'Well I'm blowed,' the master said in mock despair. 'Have we got to carry these things out? Meg, this is all your fault. You've made them too happy here. Bob, what do you suggest? How can we get 'em out easy without upsetting 'em?'

'That's simple. Prop the doors open and go away. They'll come out fast enough if they think they're sneaking out and escaping from us!'

'By gum, you're right, lad. You've got more brains than any of us. We'll do that! Block the end of the alley, and they'll have to go the other way and through the little gate into the orchard. If it takes 'em all morning to make up their minds it won't matter.'

'When these calves have gone out, Bob, you can get all the muck out of the boxes,' said Meg. 'Then I can get them whitewashed ready for the autumn. I want to finish them before the Coronation.'

'I sometimes wonder who's boss on this place,' said her father. 'I'd like Bob to do something for me over the next day or two. I hope you don't mind, Miss Ratcliffe!'

The mangolds were drilled on the ground adjoining the potatoes, fences were repaired here and there, and then Mr Ratcliffe announced an all-out attack on the winter's accumulation of manure in the fold-yards and boxes.

'We want to get it all out and in a heap on the land before we start hoeing and shearing. What's in the muck-hole can stay until we want it–it's not doing any harm there–but three yards and the calf-boxes want cleaning right out so they can sweeten up for the summer. Queen Meg here has specially requested your help in the little boxes, Bob; so you can get cracking on that. It'll all have to be wheeled out with the barrow–that passage is too narrow for the carts. We want to get the job over as quickly as possible–there's always a hell of a stink round the place while it's being shifted.'

The May sun, shining down on the roof of the confined space, made Bob sweat as he dug out the firmly-trodden mass of straw, hay and dung and transferred it to the barrow. He wiped his brow as he saw Meg approaching.

'If you're coming in here Meg, you'd better get a fork and help. I'm not going to stand and talk. It's so blessed hot in these little places that I want to get finished and away.'

'That's enough of that cross talk, Bob. Don't jolly well jump to conclusions. I'm not sure that I want to talk to you now. As you're on such a warm job, I came to see if you'd like a jug of tea which I'm just going to make. Or some home-made lemonade, which is cooling in the cellar.'

'Oh–er–well–in that case–.'

'That's made you sing a different song, hasn't it? But don't let me interrupt you. Don't lean on your fork like that, for goodness' sake–you might miss a forkful or two. Well, I'll fetch you a drink, but you don't deserve it.'

'I think I'll have the lemonade, Meg.'

'You'll have what's brought to you,' she shouted back.

'Bring me a drink, too, Meg,' ordered Sam. 'I don't see why Bob should have it all. And don't hinder him with your chatter.'

'He's just told me that himself. You men are all alike.'

'Good for him! Now what about that drink?'

She disappeared into the kitchen and almost immediately returned with a half-gallon earthenware jug and three mugs.

Ernie was bringing his loaded cart from the fold-yard and paused to share in the refreshment. Bob hastily loaded another barrow and trotted along the passage with it. But Meg did not at once offer him a drink so he returned disconsolately with his empty barrow. But Meg followed, jug in hand.

'Now, Bob, don't look so glum. I hadn't forgotten you! Stand away from that wretched barrow a minute and drink this.' She offered him a pint mug of lemonade which he emptied with great gulps.

'Thanks, Meg. That was lovely, and so are you to bring it out here.'

'I want some help from you Bob, or some suggestions, at least.'

'What about?'

'Don't you sound so suspicious. There's a meeting in the Village Hall tonight about the Coronation celebrations.'

'But that's still weeks away! Twenty-second of June, isn't it?'

'Yes, but we must start planning. Mum is on the general committee and they've roped me in too, along with two or three other girls, to make suggestions for the school-children's entertainment.'

'But I don't know anything about these things!'

'Neither do I. That's why I'm asking!'

'Oh well—how many kids are there?'

'About sixty; all ages.'

'You'll have all the usual races, I suppose—sprinting, sackrace, egg-and-spoon and three-legged race. And the kids'll need dividing into age-groups—not more than ten in any race so most of 'em get prizes. In a do like this I think every kid ought to get a prize as well as a Coronation mug. After the main sports there could be special events for those who haven't won anything. And if there's going to be a meal, it'd better be after the races and not before. They won't want to run on full stomachs.' He thought for a moment 'If you can get a few extra side-shows, so much the better. Coconut shies, Punch-and-Judy, hoop-la and so on. People from other villages might turn up if Hartnall's a bigger show than their own.'

'I'm not sure if we want that. Anyway, thanks Bob. You've given me something to think about. I'll leave you to get on with this muck.'

At supper-time that evening in the cool kitchen Mrs Ratcliffe described the proposed festivities.

'We've decided to have the first tea at five o'clock, that will be for the village school-children and the old people—at different tables of course. Then at six o'clock we'll have our tea—the helpers, I mean. It's to be a good sit-down meal—meat and salad and so on, followed by jellies and cakes.'

'Who's going to provide the money for all this?' enquired Mr Ratcliffe.

'We're taking it for granted that the farmers and tradesmen will pay for most of it. Certainly the butcher has agreed to provide half the meat and the baker will give all the bread, if the cakes are bought from him. The vicar's wife is going to arrange the finances, and organise a collection so that everyone can feel they have helped to pay for it. The Territorials will send their band—I expect Colonel Ratcliffe has had something to do with that—at about seven and they'll play for dancing until the fire is lit. The Boy Scouts will form a sort of guard-of-honour round the fire. You'll be pleased you've joined them Arthur, as they're going to help organize the children's sports.' (Arthur didn't look too sure.) 'There's the question of prizes for the kids, too. They'll get a mug, of course. But Meg insisted that every child should have a prize of some sort, and after a lot of discussion they all agreed with her. So the vicar's wife and the teachers are going to get working on it . . . '

'Yes, and they've co-opted me and Phyllis Bailey to help,' interrupted Meg.

'I'm not at all sure it's a good idea to celebrate this coronation,' interposed Sam.

'Oh, shut up Sam,' cried Meg and Arthur, almost in unison. 'Don't be such a spoil-sport.'

'Well, it's on June 22nd—haymaking time. We don't want to stop just because the government have ordered it to be a public holiday. What do you think, dad?'

'You're worrying unnecessarily, Sam. We don't often start haymaking before that date. There isn't much hay picked up in June you know—not so much as there ought to be, really. July's generally on us before we get into the swing of it. But if the weather's really hot, we can mow a field a day or two before the coronation, and the haymaking and the merry-making can go on at the same time. In any case, farm chaps won't have the day off. There's no compulsion on employers to give their men the day off, although it's a public holiday. They'll finish a bit earlier, like Sunday, and join in the fun after tea, no doubt.'

'What about the grass in the sports field?' asked Sam. 'It'll be pretty long by that time—nearly a hay-crop—much too long for dancing. We can't graze it off with cattle 'cause the droppings would spoil it for the kids' races and the dancers. Their shoes would get in a right state. We can't make hay of it, because the weather can't be guaranteed—we couldn't have the sports events in a field covered with mouldy hay-swaths.'

'Oh, I'd nearly forgotten that, Arnold,' said Mrs Ratcliffe

apologetically. 'That was brought up, and it was decided that as you were the only farmer in the village with sheep, you'd be asked to put 'em in for a while, and see that the grass is at its best for the actual day. I was asked to invite you to do it but I hadn't got round to it.'

'Well, I like that! The most important thing to come out of that meeting and you bring it out casual.' He made a rapid calculation. 'We'll put all the ewes and lambs in immediately after shearing. We can't put 'em in with the wool on 'em—they'd get round the bonfire and leave hanks o' wool dangling from the thorns. So we put them in after shearing, say the end of May, leave them in for about ten days, then move 'em out, chain harrow and roll the whole field. There should be a good covering of young thick grass by the day. Did you decide anything else?'

'Mrs Bagnall is going to look into the matter of side-shows. But as she says, there'll be similar events all over, so we might only get second or third-rate stuff.'

'That's better than nothing,' remarked Meg.

'That's true; they'll not need much amusing, Meg—at least not in the evening. I understand the squire's going to send down a barrel or two of harvest beer. Have you heard that, Maggie?'

'Yes, that was brought up. Some of the women were a bit dubious. What do you think, Arnold?'

'I don't know. But it's not going to bother anyone in this household very much. Mind you, a pint or two of weak beer is quite an encouragement to the men at haymaking time. I've never bothered because none of us here drink it. I suppose I could get in a firkin for old Ernie, . . .'

'There's one other thing. I said you'd send down a dray the day before to cart the chairs and tables and things.'

'Well, I suppose Bob can do that—Sam's time is too valuable for furniture removing. But what's going to happen if it's a wet day?'

'We've thought of that, too. We'll set up another lot of tables in the Jubilee Room, and if it rains we'll go there for tea. But a sudden thunderstorm while we're at tea in the field could spoil everything.'

'That's not likely in June—too early for thunderstorms,' Sam said. 'But it seems to me it'll be a good thing when it's over.'

'I don't see why, Sam. It's over six weeks yet. Time enough to get the rest of the muck out of the yards, then do the hoss-hoeing and shear the sheep. If we get decent weather, we should have the work well in hand. If the Coronation goes well, it might be an indication of a good summer. I hope it will be a success, because it should be the last Coronation for many years.

King George is still in his forties—quite young. Why, he's a year younger than I am!'

His three children exchanged surreptitious grins.

After a damp start to the month, the dry weather returned and Bob led Major on the horse-hoe which Sam steered dexterously between the tiny mangold plants just showing above ground. On the first morning Bob suggested using Diamond instead of the larger horse for this comparatively light work.

'What would be the advantage of that?' demanded Sam.

'Diamond's feet are smaller than Major's, so there'd be less chance of him stepping on the plants. And it might make Diamond more manageable to be led about for a day or two.'

'Right you are, lad. Sounds sensible. It's your idea so you can get Diamond in from the paddock before you come in to dinner.'

Then they had a horse-hoe each, driving through the banked-up rows of the less vulnerable potatoes. Bob liked this job. Guiding a spirited horse between the rows of peeping potatoes, stirring the soil to destroy the seedling weeds, seemed so worthwhile. The soft, disturbed soil was as comfortable to walk on as a thick pile carpet.

Towards the end of the month the sheep-shearing machine was taken down from the loft above the tool-shed and the packets of newly-sharpened blades from one of the kitchen cupboards. Everything was fitted up and tested, and a pen built in a corner of the Home Paddock. The sheep were brought there from a distant field, and as the farm did not possess a dog Meg turned out to help pen the ewes, which became more recalcitrant each day.

Sam was an adequate shearer but not very swift, and Bob found he had to turn the little cranked handle briskly for at least ten minutes for each ewe. It could have been boring, but he found a spark of interest in watching Sam closely, and tilting the top of the machine backwards or forwards if the ewe changed her position.

'Can I have a go, Sam?' he asked on the second day.

'No you can't, Bob, not this year. It's not the shearing that's so difficult, it's holding the sheep. You haven't handled sheep enough to be able to hold one properly for this job. The ewe 'ud certainly escape with her broken fleece, chase all over the field, and we'd be a laughing-stock, because it would get about in the village.'

Bob thought for a moment.

'We could easily avoid that. Make a little pen with four hurdles and shear the sheep inside it. She might get away from me, but she wouldn't get out of the pen.'

'Trust you to come up with an answer. You never bloomin' well fail, do you? But you can have a go next year. I daresay you'll be here.'

The hot sun, so desirable for smooth, neat shearing, also gave them a rich thirst, and Meg visited them at least once a session with a jug of home-made lemonade.

On one of these occasions Bob broached the subject of mowing, which now loomed close in the calendar.

'If I can't do some shearing, can I do some mowing, Sam?'

'Mowing? No, by gum you can't. You've got to be able to drive a pair o' hosses dead straight, and watch the knife as well, to see that you don't hit anything. If you drive 'em too far from the standing grass, the heel of your knife will block up with the cut grass in the last swath; and if you drive too close in you'll likely miss a strip which won't be noticed until after the hay's cleared. Then it'll show up until the end o' the summer. We'd never hear the last of it.'

'Take no notice of him, Bob,' said Meg. 'He's always trying to make things out to be harder than they are!'

She realised her mistake too late and tried to jump back, but Sam grabbed her wrist and pulled her down across his knee as he sat on the corner of the hurdle. He raised his hand as if to spank her.

'How dare you, Sam? Let me go at once you horrid thing! Can't you take a joke?'

Sam let her go with a grin, much to Bob's relief. She was flushed and shaking with fury.

'Look at the marks you've made on my arms with your grubby hands. And my apron—you've ruined it with your greasy, shearing clothes. It was clean on this afternoon.'

She stamped her foot and turned away, trying to hide her tears.

'Teach her not to be so cheeky,' said Sam with an uneasy grin. 'Must say I didn't think about her clean apron on these mucky trousers. Turn up, Bob.'

'I can't do any mowing then?' Bob said, to change the subject.

'Tell you what—later in the summer we mow the thistles in the grazing fields—sort of trimming 'em up. You can have a go at that with Major and Diamond and the old machine. If you can cut thistles without missing any strips, you might be able to mow a field of hay next year.'

After the shearing all hands busied themselves hoeing in the root field. The task seemed endless to Bob. His lack of skill made him lag behind the others. In his efforts to keep up he aggravated the backache which the half-bending position inflicted on him. Every day he longed for dinner-time, and then for milking-time. In spite of the flies, to sit down beside a hot cow with swishing tail was absolute heaven.

He was intensely relieved when on the morning before Coronation day Mr Ratcliffe gave him different instructions at breakfast time.

'Take Major and the dray and shift some tables and chairs from the village hall to the sports field. Meg'll go with you for the first load to show you what's wanted. She's on the committee, and knows where things have to go. As a matter of fact, she'll be on the field supervising something most of the day, so don't come back at dinner-time without her or you'll never hear the last of it. Thank goodness the weather's fine. It'll be hot tomorrow too, that's certain. There's no sign of rain at all. If it keeps like this it'll suit me.'

Bob could hardly harness Major quickly enough. When he brought the dray round from the rick-yard Meg was waiting for him, a small basket of refreshments in her hand.

'What's that? I thought we were coming home to dinner.'

'It's for Sam, silly. He's been mowing since before five o' clock, and he won't be home until dinner-time. He likes to do as much as he can in the cool of the morning. Better for the horses.'

She settled down on the front corner of the dray beside Bob and Major trotted with long-ranging strides out to the road. In the field opposite the farm-entrance Sam had paused in mowing the thick crop to change a knife.

The heavy fragrance of the newly-mown grass, the tang of the perspiring horses and the hot oily smell of the machine seemed to fill the air. Sam met Meg half-way to the gate and sent her quickly back. Bob hurried Major through the village to the little hall where all the social events were held, and Meg directed him to the stack of equipment which he was to move to the field.

'Only take a few to begin with. I want to get down there as quickly as possible. They might be waiting for me.'

The field was the scene of great activity. Knots of women were in earnest discussion. A couple of fair-ground men were unloading a coconut-shy from their shabby waggonette. A gang of the squire's estate hands was erecting a small marquee in the corner of the field opposite the gate. In the distant corner of the field the bonfire towered, conical and black.

Bob was interested in everything going on, and proud to be involved. He would like to join in all the celebrations, but was resigned to the fact that he could attend only when he had taken the milk. The holiday was really only for the children, house-wives and well-to-do folk. Ordinary people had their normal day's work to do. But he made the most of his presence on the sports-field, enjoying his short trips to and from the village hall, appreciating the help of some of the villagers. Meg and Bob went home to dinner together, and back to the field until four o'clock. Most of the work had been done by then, and the helpers drifted away to be replaced by school-children, who came excitedly to inspect the arrangements.

At supper that evening Mr Ratcliffe gave his final instructions for the next day's work.

'Sam, you, Bob and Ernie had better keep on at the singling tomorrow. See if you can finish it, but don't stay too late in the afternoon. You want to start milking a bit earlier, so you can come down to the fair. Bob'll be later, 'cos he'll be taking the milk. A pity, but it's got to be done. You should be back in time to get there by seven o'clock, Bob. I've got to be there all day, unfortunately, and Meg and Mrs Ratcliffe, so you'll have to get your own meals for once. I'm sure they'll leave you plenty. Sam, you'd better ask Ernie to come in to meals with you as he'll be on his own too. Mrs Wagstaff'll be there helping with the teas. When we get this blessed Coronation day over perhaps we can settle down to some steady haymaking.'

Chapter Seven

Meg and Arthur were wildly excited the next morning, and Mr and Mrs Ratcliffe only slightly less so.

'We've left you plenty of food, Sam,' his mother said. There's cold meat all ready carved; Meg's made a great bowl of salad, and there's gooseberry pie and a couple of rice puddings. Now help to take out these boxes and baskets and put 'em in the trap –Bob's just brought it round. We'll expect to see you down there some time after tea. My, but it's hot, and going to be hotter, I think!'

The farmer and his wife drove off in the heavily-loaded trap while Arthur, proud in his new Boy Scouts' uniform, Meg and Bob walked across the fields and round by the churchyard wall. Bob's task was to bring back Bluebell and the empty trap; he felt very low as he left the bustling scene. Never had hoeing seemed less rewarding, or more painful. The hot sun scorched his neck and the day dragged slowly on, broken only by the stop for dinner, which was eaten rather less tidily than usual.

At half-past three Sam said, 'That's enough! We haven't quite finished 'em, but the rest can stay until tomorrow. Get the cows in Bob, and let's get done; then you can go down to the sports if you want.'

During the meal he offered to drive the milk to the station. 'You'd get down to the sports an hour earlier, Bob.'

'No, thanks Sam. It's my job, and your dad expects me to go, so I'd better do it.'

'Just as you like, lad. But I might not be going down to the village at all, myself. I want to sharpen a couple o' knives for the mowing machine tomorrow, then walk round the outlying beasts. This hot weather's beginning to reduce the grazing a bit.'

'Well, I'm certainly going down,' said Ernie. 'I want some o' the squire's free beer–as much as I can get, if the Missus keeps out o' the way.'

'Finish your tea, Bob. I'll go and put Bluebell in the float, and Ernie n' me'll load the churns for you so you're all set to go.'

The farm was deserted when Bob returned from the station. He banged down his empties, hustled Bluebell into the paddock, and rushed upstairs to change. He was soon jog-trotting along the footpath towards the churchyard stile. Sounds of merriment filled the warm evening, and he heard a few notes of music as if bandsmen were practising. The field hedge was thick and high, and until he reached the gate he could see nothing of the festivities.

He was surprised at the crowds. There seemed to be several hundred—far more than the whole population of Hartnall, he thought. The squire's generous gift of free beer to all comers had obviously attracted ale-lovers from other villages, for there were dozens of bicycles sprawling at the foot of the hedge.

The long trestle-tables, which he had helped place there yesterday, were now bare of food, but groups of mugs and glasses were there to be used by anyone who thirsted for the squire's beer. A row of barrels were set on stands under the huge cedar trees in the hedgerow, and relays of Hall servants dispensed the drinks. Further along, the squire's coloured marquee had been roped off, presumably to keep the crowd at a distance. As he sauntered by, Bob glanced through the open flaps and could discern tables and chairs, and glasses in abundance, as well as crates containing bottles of drink, obviously stronger than beer. Also within the roped enclosure a smart chestnut horse and varnished float belonging to the Hall stood patiently, waiting to carry away the remains of the evening's drinking.

Further along the coconut-shy was still doing desultory business, but the stock of nuts seemed small. Wandering round in search of Meg or Arthur, Bob paused at the coconut-shy and invested sixpence. He took eight balls and threw with all his might. Though his aim was true—he struck a coconut with each alternate throw—he failed to dislodge a prize. He wondered how anyone could possibly knock down a nut with such incredibly light balls. He now realised why he had not seen anybody carrying a coconut.

Bob gravitated towards the towering bonfire and inspected its layers of straw, twigs and branches. A few broken gateposts and old fencing-rails had also been added to give staying-power. It was to be lit at eight-thirty, according to the hand-written programme. Bob consulted his watch, but it was still only twenty-past seven.

He moved on, continuing his circuit of the field. Under a huge oak tree a group of Territorial bandsmen were preparing to play, and from the interest shown by the surrounding people, it was clear that they were expecting to dance.

After a good deal of testing of instruments, the band finally struck up the Exeter Polka. Some of the villagers paired off and attempted the one-two-three-hop of the lively dance. On the uneven ground the result was sometimes comical. By now some of the men had consumed plenty of beer, and collisions were frequent; but it was all taken in good part. Bob was not yet a dancer. The two occasions when Meg had tried to teach him the steps had produced no noticeable result, and he did not know any other woman well enough to ask her to tolerate his clumsiness. Bob hung about on the fringe of the crowd looking for any of the Ratcliffe family.

He wandered round the other side of the dancing area and then caught sight of his employer sitting on a schoolroom form in the centre of a group of men. The grave set of their features showed they were almost certainly discussing farming. A short distance away, at the end of another long table, a small group of women were chatting together, among them Mrs Ratcliffe. But of Meg there was no sign.

The band persisted with the polka until all the dancers were showing signs of fatigue. Some of the couples staggered a few yards and then sank to the ground to recuperate, but the more robust men seized empty glasses and marched in the direction of the beer. Almost immediately the band struck up the Emperor Waltz. Now those who had not taken part in the hectic polka glided sedately over the crushed grass. Mr Ratcliffe left his cronies and walked across to his wife. She rose from her chair with a wry face, which quickly changed to a smile of pleasure, and they joined the growing number of dancers. Some of them had appeared from the direction of the squire's enclosure, and Bob was delighted to see that Meg had joined in. How attractive she looked in her blue dress. Her partner was a tall, willowy young man with aristocratic features. Bob sensed that this was Mortimer Ratcliffe, the squire's son.

The boy moved away disconsolately, feeling slightly jealous. He was aware that Meg's parents had great hopes for her, but surely these did not extend to the squire's family. He wandered away in the direction of the bonfire and walked slowly round it. Beyond the fire the field extended in a long curving tongue to his right and in the distance it seemed to merge into the thick shrubbery on the Park boundary.

He left the fire and sauntered back towards the band, which had just played itself out on the fourth successive rendering of the Emperor Waltz. The evening was hot and some of the bandsmen were beginning to look the worse for wear. The tired dancers dispersed, and Meg walked away, still with her partner. Mr and Mrs Ratcliffe had rejoined their friends and resumed their conversation. Mr Ratcliffe had danced lightly for such a heavy man but he mopped his brow and neck in some relief.

After a short rest, the bandsmen started up again, this time with the flowing sequences of the Blue Danube. A few couples could not resist the lure of the music, and resumed dancing. Bob noticed Meg and her tall partner among them. He gazed at them, fascinated by their graceful movements. More dancers joined in for the last waltz of the evening. As the music swelled to its flourishing finale, Mr Ratcliffe picked up a bucket containing two sticks, and approached the fire, round which Arthur and his fellow-scouts had already formed a neat circle.

Most of the crowd surged after him, and Bob allowed himself to be pushed along with the press of humanity. Bob wanted to see the fire, but he also wanted to keep an eye on Meg. He thought she had remained with a few others to dance out the last few bars of Strauss.

Mr Ratcliffe drew one of the sticks from the bucket. A little bundle of sacking secured to the end of it was dripping with oil. He struck a match and lit the torch. It burst into life with a long smoky flame. The farmer held it high to announce his intention and then hurriedly applied it to several places round the base of the great heap, completing the circuit just as the torch failed. Huge pillars of fire grew from each tiny flame, spurting up through the tightly-packed thorns and straw. Some green holly had been included in the heap and still retained its explosive qualities. As the flames leapt up, thousands of tiny reports merged into a loud crackling sound. The heat was intense and made the crowd move hastily backwards. The light pushed back the dusk and darkened it. The crackling became a powerful roar as the fire ate into the heart of the stack, where heavy chunks of timber weighed down the lighter materials.

Bob stood spellbound. He had never been close to such a huge fire before, and was slightly alarmed at its intensity. He fell back into the crowd, remembered Meg and looked across to the dancing area. But all the dancers had dispersed. She was not to be seen. Nor could he spot her on the edge of the crowd either. She and her companion must have walked off into the semi-darkness. He edged through the crowd, his mind concentrating on the girl. The fire was still noisy, with a constant dull roar and an occasional wild crackle. The throng was getting noisy too. Groups were chattering together in excitement, and one or two a little drunker than the rest tried to start up a patriotic song.

Above this mild pandemonium Bob was startled to hear, very faintly, a woman's scream. He stood still, all his senses alert. Perhaps he was mistaken. No-one else was taking any notice, but they were intent on the celebrations. He squeezed through the crowd as quickly as he could in the direction of the scream.

Behind him the glare of the fire was dying to a redder glow, its roar drowned by the babble of voices. Then in front of him he heard the woman's voice again–a sobbing scream. 'Don't! Don't! Oh please, don't! How dare you! I won't let you– I won't!'

Meg's voice! Bob gasped in anger. He broke into a headlong run. He felt the struggle as he covered the ground. He came upon the pair scuffling on the grass just inside the shrubbery. Meg was on the ground, her clothing disarranged, her dress pushed up round her waist. She was vigorously fending off the squire's son, who was on top of her and trying to subdue her struggles.

A strange sound burst from Bob's lips—anger, concern, an overwhelming desire to wreak vengeance on the attacker.

'You swine! Leave her alone!'

Rage crossed the features of the young man as he turned and stood upright. In a flash Meg was on her feet and fled.

'You insolent yokel! How dare you address me in that fashion. Be off and mind your own damned business!'

'I'll teach you,' said Bob, setting his teeth.

'Damn your impudence. By God, I'll teach you a lesson.'

He was much taller than Bob, with boxing skills learned in gymnasiums. He stepped forward and flicked out his fist. Bob tried to dodge, but moved too slowly, and took the blow on his lips. He put up his hands and tried to parry the blows his adversary rained on him, but he was too slow on his feet, and his arms too short. He took a blow on the nose which started the blood pouring down his face, and another on the upper lip, which split it, and he caught the taste of blood in his mouth. He retreated slightly, but with firm steps. Mortimer followed, hitting the shorter youth as he pleased. He did not put all his strength behind the blows—he intended to delay the knock-out as long as possible.

Bob was not a natural fighter, but he thought rapidly. Unless he could outwit this giant he would be utterly humiliated. He was convinced that Meg had paused to watch the struggle from an unseen position in the gloom. No-one else came near, nor was likely to. The crowds still jostled and sang round the glowing bonfire. He must not panic he told himself, as he took a right-hook on his eyebrow. He scarcely felt the pain, so fiercely did his anger boil within him. Very well. If he could not dodge this punishment, he would go in and get close enough to give one savage blow. Four months of rolling milk churns and wheeling barrows of mangolds had developed his muscles until they were as tough as Sam's plough-lines.

He put his right foot down firmly and stepped forward, connecting at once with a forceful blow, again on his left eyebrow, bringing more blood. The squire's son was surprised when his target moved towards him, and shook his right hand ruefully. Quickly recovering, he snaked out his left for Bob's jaw, but Bob moved forward a step and at the same time nodded his head leftwards. Mortimer's blow slid along his chin instead of making full contact on the point of the jaw, as intended. Bob saw his chance, stepped forward quickly, and while Mortimer was slightly off balance, shot out his right fist with the force of a steam piston. It connected just below the centre of the chest. All Bob's fury, concern for Meg, and revenge for the blows he had taken were in that blow.

The squire's son reeled, made a strange groan, and staggered back, dropping his hands. Bob lunged forward, delivered a left-hook just below the jawbone, and brought his right fist round fiercely to the other side of the jaw. The stricken young man slumped to the ground, gasping.

'That'll teach you manners,' said Bob with satisfaction, spitting out some blood.

'You insolent oaf!' said the young squire between gasps. 'How dare you assault me!'

Bob turned and walked away quickly in the direction Meg had taken, but like her gave the fire a wide berth. It was still glowing fiercely but was now reduced to a huge mound of embers. He felt its great heat although he passed sixty yards away. Some of the crowd had drifted over to the gate in the far corner of the field, but a good sprinkling still remained, making the most of the fire's dying light, some singing, some trying to dance. He veered off still wider to avoid them. His face began to hurt now, and felt as if great patches of skin had been torn off. He realised that his features were caked with blood, and shrank from the idea of anyone seeing him. Hurrying to the corner of the field he climbed the fence onto the road. He crossed the road and climbed over a rail-place in the opposite hedge into another grass field, aiming to make a wide detour of the village. As he did so, the band struck up the National Anthem with great gusto.

He walked on quickly through the deep mowing grass. He was very tired. The fight had taken more out of him than he had realised. After a few minutes he discovered he was in his employer's river meadow, approaching the fattening bullocks. They looked startled to see him approaching at that hour. They stood watching him warily. He paused to reassure them, and now the only sound breaking the silence was the gurgle of the river at the drinking-place. It was a comforting sound, and he made for it. He lay on his front where the water was deeper, and washed the dried blood from his injured face.

He felt cleaner for his wash. But the knowledge that his lips were split, his nose out of shape, his cheeks puffed, both eyes probably blackening, and one eyebrow cut made him dread going back to the farmhouse. But go he must; they would wait up for him and eventually search. He walked slowly up the pasture and into the field Sam had mown the previous day. The juicy aroma of the freshly-cut grass was already giving place to the fragrance of new hay. Crossing the road and dawdling up the farm drive he recalled how, four months ago, he had walked that same drive for the first time, slowly and nervously. He was nervous now, but for a different reason. Passing the lighted kitchen window, he glanced in and saw the family at table about to start supper. His own place was laid, with a helping of cold meat awaiting him. A surge of gratitude passed through his mind.

He entered the back door, walked through the scullery, and into the kitchen. They were all busy eating, but from the far corner Arthur looked up; 'By gum! Look at Bob's face!'

The heads of the others turned in his direction at once, three in wonderment and one in concern. As he passed behind Meg he thought she shivered slightly. Bob said nothing but sat down in his chair and reached for the pickles.

'What the devil have you been up to, Bob?' asked the farmer. He spoke with an anger which he had not previously shown to the youngster. 'Coming home with your face looking as though you've had a fight with a windmill. Who the devil did you fall out with to get busted up like that? A damned disgrace, I call it. This was supposed to be a day of national rejoicing, not drunken brawling. All those gallons of cheap beer! I knew there'd be too much drinking. I want to know who it was Bob, and why! Come on, now, out with it!'

'I can't tell you,' Bob said, but his damaged lips trembled.

'You've damned well got to tell me! You're living in my house, and I will know the reason for this behaviour. I thought better of you, Bob!'

'Oh, shut up, Dad!' Meg broke out, pushing back her chair and fleeing into the drawing-room. Bob got up too, pushed his chair under, and walked out into the farmyard.

'Well, I don't know!' said Mr Ratcliffe in exasperation. 'What's got into this house and what's between them two? Seems we were mistaken about Bob after all.'

'Let it drop, Arnold,' his wife said sharply. 'And don't pass judgment until you've heard all the facts. There's more in this than meets the eye.' The farmer shrugged and continued his supper. Arthur jumped up from the table and made as if to follow Bob. His father stopped him.

'Sit down and finish your supper Arthur, and then get off to bed. This is nowt to do with you, and you're best out of it.'

Mrs Ratcliffe followed Meg into the drawing-room, and found her lying on the sofa sobbing. Her mother pulled her to a sitting position, sat down beside her, and put an arm round her shoulders.

'What ever is it, Meg? Don't cry so, child! Tell me all about it. Bob hasn't been bothering you, has he?'

'Oh, no, no, Mum, no!' Meg stopped crying and looked wide-eyed at her mother. 'No. Just the opposite. He rescued me. Dad was so horrid. I felt too ashamed to say anything.'

'But what happened, love? What did he rescue you from?'

'It was Mort Ratcliffe, Mum. I'd been dancing with him a lot before Dad lit the fire. He said we didn't want to get among that crush; why not go for a walk down the long slip. Well, I wasn't very keen, but I thought as he was a gentleman it'd be all right. But when we got past the fire, he started making suggestions and being familiar with his hands. I screamed and Bob must have heard me, though I don't know how he could in all that din. Then Mortimer got violent–I think now he must have been supping wine all day. He got me down on the ground–and my clothes up. I screamed and told him to stop. I tried to keep lady-like at first, but when he persisted I started to get mad and fought. I think I'd have managed him because he's not that strong–not like us. But then Bob came charging up. I felt awful. Me there with my dress around my waist, showing all of my drawers and everything.'

'At least they were clean,' said her mother trying to lesson the dramatic impact.

'Oh, Mum! Bob's face was white with rage. He told Mortimer to leave me alone. When Mort got up to face him, I scrambled up and ran off. But I stopped to see what would happen. Bob stood his ground. But Mortimer hit Bob all around the face. Bob didn't flinch. Oh, Mum, he took all that Mortimer could hand out. His face was covered with blood–he couldn't see properly. But he went in even closer, and then flattened Mortimer with two thumps which would have knocked a bullock over. I came away then. I was ashamed to meet Bob, him having seen me like that.'

'There, there, child. That feeling will pass. What an outrageous way for young Mortimer to behave. Must have been drunk. Your father will have a word with the squire. It's a mercy Sam didn't see it. He'd have killed him. He might try to still.

'Now love, you'd better not come out into the kitchen again tonight with your face in that state. Go upstairs, have a wash and get to bed. You'll feel different in the morning. Don't worry about Bob. Dad'll make it all right with him. He's a brave lad and tough. Now off to bed, lass. What an ending to the day we were so excited about!'

She returned to the kitchen, where her husband and elder son were finishing their second helping of cold beef.

'This is a fine state of things, Arnold. Young Mort Ratcliffe tried to interfere with Meg. Got her down on the ground and all! Outraged her modesty and frightened her, but I think that's all. But it might not have been if Bob hadn't come along and seen her struggling. He sailed into Mortimer, but Mort punished him terrible. Bob took it all until he could get in a blow which knocked Mort out. It's upset Meg. I'm afraid she'll need careful handling for a day or two.'

Sam sprang to his feet, clenching and unclenching his fists with such fury that his muscles threatened to burst through the skin.

'By God, I'll murder the bugger. Ah'll smash him into little pieces.'

'Shut up, Sam, and don't talk so wild,' said his father, a little frightened at his son's vehemence. 'There'll be enough trouble over this without murder being done. The cheek of it! Treating my daughter like a gipsy wench. But I should o' thought our Meg'ud 'a been strong enough to fend off that streak o' nothing!'

'I think she was too surprised and scared and lost her wits. By the time she realised, Bob was on the scene. You owe that lad an apology, Arnold.'

'By gum, yes. The way I went at him. I'll go out and fetch him in.'

He went through the scullery and out into the cowyard. The soft summer darkness shrouded the empty cowsheds and the untenanted stable. He loved the tang of the farmyard which was the breath of life to him, and every square foot of it too, as he had done ever since he brought Maggie here as his bride twenty-two years before. Perhaps he would spend another twenty-two years here. Sam would probably be farming it then, he thought, and Meg he hoped would be married to a successful farmer, possibly in the near neighbourhood. Meg! He suddenly remembered why he had come out here so late. He wandered slowly down the concrete yard, round the manure pit and peered into the stable.

'Bob! Bob!'

There was no answer. He completed the circuit of the cowyard, passed by the kitchen window and into the rick-yard. There was no sign of the boy.

He turned back and walked up the alley to Meg's calf-boxes. Then he distinguished the silhouette of the lad at the far end, leaning over the bottom half of the door. The farmer sensed that Bob had been crying.

'Why, there you are, Bob.' He walked up and put his hand on his shoulder. 'Don't upset yourself, lad. Come on in and finish your supper. Meg's told her mother all about what happened.

I'm sorry I said what I did. Jumped to conclusions. I should have known you better.

'You acted splendidly lad; I'm right proud o' you. Sailing into a chap, taller and quicker than you. And a trained athlete as well. You did the same as my sons would 'a done to save their sister. It was grandly done, Bob and I'm glad to think you're a member of my household. But let's go in and decide what we're going to do in the morning.'

'I can't go in like this,' protested Bob, snivelling slightly, but now with relief.

'That's all right, lad. What's a few tears. You must 'a been cut to the quick by what I said. And you made no attempt to defend yourself against me.'

'Well–I thought–er–I didn't know whether–perhaps Meg wouldn't want it generally known.'

'That makes it all the more creditable Bob. By gum, there's more of the gentleman in you than in Mort Ratcliffe, that's certain. I'm glad it was you and not Sam. He'd a' killed the young squire and then we'd 'a had a murder to sort out.'

He ushered the boy into the kitchen where Mrs Ratcliffe put a fresh mug of cocoa in front of him.

'Meg's grateful to you, Bob, and so are we all,' was her only comment.

'I'd better take the milk for you Bob,' said Sam clumsily. 'For a week or two at any rate. You don't want to be seen in Willington with a face like that, or people will get talking and asking questions. Nobody knows owt about it except us and the squire's family. For Meg's sake it'd better be kept that way.'

'You're right there,' said his father reflectively. 'But summat's got to be done. We can't let it pass. That drunken young rip's going to come up here and apologise to Meg, or my name's not Arnold Ratcliffe!'

'No, Arnold, that he will not do! I'm putting my foot down on that idea. Meg does not want to meet him face to face for a long time. But you must see the squire and tell him what his son gets up to.'

'All right, Maggie. If you say so as stubbornly as that, I'll not go against you. Tell you what, in the morning Sam and I will go down to the hall and have it out with the squire. We'll take Bluebell and the best trap, Sam, and wear our market clothes. Make a show of strength. You can stay outside with the mare in view of the study windows while I go in and see Colonel Ratcliffe. Some protest must be made. But first we'll sleep on it.' He settled down in his fireside chair and started to take off his boots. 'These blessed boots are killing me,' he grumbled. 'What a day it's been!'

Chapter Eight

Colonel Ratcliffe had an early breakfast and secluded himself in his study. It was an enormous room at the front corner of the mansion, with a bay-window looking out along the drive, which wound down between iron railings through the park. On one side the squire's hunters and bloodstock grazed, and on the other the cows and calves of his pedigree herd of Beef Shorthorns. The Home Farm was reserved for his beef cattle and his horses, in both of which he had a personal interest, preferring to have them under his eye.

The walls of the study were covered with large-scale maps of the estate and book-shelves closely stacked with works on agriculture and estate management as well as herd and stud books. There was a little lobby with a side entrance so that the squire's business callers did not need to apply at the imposing Georgian front door of the Hall.

Mortimer Ratcliffe also rose early, although he did not feel like doing so. His chest showed a great blue-black bruise where Bob Felton had landed his telling blow, and his jaw and neck hurt badly. But he knew his father's habits, and he knew the villagers knew them too; if any complaint were to be made about last night's scrimmage, it would be done this morning while the squire was in his office.

The young man entered the breakfast room just after his father had left it, and helped himself to several cups of black coffee and a piece of toast. He was not hungry but had a raging thirst. He was angry with himself for not realising that the girl he had been dancing with was the daughter of Farmer Ratcliffe, his father's favourite tenant. He had assumed her to be a village girl. And then to be worsted by that young farm lout.

His father looked up in surprise when the young man entered. 'Mortimer! It is unusual to see you up so early. Are you going out riding? If so, you can go out to Hockley and deliver a message to Maunders.'

'No Father—I think I will return to Cambridge today. But there was a bit of bother at the fete last night which I think I ought to tell you about.'

'Oh, indeed! Go on.'

'That fair-haired girl I was dancing with – I suppose you saw . . .'

'Yes, indeed. Margaret Ratcliffe—a remarkably pretty girl.'

'Quite so. But I didn't realise it was Arnold Ratcliffe's

daughter. I thought she was one of the village girls. I–er, tried to make love to her. I'd had a few drinks–perhaps I went a bit far. She struggled a little and screamed–and I'm hanged if Ratcliffe's milk boy didn't turn up and pitch into me, by Jove! Confounded impertinence! I decided to teach him a lesson, and punched him round the head a few times. But I was careless. I allowed him to get too close to me, and he hit me in the chest like a battering ram. I think he must have had a chunk of lead in his hand. Anyway, I went down. It wasn't until afterwards that I realised who the girl was.'

'Well, this is a fine catalogue of mischief. Mortimer, what were you thinking of? You get half-drunk in public, try to seduce the daughter of my oldest and best tenant and then brawl with one of his employees.'

'It was only a bit of fun,' muttered the young man. 'It was all a mistake.'

'A grave mistake to behave so irresponsibly. Disgraceful. We are not living in feudal times. This is nineteen-eleven! The village girls are not there for your amusement, and for you to annoy a farmer's daughter–one of my own tenants–was unpardonable. It's a good thing that giant son of Ratcliffe's was not there, or you would have been beaten to a pulp.'

'That milk boy hit hard enough. My chest feels as though I've been charged by a bull.'

'Serve you damned well right, my son. Perhaps you'll learn to behave yourself. But why are you telling me all this?'

'I thought perhaps Ratcliffe would turn up this morning and make a complaint . . . '

The squire looked out of the window. 'So you thought you'd get your story in first? You're right. Here comes Ratcliffe now, and his eldest son with him too. Leave the study now, Mortimer, but do not leave the house. I will ring if I want you. You had better return to Cambridge after lunch. I will consider the possibility of applying for a place for you at Sandhurst, so that you may learn to fight in a rather different sphere. I daresay I still have some influence with my old regiment.'

The squire scanned his visitors through the huge window. Sam remained in the trap while his father strode firmly to the door, which was opened by Colonel Ratcliffe himself.

'Good morning, Mr Ratcliffe. Do come in.'

'Good morning, Squire. It's always pleasant to see you, sir. You may not be so glad to see me when you hear my complaint.'

'Do sit down, Mr Ratcliffe.' The squire took his usual seat in the commanding position behind the massive flat-topped oak desk. 'How splendid that the fine weather continued for the Coronation. It will be hot again today, and possibly for several days. All the signs point to it. We shall soon need a long and steady rain to keep the grass growing.'

'Yes, we can do with a day's rain now and again, even during the haymaking,' replied the farmer, wondering how soon he could return to the subject of his visit. But the squire solved the problem for him.

'I can guess the reason for this sudden visit, Mr Ratcliffe. My son has confessed this morning that he annoyed your daughter last night. On his behalf I wish to apologise for his outrageous behaviour.'

'It went a great deal further than annoying her, Squire. It was an assault of her chastity. That is a serious matter for such a young girl.'

'At this point I must say, Ratcliffe, that Mortimer did not know that it was your daughter. He has been much away from home lately, and Margaret has developed into a magnificent young woman. It is not surprising that he failed to recognise her. She is the most attractive girl in the parish. But I am surprised when you say she was in danger of lustful assault. I have seen her working on and about the farm on several occasions, and she impressed me as being strong enough to be capable of protecting herself.'

'No doubt, Squire. Meg's strong enough. But although she's a farmer's daughter, she's not very worldly wise in these matters. I'm not sure that she would realise at first what she had to protect herself against. She'd be so surprised, sir—especially coming from Mr Mortimer. We've always looked up to your family, Squire.'

'Yes,' said Colonel Ratcliffe sadly, although he had reservations about Meg's alleged lack of knowledge. 'I can only plead in extenuation that he had foolishly had too much to drink—far too much. He could not restrain himself and lost his head. It will not happen again, I can assure you.'

'I believe you, Squire. But there could have been serious consequences. If my son Sam had found someone mauling his sister, I think he would have been capable of killing the man responsible. He doesn't know his own strength!'

'I agree, Mr Ratcliffe, and I am sure this point will not be lost on Mortimer. I must congratulate you on the splendid physique of your son. But she was not without a champion, it seems.'

'Ah, yes, you mean my farm lad, Bob Felton. He heard Meg calling for help, rushed to the spot, and took on Mr Mortimer. Mr Mortimer's a bit of an artist with his fists, and punished the lad something cruel about the face. But Bob stuck it until he could get close enough to land one telling blow.'

'So it would appear. According to my son he has a punch like the kick of a mule. But I regard it as most unedifying that my son should embroil himself in a fight with a farm-boy employed by one of our tenants. Not that I blame your lad. He is obviously a loyal and devoted servant to sustain a beating for the sake of his employer's daughter. I think I have seen him once or twice —a fresh young fellow with an open countenance, is he not?— driving the milk with your splendid roan mare. By the way, if you ever wish to sell her, Ratcliffe, I am a prospective buyer.'

'No, I shan't sell Bluebell, Squire. She's the fastest thing on four legs for miles round here and still young—not seven years old yet. I'll keep working her for another three or four years and then breed her to a thoroughbred stallion.'

'Excellent idea! Remember, when the time comes you may have the choice of my two stallions. But I think you know that!'

'Well, thank you, squire . . .'

'But with regard to this boy Felton, I must say I applaud his courage and if he was badly punished at least he emerged the victor. A pyrrhic victory, I fear. As long as England can produce such youngsters we need not worry about our country's future. I would like you to give the lad this sovereign from me—not as compensation for his bruises; if he's the lad I think he is, the fact that he has championed his employer's daughter will be compensation enough. But as a memento from me, as a token of my admiration for his pluck.'

'Thank you, Squire, I'll tell him what you say.'

'Is there anything further to say on this matter, Mr Ratcliffe? I do most sincerely deplore the whole thing, I can assure you. Would you wish Mortimer to apologise in person to you or your daughter?'

'I think not, Colonel; there's no need to extend the unpleasantness. Your assurance is good enough for me, and I feel the air is cleared. I'll bid you good-morning and get back to my farming, which'll be mainly hay-making if this weather holds.'

'Yes, I see you have cut one of the river fields; there appears to be an ample crop. I hope you secure it in good order. I regret the errand which has called you away from your hay-making. Good-morning, Mr Ratcliffe.'

From his window he watched the burly farmer stride away with a satisfied air. His weight made the trap almost heel over as he put his foot on the front step. Sam turned the mare round with a slithering of hooves on the gravel, and bowled away at a smart pace.

'What a great pity this has happened,' mused the squire. 'Why bring that gigantic son with him? Surely not to intimidate me. He needed someone to watch the mare of course, and he wouldn't bring the lad or the girl. There is the labourer, Wagstaff, of course. Perhaps Ratcliffe preferred to keep the whole matter within the family. Damn Mortimer for causing all this upheaval! Things can never be the same again between Arnold Ratcliffe's family and my own.'

The farming Ratcliffes had their own problems. Bob's face was such a mass of bruises that it would be bound to invite questions—not least from Ernie Wagstaff and his wife Elsie during her regular morning work in the farmhouse. Mrs Ratcliffe and Meg agreed not to mention the incident in Mrs Wagstaff's presence. But Ernie was a different problem. He worked with Bob, and was curious to know how his young companion had become so badly damaged. Unwittingly he supplied the subterfuge himself.

'Bah gum, Bob, what ever's thee done to thi face, lad,' he said the next morning as they were hoeing together. 'Thee looks as if thee'd run full tilt into a brick wall—and not a very smooth one at that. Or else one o' the 'osses 'as put its foot on your face when you were asleep!'

Bob gave no explanation, as he could not think of anything suitable to say, and Ernie went on to jump to a convenient conclusion.

'Oh, Ah see now, thee's had a row wi' Sam. Must 'a bin after the bonfire, I reckon. That wasn't a good thing to do, Bob. After all, he is the young gaffer, and likes his own way as far as the boss'll let him have it. And you're living in the 'ouse too, which meks it wuss. They wunt want to keep a lad who scraps wi' the boss's son. It were a daft thing to do, anyway, Bob. Sam's a hell of a strong chap, and he's made a mess o' thee, while you've hardly touched him. In fact I can't see that you've touched him at all. It's a bad business. Ah've taken a liking to thee, and hoped you were going to stop wi'us.'

'It won't happen again, Ernie,' Bob said ambiguously, but with such sincerity that his companion was impressed.

Bob caused some amusement at dinner-time when he repeated Ernie's suspicion.

'Better play along with it,' the farmer said smiling, 'Perhaps it's the easiest way out. You remember that, Arthur.'

But Sam was not too happy to be cast in the role of the bully, especially when the object of his alleged bullying was a lad for whom he had an increased liking. Meg said nothing, she had not yet recovered.

Bob did not refuse the squire's sovereign. His life as the son of a shopkeeper had not encouraged any notions of false pride. He had never considered it humiliating to accept a tip from his father's customers. But he did not spend this coin. Instead he wrapped it in an old envelope and placed it in the back corner of his bedroom drawer. He would cherish it as a talisman.

Meg and Bob were reserved with each other when they met. Bob had no doubts about his feelings. He was glad he had floored the lecherous bully, even though there might be repercussions. He was proud that he had suffered punishment on the girl's behalf. But when Meg looked at the quickly-healing bruises on Bob's face her feelings were a mixture of pity, shame and irritation, with only the faintest touch of gratitude. She could not quite understand herself. But the urgency of haymaking soon took precedence over personal feelings.

The afternoon after the Coronation Bob was shown how to use the swath-turner and turned the hay in the First River Field with Diamond. The boy was fascinated by the efficiency of the curved, revolving forks, each pair dropping into place as they turned on their spindle. He could not see them working as he sat in front of them, and had to give his full attention to the self-willed horse. But as he drove round the field, he could observe the neatness of the rows already turned, the grey-green of the exposed, cured hay being replaced by the sickly yellow-green of the upturned swath.

The following day was Saturday and Mr Ratcliffe announced his plans for the weekend. In the absence of Sam, who was on one of his early-morning mowing sessions, his directions were accepted without demur.

'Going to be another scorcher again today,' he said as they sat at breakfast. 'And tomorrow too, by the looks of it. That first field o' hay will be nearly ready for picking up tonight, but not quite. But by Monday, if this heat continues, it'll be over-made. So I want all hands out today—after dinner. And that includes you, Maggie, and Meg and Arthur and Mrs Wagstaff. We'll rake that field into windrows—and then we'll cock up the whole field before nightfall. That'll stop it spoiling with too much sun. And if it rains the cock's will keep the rain out. But it won't rain. We'll carry that field on Monday in perfect condition.'

The wooden hayrakes were taken down from the rafters of the tool-shed and in the broiling afternoon sun the team of eight made an impressive show, walking round the six-acre field with firm steps, shuttling the rake backwards and forwards. Two rows were pulled in together by each haymaker. At the end of a complete circuit, they all turned about and raked round the field in the opposite direction, pulling two more rows in to join the first. Conversation was desultory, each making an occasional contribution. Meg began to recover her pertness and Bob to lose his self-consciousness about his bruised face.

The evening was given over to building the thick rows of hay into conical heaps—each one the correct size for the pitcher—to conserve the hay until it could be loaded on to waggons. They all took part except Sam, who drove the milk to the station. Bob's feelings were mixed as he watched Sam drive away with Bluebell and the float. He felt faintly aggrieved that Sam should usurp this job, which he had come to regard as his own.

At the hay-cocking Bob found himself at a disadvantage. He had managed to keep up while raking, but the building of hay-cocks required a deftness which the others, even Arthur, possessed and he had not yet acquired. But the field was finished as twilight fell, and as the haymakers gathered at the gateway, they paused, leaned on their forks, and surveyed the result of their labours. Hundreds of rounded grey-green cones covered the pale surface of the cleared field.

On Monday afternoon the four men drove to the field, with Major and Violet each pulling a mophrey which had been fitted up by Mr Ratcliffe and Ernie during the morning. This was a conversion of an ordinary cart into a waggon. The cart-body was released from its position on the shafts and tipped back, while the shafts were removed from the axle. An undercarriage, with steerable wheels each side of a central member, was hooked on to the middle of the axle. A cross-piece above this supported the cart when it was returned to a level position, the shafts were re-attached to the front of the added portion, and a platform fitted above at the level of the top of the cart-body. Extensions, referred to as raves and gormers, were then added to allow the load to be built wider and higher. The resulting manoeuvrable waggon impressed Bob, who had seen nothing like this on the farms of his Mill Hill paper-round.

Sam and his father were equipped with towering-pitch forks seven feet long, while Ernie and Bob had short hand-forks for loading. The farmer motioned Bob into Violet's waggon, and instructed him in the art of loading.

'Now Bob, I'll show you how to do this, and take it all in because, I'll not show you again. You start at the front and lay the corners first, then put a big forkful between 'em to hold 'em on. Then, working backwards, you place a big forkful next to the corner one, each side, then one in between 'em again and so on. When you get to the middle of the waggon, you turn round and go to the rear-end, and start there, working back, towards the middle again. In fact, I'll place the main wads for you, all you'll have to do is hold 'em in place while I pull my fork out. Always keep your middle full, or the side'll fall inwards, but not too full, or the sides'll drop out. When I shout "Howd yer" it means I'm going to lead the mare on. You may not think it's necessary when we're starting the load, because you can see what I'm doing. But when you get higher up and are working at the back end, you're right out of sight of the hoss.'

Bob thought much of this unnecessary–he had often seen loads of hay being built. But he made no comment as he tried to surmount the huge cocks of hay which Mr Ratcliffe impaled on his fork and placed carefully in the appropriate place on the waggon. A towering load was built and Mr Ratcliffe surveyed it critically from front and rear.

'Will it want a rope on?'

'Yes, it jolly well will, Bob. You've made a fair job of it, but I'm not risking it coming off. We're working alongside a public road, remember, and we've got to cross it to get home. If a load came off, somebody'ud be sure to spot it and everybody in the village 'ud chuckle. Waste a lot o' time too. Now I'll throw the rope up, and you can cast it by criss-crossing the load five times. You pull from the top on each crossing while I tighten it round the hook. Then slide down the last rope, snatch the dangling hay from round the wheels, and we're away.'

The waggons were quickly unloaded, Sam throwing off the hay in mighty forkfuls while Ernie built the stack, assisted by Mr Ratcliffe and Bob. At first Bob was frequently buried under the tumbling avalanche thrown down by the energetic Sam. He liked haymaking, the smell and the feel of it, but the seeds and dust in his hair and down his shirt were not so pleasant. He was scrambling from under one extra-large load to find himself facing Meg with a jug of lemon squash in her hand.

'You're supposed to move the hay with your fork, Bob, not your head. If you're going to carry on doing it that way, take care to get all those seeds out of your clothes before you go to bed. I don't want to have to clean all that stuff from the floor of your bedroom.'

Her eyes twinkled as she said it, and Bob was so pleased to see this evidence of a return to her normal self that he stood there gazing at her mischievous face. Another huge mass of hay was thrown from above, this time with deliberate aim, and he disappeared under it as Meg giggled again.

'There's no need for that, Sam' said his father testily 'And as for you, Bob, you must learn that you've got to keep your eye on the unloader, especially when the stuff's being thrown downhill, or you'll always be getting smothered. Meg, you can get on here and help Ernie for the next load, while Bob and I go out for another. And after tea Arthur can help as well. Come on, Bob. Back Major out o' there and we'll get off. I'll have a swallow of that lemonade first though.'

When Mr Ratcliffe and Bob left the field with their second load, Sam and Ernie had already arrived and started to reload their vehicle. In the yard Meg was waiting by the growing stack, flushed and perspiring, but with scarcely a trace of hayseeds in her golden hair. She climbed on the stack with her father as Bob untied the ropes.

'Get up and chuck that load off, Bob,' said the master. 'You loaded it, so you should be able to find the layings better than anybody. While the unloading is downhill, try and throw it as near to the middle of the stack as you can.'

Bob reversed the process, but found that the great wads of hay took more pulling out than he had thought. He threw it as far on to the stack as he could, but noticed that wherever it landed, Meg was always just clear of the falling mass, and while he turned to drag out another forkful, she transferred the previous one to within reach of her father's fork. Every movement was neatly timed to avoid discomfort and unnecessary effort. Bob thought there seemed no end to the things one could learn about farm-work.

July came in even hotter and drier than June, and when each field of grass was cut it dried rapidly and with the minimum of haymaking. Sam was indefatigable, rising in the dark to mow a stint in the cool dampness of the morning. Then after dinner he slaved with all the other hands at carrying, to get the superb crop under cover while the hot weather lasted. Between breakfast and dinner Bob hitched Major to the swath-turner and turned the hay ready for the women to come out later and rake it into windrows in advance of the pitchers. Immediately after tea, Bob had to leave the hayfield to drive the milk to the station, since once his face healed there was no need for Sam to deputise for him. Bob loved working in the hay in spite of the heat, the dust and the strenuous work. He was reluctant to leave it to catch the train, although he realised that dispatching the milk was the most vital job of the day and must take precedence over everything else. On his way to and from the station he passed other farmers busy in their hayfields, and they waved their arms cheerily. Bob felt he was an integral part of the farming community, a thought which gave him an inner satisfaction. He urged Bluebell on so that he could get back to the hay. Diamond, who had been purchased primarily to relieve Bluebell, was in fact rarely used for the milk-run, for he just would not stand still long enough for the churns to be unloaded.

Sometimes after a particularly gruelling evening Sam and Bob would hurry down to the Trent for a quick bathe to get rid of the dust and hayseeds. They undressed in a clump of willows in the Second River Field. The fattening bullocks were grazing there, and on the first occasion Bob left his clothes on the ground. A few minutes later he looked across from the river and saw that the bullocks had congregated there and one had the sleeve of his shirt in its mouth. He splashed to the bank as quickly as he could and chased away the offending animals, which stampeded to the far corner of the field. Bob's shirt went with them, until the beast carrying it opened his mouth to bawl in ecstasy, and dropped the garment. When Bob retrieved it, the sleeve was wet with saliva and the front marked with hoof-prints.

Sam chortled.

'Allus hang things out of reach if you're in a field where beasts are! You won't forget again I reckon.'

Meg sometimes bathed in the Trent too, but privately and in the middle of the afternoon, when young men could be expected to be at their work. Bob saw her making for the river when he was horse-raking the First River Field. He was surprised to see that she was wearing a long mackintosh and her hair was tied closely to her head. When she paused beside the horse-rake, Bob saw her bare ankles, and realised she was probably wearing a bathing dress under her coat. She would not risk undressing in the open country, not even in the seclusion of her father's farm.

'Hope you find the water warm Meg.'

'I expect I shall. The sun's hot enough to set the water boiling, I should think.'

'Wish I could come in with you. Better than being cooked on the seat of this blessed old rake.'

'Don't you be so bold, young Bob! Mixed bathing may be allowed in London, but we don't have it in the country yet, at least, not round here.'

Diamond was already fidgeting to move on. Meg took her cue from the horse and sauntered on over the shorn grass.

'Don't you dare come and see me in the water, Bob Felton.'

'I can't leave Diamond, can I?' Bob shouted to her over his shoulder. 'If I had one of the other hosses, I would,' he added daringly; but she did not look back.

The hot weather enabled the hay to be made at such a speed that now and again the carrying of the crop caught up with the mowing. This gave a welcome pause in the tiring sequence of operations. The warm fragrance of the settling hay permeated the whole farm. It even filled the house, penetrating to Bob's bedroom on the top floor, although the window was on the side of the house furthest from the rickyard.

But if the hay was being gathered in quickly, the endless drought was causing problems in the grazing fields, where growth was negligible. As grass became scarcer the milk-yield fell. Sam and his father tried to work out varying permutations of stock in the pastures.

'One thing's certain, dad,' said Sam in his positive way. 'We've got to get the sheep away from this side o' the farm. They'll soon be starving the milking cows, and we might have to start feeding hay to 'em in the shed at milking time.'

'Oh, yes! That would be a grand thing to do, wouldn't it? The cleanest and sweetest hay I've ever made in my life, and you talk about having to start feeding it in July! That won't do Sam.'

'Some people're doing wuss things than that, dad. I've heard tell of some farmers who're cutting off the potato-tops to carry to the cattle in the field. Must be a funny diet for 'em and not much milk in it, I reckon.'

'Well, thank goodness we haven't got to that stage yet. The river meadows have still got a bit o' keep in 'em. I suppose we could put the ewes and lambs down there with the bullocks. The lambs ought to be weaned, but there's no fresh field for 'em, so they'll have to stay with the ewes for the time being.'

'Can't we get rid of a few, dad? I'm sure there's a bullock or two ready, and there must be some lambs nearly fat too.'

'You're right, Sam; we must sell some. But I don't fancy driving fat-stock to Burton or Derby this weather. I tell you what, I'll see Goodhead and try and get him to take a bullock a week straight in to his slaughterhouse and maybe four or six lambs too—we could take them down in the float. I must say the stock have done well this year.'

'Don't they say, dad, that all grazing stock need to make 'em thrive is plenty o' room, hot sun on their backs and unlimited clean water?'

'They do say that Sam, and this year's certainly proved it. And if the grass hasn't grown as much as we would have liked, the thistles certainly have. The pastures are beginning to look very untidy.'

'Yes, I wanted Bob to do a bit of thistle mowing with the old machine and the two light hosses, just to get him used to the job—sort of.'

'I remember you mentioned that before. But you know, Sam, I'm not at all sure that it'll be a good idea to do a lot of thistle mowing this year, so long as it keeps dry. If we trim off all the top growth, we might let the drought into the roots of the pasture and check growth even more!'

'I suppose that's possible,' said Sam doubtfully. He had an even tidier mind than his father. 'But the beasts will eat the thistles when they're wilted.'

'Oh, yes, sure. But only a fraction of 'em. When you trim off a field, ninety per cent of the thistles'll get prickly and crisp long before the cattle can eat 'em all, especially in this confounded heat-wave.'

The whole family were seated round the table, and Bob had been following every word, absorbed in the problem.

'Mr Ratcliffe, can I suggest something?'

'Of course you can, Bob. But I don't think your experience is quite equal to what we're talking about.'

'I know, but I just thought that if we're short of keep, and if the stock'll eat thistles a day or so after they're cut, but at no other time, why not cut a little piece in each field every day. The cattle 'ud be more satisfied, the fields 'ud be getting trimmed gradually, and we'd be making the most of all the keep we've got.' He stopped as if doubtful of the worth of his suggestion, and dropped his eyes to the table.

Mr Ratcliffe looked across in some surprise at Sam and then back across at Bob.

'Well, I'm damned! Bob, you're a genius! I think you'll make a better farmer than any of us. That's a clinking idea. Don't you think so, Sam?'

'I do! Why didn't we think of it? Seems simple enough now Bob's suggested it. It'll be a bit time-wasting moving from one field to another three or four times a day, but this is an exceptional year. We've got a genius in the house. I think we'd better start tomorrow; since it's Bob's idea, he can carry it out right through!'

These joking compliments made Bob look away in embarrassment. In doing so his glance took in Meg's features. He was thrilled to notice that she was smiling at him with understanding, and, he thought, proudly as well.

Chapter Nine

After morning milking Bob eagerly harnessed Major and Diamond, and hitched them to the old Bamford mowing machine which had been dragged out from the recesses of the cart-hovel annexe. The machine almost blinked when it came out into the light, and he hastily dusted off the whorls of poultry manure which some wayward hen must have dropped from the rafter above. He clanked by the kitchen window, hoping Meg would see him riding in state. Sam accompanied him to the East Pasture, occupied by the milking cows, and showed him how to lower the bed and insert the knife.

'You're all ready now, Bob. Keep her well oiled, and you'll be all right. Do a few rounds here and then go in to Rickyard Pasture and cut a bit for the big calves. After that, go down and do some in the Third and Fourth River Fields. After tea, I'll show you how to sharpen the knives. Keep the hosses moving. It'll do Diamond good to do some real work–he's been an ornament most of the time sin' he came to this place.'

Bob was proud of his responsibility and delighted with the job. It was much pleasanter to ride on the shaped iron seat watching the knife shuttle to and fro, cutting all in its path, than to be out in the mangold field with the others at the back-breaking second hoeing. At first he was nervous in case he should injure the cows with his lethal chariot. But he found that they kept out of his way and ignored him as long as he kept moving.

In the afternoon he cut a stint in each of the two fields bordering the Trent. He kept his horses well away from the edge, dreading what Sam and the gaffer would say if one of them went over the bank, which was three feet higher than the river in some places.

After tea Sam merely said 'Come on, Bob' and got up from the table, Bob making to follow. Meg said suspiciously, 'Where are you two off to? There's no field work tonight.'

Sam did not deign to reply, but Bob having no reason to be rude to the girl explained 'He's going to show me how to sharpen my knives for tomorrow.'

'H'm, getting quite a waggoner, aren't you?' she said and turned her back on him to clear away the tea-things.

In the tool-shed Sam showed Bob how to clamp the knife in the sharpening trestle and file a new edge on the twenty-four triangular sections of each knife. It did not take Bob long to grasp this simple task, and he had sharpened three sections to

Sam's satisfaction when Meg appeared in the doorway.

'Sam, you can clear off now,' she said imperiously. 'There's no need to stand over him while he files every section.'

'Well, I don't know! Have you got something secret to tell him? I'm off down to the village.' He pushed by her unceremoniously but chucked her under the chin as he strode past.

'Haven't you got anything to do indoors?' asked Bob bluntly.

'Don't be rude, Bob. As a matter of fact, I came out to teach you some more dancing steps. We haven't practised since before haymaking.'

'I'm not sure that it's a good idea. I mean—I'm pretty stiff from sitting on that bouncing iron seat all day.'

'Nonsense! If you're stiff, a few minutes' dancing will wear it off.'

'There's no music.'

'You can whistle the "Blue Danube".'

'Don't know it well enough.'

'Then I'll whistle it!'

'Girls don't whistle.'

'I do, when I think I will!'

There was no arguing with Meg.

'And I want you to do some mowing in the orchard tomorrow. Why shouldn't my young calves have some dying thistles to eat?'

'You know I can't do that unless your dad tells me. I can't go just anywhere I like! And in the orchard! There are too many tree trunks and I might not be able to miss 'em. And I'd have to watch the low-hanging branches so as not to drive the hosses' heads into 'em. Better leave it for Sam.'

'Don't be mardy, Bob. Of course you can do it!'

'Well, I won't do it unless I'm told,' he said stubbornly. 'But to change the subject, do you know why your dad has taken the milk tonight?'

'Don't worry. He's not going to do you out of a job! I think he wanted to see how Diamond is shaping. Dad's terribly disappointed about that horse. He doesn't seem to be any good at all for float-work, which is what he was bought for, mainly!'

'I know. He gets worse instead of better. Heck of a nuisance having to take a halter and tie him up every time you want to stop somewhere.'

'I think you'll have to put up with it, Bob. Dad's too stubborn to sell him. He can be very stubborn at times, can dad.'

Bob was about to say 'And so can his daughter' but thought better of it. Instead he remarked, 'Well, that's the last section of the second knife. Now, how about this blessed dancing lesson?'

He put away the trestle and walked stiffly out to the concrete surround. Meg showed him precisely where to put his hands.

'Hold me at arm's length, Bob. It's too hot to dance close together. Besides, it's not done! Now, you step forward with the left foot, come up with the right, then mark time sort of step with the left, then a bigger one with the right in the opposite direction, up with the left—tiny step again, turning all the time.'

'Better keep away from the muck-hole wall, then. I might get giddy and tumble over it.'

'Don't you dare get giddy when you're dancing with me. If I can keep upright, so can you.'

Bob could not keep the admiration out of his eyes as he looked his partner in the face. Her silky hair, shining like polished gold, taken back cleanly each side, revealed her wide brow. A few faint freckles separated the startlingly-blue eyes and the neat nose was in perfect balance with the expressive mouth and firm chin. He became embarrassed and looked away. But Meg was not averse to having her features admired.

'Look at me all the time Bob, and concentrate—or you'll get out of step more than you are already. Oh bother! Here's Arthur coming out to giggle at us.'

But at the same time the familiar rattle of the milk float was heard, and Mr Ratcliffe drove into the yard, turning through the gate at full trotting speed.

'Whoa! Whoa! What's this I've come home to? A dancing lesson? Here Arthur, take hold of Diamond while I show Bob how it's done.'

He jumped over the back of the float and strode down to where Meg and Bob were still hesitantly gyrating.

'You're making an awful poor do of it, Bob. Here, let me show you.'

He commandeered Meg and fell instantly into the rhythm of the waltz, humming the accompaniment at the same time. Bob looked on enviously as father and daughter revolved in harmony.

'You've got to live the waltz, Bob,' the farmer called as they reversed close to the onlooker. 'Feel the music flowing through your limbs and directing the steps. But, by gum, that's about enough, now Meg. Phew! Fancy dancing with hob-nailed boots on concrete on a July evening. Might as well do the clog-dance I reckon. It'd be just as fitting.'

They walked up the yard together.

'Dad, can Bob mow some thistles in the orchard tomorrow?'

'Bob's got plenty to do round the other fields. Why is the orchard so particular? We can do that at odd times—wet days, for instance.'

'Wet days? When are we going to get them? There are a lot of thistles out there and some are so tall you can hardly see the calves.'

'Then they've grown a lot since I was out there on Sunday,' said her father drily. 'However I suppose I shan't get any peace unless you have your own way. Go out there first tomorrow, Bob, and knock 'em down. It's not a very big patch.'

'But what about all those trees, Mr Ratcliffe?' Bob said anxiously, ignoring Meg who was making faces at him from behind her father's back. 'I'm not sure that I can drive well enough to miss 'em. And young calves are inquisitive. They probably won't move out of the way.'

'You'll manage all right, Bob. I can trust you not to drive into a tree, surely. But if you're doubtful, just drive your hosses once up and down each avenue, and then across. Meg can be there to chivvy the calves out of your way. As a matter of fact, Meg, you can go there a few hours each day and cut the thistles close in to the trees.'

'Oh! Why can't Ernie do that?'

'Because he'll be busy in the mangolds for another week or ten days. But put Diamond away Bob and then stroll through the orchard to see the lie o' the land. There's a tree stump or two to watch out for.'

Mr Ratcliffe was gratified when he returned from market the following Friday.

'I knew that farming news travelled fast and far, he said at tea-time. Several farmers have taken to Bob's idea of cutting the thistles a few at a time. You'll make a reputation, Bob. Anyway, keep mowing as you are doing for the next fortnight. You'll get round all the pastures by then, and it'll help to bridge the gap. We'll be cutting the oats by then.'

'There'll be a bit more keep when the sheaves have been carried, won't there?' Bob ventured.

'I don't see how unless it rains.'

'I thought you'd turn the cattle on the stubbles.'

'Whatever for?' interposed Sam. 'I don't like the idea behind that. We've no weeds and twitch in our corn for the beast to get a living on. Our stubbles are clean, young Bob.'

'I was thinking of the verges round the fields, Sam. It's only a foot or two wide and a bit in the corners, but there must be some keep there. It's been growing untouched since the spring.'

Mr Ratcliffe digested this while he helped himself to more salad.

'You mean, turn the beast into the cleared corn-fields so that they can eat out the hedge-bottom? Bob, you're full of bright ideas. There's no reason why we shouldn't do as you suggest. There's no water in the arable fields, but they could run back to the nearest grass to drink. What about it, Sam?'

'I think it's a good idea, dad. Every little bit o' keep helps in this weather. The heifers and the dry cows could go there—maybe it'd keep 'em happy for a week or two. This has been a summer, hasn't it? I don't know what we'd 'a done without the riverside meadows.'

'I don't know what you'd have done without Bob!' interposed Meg swiftly. 'He has all the bright ideas on this farm.'

'I thought it about time you chipped in,' said her father in the bantering tone he reserved for his daughter. 'You can't keep quiet for long, can you? Now you've made Bob blush! Never mind, Bob. I'm glad to have your suggestions, lad. One good idea is worth more than a barrowful of Meg's cheeky remarks.'

Sam steered the conversation back to farming.

'Have you seen Goodhead yet about the bullock and lambs, dad?'

'I did—saw him in Derby today. He agreed to take the fat beast two at a time at two pounds a hundredweight, and the lambs five or six a week at tenpence a pound deadweight. We can take them down in the float and drive the bullocks down at the same time. So we shall reduce our stock, relieve pressure on the grass, and get some money in at the same time. We can do with it, too! It'll soon be rent day. I've got to find two hundred pounds for Colonel Ratcliffe at the end of September.'

The family sighed. This was an attitude which recurred twice yearly.

'You've been finding it for a good few years now, dad,' said Sam.

'Maybe. But I'm not finding it any easier. It'll be your problem one day, and don't you forget it. I've half a mind to apply to the squire for a reduction in rent. I wonder how he would take it.'

'Oh, come father, grumbling about the rent,' Mrs Ratcliffe said. 'I hope you're not going to keep on from now until Michaelmas. You've got the harvest to get out of the way before rent-day, and if this weather keeps on you'll get it good—clean straw and not too much handling of the sheaves. Stop grumbling until you've got something to grumble about.'

'Well, that's all the sympathy I get from my family,' sighed the farmer as he moved away from the table, sat down in his armchair and snatched the *Farmer & Stockbreeder*.

The rain was falling steadily on Monday morning when the first consignment of bullocks and lambs was to be delivered to the slaughter-house in the village. They all got wet and Bob had a private grief at sending such vigorous animals to their death;

he was not yet hardened to the harsh economic facts of meat production.

The rain lasted three days, and then the sun returned, mildly at first but gradually building up into another heat-wave. Mr Ratcliffe announced his intention of cutting the first field of oats, and Sam dragged out the Hornsby binder with the eager assistance of Bob and Arthur. The machine had been purchased new the previous year and the paint and maker's name were still smart. The thrill of starting the harvest affected everyone at the farm, Arthur with the enthusiasm of youth, Sam with the confidence that the new machine would cope with the crop. Mr Ratcliffe was quietly satisfied at the approaching culmination of the farming year, and Meg looked forward to her visits to the harvest fields. Even Mrs Ratcliffe remarked 'Funny how harvest gets you excited, like. On a cow farm, the value of the corn doesn't amount to much, compared with the milk, but it seems important out of proportion. Must be childhood memories I s'pose, when we rode home on the waggon-loads of sheaves—and gleaning too when I was a girl. There were no binders then. All cut by reapers and scythes and tied up by hand.'

Bob was soon to learn how to bind sheaves by hand, as he was sent to help Ernie 'open out' the field—that is, to clear a strip sufficiently wide so that horses and machine could make their first circuit without over-running the standing corn.

The old man showed him how to make a bond by taking two handfuls of straw and splicing them together at the ears without tying, which would have rubbed out some of the grain. Bob experimented with his bonds, but failed time and again to make a suitable join. He fell further and further behind the scythe, so he decided to use his own method. He selected the very longest of the straws, prepared a smaller sheaf, and tied it quickly with a single length. Ernie eyed him askance when the boy caught up with him as he sharpened his blade.

'You're a reight 'un young Bob. Show you how to do the job properly, and you find your own way and do it quicker. Well, I don't know! These lads! Onyway, if you're going to use single bonds I'll show you how to tie 'em without stripping off all the oats, which is what you're doing now.'

The following morning Sam hitched Flower and Violet to the pole of the binder.

'Put the sling gears on Major and bring him along,' he ordered Bob. 'It needs three hosses to pull this machine for any length of time.'

Arriving at the field, Bob tried to memorise the sequence of operations necessary to convert the machine from its travelling position on the road to the working position in the field. Mr

Ratcliffe mounted the high seat of the binder and from that position manipulated the assortment of levers, in addition to driving the two mares.

'I'm getting too old and heavy to walk about stooking,' the farmer informed his staff. 'So I'll do the riding—for a time, anyway.'

The binder was fascinating in its precision, Bob was mesmerised by it. He had never been so close to such a machine before. The upright corn tumbled backwards on to the cutter table, travelled laterally and rapidly up into the body of the machine where the mechanism automatically bound it into a sheaf, tying a safe knot with unerring accuracy. Every few feet the ejector fork made a complete circle and flung out a neat, tightly-bound sheaf. A straight row of these was left down the length of the field.

'Isn't it grand to see it in action, Ernie?' asked Bob as they stood watching the machine recede from them, its clatter getting fainter. It reminds me of my mother's sewing machine.'

'Ah, 'er is running well today. And so 'er should. 'Er's a new machine for one thing, and Sam coddled it up like a babby when 'e put 'er away. And it's a clean, standing crop—generally is in a dry summer. There's been no storms to knock it down and tangle it. Bindering can be a terrible job in a wet year, with the corn bent over and lying in all directions, full of thistles and other rubbish. It's miserable then, I can tell you. Sprawling sheaves, three or four joined together, badly tied and some not tied at all. The straw winds round the knotter you see, and blocks it. But we shan't see any o' that this year, thank the Lord!'

'Well now, Bob, the Gaffer said to show you how to stook, so we'd better get started. Not that we can do much until they've bin round a few more times. We generally put five sheaf rows into one shock row. You pick up a sheaf under each arm, like this, stand in between 'em, and ram 'em down into the stubble hard. The ears leaning in together, and the knots out'ards. Then they wunt fall down. There's no more miserable job than setting up sheaves that've fallen over.

'You put six sheaves to a shock in a light crop, and eight or ten in a thick 'un. And the shocks 've all got to run the same way North to South.'

'Why's that, Ernie?'

'Well, the idea is that each side of the shock gets the same amount o' sun as it moves round. If the shocks ran east to west, the south side wouldn't ripen so well.'

'Think there'll be any rabbits here, Ernie?'

'Oh—ar, sure to be. They come in from the spinney on the other side. The Gaffer's bound to bring his gun out after dinner.'

'What, and shoot from the seat of the binder?'

'No, he wunt be on there then, Bob. It's Wednesday, and Arthur'll lead the chain 'oss and the gaffer'll do the shootin'. P'raps the squire'll come down with his gun. He often does when we're corn-cutting.'

Arthur was furious that harvesting should have started before school broke up.

'Don't cut any more before next week, dad,' he begged at dinner time.'

'I'm not likely to, Arthur. The other field of oats won't be ready until Monday, and the wheat'll be a week after that. You can lead Major this afternoon.'

As the binder had to halt for dinner, so it also had to stop for milking.

'It's a temptation to carry on and finish it,' said Mr Ratcliffe, surveying the neat rectangle of standing corn. 'There's only about two hours' work left. But somebody's got to do the milking, and I want everybody here when we finish it, to make sure no rabbits get away.'

'How's it going, Arnold?' asked his wife during their quick after-milking tea.

'The sheaves are leaving the machine nicely, but there just aren't enough of them. But we couldn't expect a much better crop in such a dry summer. Will you and Meg come down to the field after tea, and help beat the rabbits out? And bring Sam's gun with you. He might as well have it there in case the rabbits are too many for one. Bob, get off with that milk and be back as quick as you can. Bring the float straight into the cornfield as you come back. We shall be near to finishing then, and I want you there for the rabbits.'

Bob felt outraged that he had to leave the harvest field for the lonely trip to the station. But common sense told him that nothing must prevent the dispatch of the milk. When he returned, driving Bluebell into the field at full trot, he rejoined Ernie who was striving with the stooking on his own.

'We shall never finish all these tonight,' said Bob, looking with dismay at the endless rows of sheaves.

'Don't expect to, lad,' replied Ernie. 'It takes four or five stookers to keep up wi' binder. But there's all day tomorrow, isn't there?'

As the strip of standing corn got narrower, a few of the more venturesome rabbits peeped out of the corn warily, then suddenly made great bounds for the haven of the spinney. But Mr Ratcliffe was waiting in a strategic position, and rarely missed. When only a twenty-yard strip remained, Sam stopped the binder, took his gun from Meg, and stood between the standing corn and his father. Ernie, Bob, Arthur and the two women walked slowly and carefully a few feet apart through the remaining crop. The half-dozen or so cautious rabbits still in hiding were startled out of their cover and set off in a wild dash across the stubble. But they were confused by the rows of sheaves. Those which Sam missed were accounted for by his father.

They gathered up the spoils, and when they packed up the binder in the dusk and returned to the farm, the bed of the machine carried twenty dead rabbits.

'Take two for yourself, Ernie,' said Mr Ratcliffe. 'The rest can go to Goodhead in the morning. They'll bring in a bit. It'll all help to pay the wages. Bob, help Meg to gut those rabbits when you've put Bluebell away, and hang 'em up in the wash-house. You can run 'em down to the village in the morning.'

'This is a messy job,' said Bob later as he watched Meg paunch the carcasses and fling the entrails over the muck-hole wall.

'You'd find it messier if you did some and not leave them all to me,' said Meg. 'And when we've finished get a fork and cover up all those guts with muck, otherwise the house'll be full of flies for the next few days.'

'They sat down to a lamplit supper which they all thought was well earned. 'A successful harvesting day makes you feel that way,' Mrs Ratcliffe said, to no one in particular.

'I'm surprised the squire didn't turn up for the rabbits,' remarked Mr Ratcliffe thoughtfully.

'Did you let him know?'

'No, but then, I never do. He must find out by instinct. He's never missed before, especially with the early fields. It's different later, when everybody's at it. He can't visit every field that's being cut. Perhaps he'll turn up next week—or young Mortimer. He's home again, I believe.'

'I don't think Mortimer will be shooting any rabbits on this farm—not this year, anyway,' said Sam grimly.

After the week-end the second field of oats was cut and stooked, and a few days later the three fields of wheat were cut in quick succession. Arthur was proud of his responsibility in leading Major, and in seeing that the traces were kept taut, which allowed Sam to assist with the stooking or relieve his father on the seat of the binder. Neither the squire nor his son turned up to join in the sport. Mr Ratcliffe was mystified, but the urgency of getting the sheaves drove such matters from his mind.

The continuing hot weather allowed the corn-carrying to go ahead without hindrance. The partly-filled bays in the Dutch barn were filled up first, then two empty bays. The last two fields of wheat were built into beautiful round stacks at the top end of the rickyard. The work went on for over a fortnight. Ernie was the stacker, as with the hay, ably assisted by Meg and Arthur, who was determined to prove that he could be an adequate farmer, whatever his possibilities as an auctioneer.

Bob loved it all, and his enthusiasm communicated itself to the others. Mr Ratcliffe, Sam and Bob did the pitching, loading and unloading while the others remained in the yard. Sam pitched sheaves to his father and then drove his waggon into the yard for unloading. Then Mr Ratcliffe pitched a load to Bob, who drove it home, while Mr Ratcliffe sometimes had a few minutes' rest before the first waggon returned.

The whole process was thrilling, satisfying and very orderly, thought Bob. The sheaves were easier to handle and so much tidier than forkfuls of loose hay. A small but defined area of the field was totally cleared with each load leaving only the short, clean stubble. It was the climax of the year's work.

Two horses were needed to haul each load from the field. Bob had Violet in the shafts and Diamond in front as his chain-horse. In this capacity Diamond was a mixed blessing. He could not wander off ahead while he was hitched in front of Violet, who waited until the word of command was given, so he compensated by fidgeting as far as the restricting traces would allow. He sometimes edged round and faced the waggon, standing head to tail with the disapproving Violet, who laid her ears back at such behaviour. Mr Ratcliffe, who was on the ground pitching, would sigh and scold alternately. But when the load was completed and roped down, Bob slid to the ground and took over the driving. He knew that Diamond would pull well enough on a straightforward haul. Proud of his growing skill, Bob drove Diamond with his left hand, and led Violet with his right. As the horses dug their hooves into the unyielding stubble, and the stately waggon creaked gently over the undulations, the boy would not have changed places with a king. The jingle of the chains, the squeak and flap of the harness leather, the thud of the horses' feet and their heavy breathing as they exerted every muscle–all were as music to his ears. He compared himself with the captain on the bridge of a ship laden with merchandise.

Sometimes the bulging sheaves on his load would brush the top of a gatepost, but as they were soft and yielding no visible damage was done to the load or to Bob's reputation as a waggoner. For part of the journey he came under the searching scrutiny of Sam, returning with the other team; but when things were going well, Bob felt himself the equal of the gaffer's son. The boy loved to drive his swaying load at a good pace through the cow-yard into the rick-yard, and pull alongside the stack with a flourish of horsemanship and a commanding shout of 'Whoa!'

Sometimes he was a little too close and disarranged some of Ernie's carefully-laid sheaves. Other times he was too far away, which meant that he had further to throw the sheaves when unloading. In the one case Ernie muttered imprecations under his breath, and in the other he chortled freely. These slips caused Bob chagrin, as he liked to do well in front of Meg, who would be watching casually from the top of the stack. The girl was amused at Bob's desire to do well, but was not particularly critical of his occasional mistakes.

During Bob's absence on the milk run, Arthur was pressed into willing service as a loader, and Ernie continued his stacking with the sole help of Meg.

Every night they sat down thankfully and wearily to a huge nine o'clock supper of cold bacon or beef, salad and potatoes, followed by the unvarying rice pudding and fruit pie. And every night Mr Ratcliffe would say as he sat down to eat, 'There's nowt like a good supper after a full day's harvesting in hot weather, when you can say you've achieved summat.'

On Saturday night he said, 'It's been a heck of a good week, everybody. The weather's been good–the best harvesting weather I can ever remember–and the progress has been good, too. We can all go to church tomorrow with an easy conscience.'

Chapter Ten

When not another sheaf could be prised under the iron roof of the Dutch barn, Ernie measured out and prepared bases for two circular stacks.

'You'd better have Bob on there with you, Ernie,' the farmer said when everything was ready. 'He might as well learn how to stack. Arthur, you can do the loading instead of Bob. It'll do you good to have a few continuous days in the field.'

'And what am I supposed to do?' asked Meg, crossly.

'You'll be wanted on the stack. Ernie'll need all the help he can get. These stacks'll be a fair size by the time he's run 'em out a bit, and there's about eight acres of sheaves to go on each one.'

Arthur, although anxious to prove his worth as the equal of an adult worker, was not at all sure of the satisfaction he would get from loading corn to his father and brother as alternating pitchers. He climbed into the mophrey without a word as his father took Diamond's reins, and extricated the horse from the tangle he had created by placing his hind foot outside the trace chains. When they had gone, Bob watched with interest while Ernie started to build the stack with the sheaves thrown from the load by Sam.

'First thing to do is to mek a little stock in th' dead centre, and then keep laying sheaves round and round it, ears uppards, until you get to the outside edge o' th' stack. You overlap each sheaf at least half-way and slope 'em o' course, so that no ears are touchin' the rick-bottom where the damp might reach 'em. When you bin right round the outside edge you start agen in th' middle. Allus keep the sheaves pitching slightly uppards so the rain can't run in.'

'I wouldn't a' thought that,' said Bob. 'Have you ever seen it happen?'

'Ah have that, lad, but not wi' ony stack as ah've built. Once you sin' the roof of a stack sodden and ruined, it learns you to tek more care another time.'

He started laying another course and showed Bob how to follow him round, laying an inner course on top of the first, so that the butts of Bob's sheaves just reached the string of those laid by Ernie. Meg stood close to the waggon as Sam unloaded, she threw a sheaf to Ernie and Bob alternately.

'It seems easy enough,' said Bob after a while.

'Ah! It's easy enough so long as you get all the outside

sheaves in the right place, and 'er settles down evenly all round. But sometimes a stack'll settle more one side than th' other, and if 'er looks likely to go over, we have to put props in to'owd her up. Now ah'm going to start running 'er.'

'Running her?'

'Ah—pushin' the outside sheaves a bit further out on each course so 'er's getting wider across all the time, and from the ground th' body o'th' stack looks a bit like a letter V. The overhang helps keep the rain away from the sides, you see.'

'Sounds pretty dangerous to me,' said Bob.

'Not if you know what you're doing, lad. But there's another thing—the butt of a sheaf isn't level, which you might have noticed. It slants across a bit, so the sheaf seems longer on one side than the other. Now, when you're building the body o' th' stack, you lay the long side uppards, while the short side is on top of the long side of the sheaf below it. That's how you push your sides out wider. But when you build th' roof it's just the opposite. You want to reduce your width, so you lay th' sheaves th' other way up, short side uppards.'

'I don't know how I'm going to remember all this.'

Sam drove his empty team back to the field, and in a few minutes Mr Ratcliffe drove in with Diamond and Violet. They all worked smoothly and silently. It did not occur to Bob and Ernie to converse in the presence of the gaffer. But Meg chafed under this self-imposed restriction.

'Now you've learned to build a stack, Bob, perhaps you'll talk to me. I'm fed up with being left out,' she said, showing off slightly in the presence of her father.

'Shut up, Meg,' he admonished her. 'This isn't a Women's Institute meeting. Let Bob concentrate on helping Ernie, and you make sure you get the sheaves across to them the right way round!'

Meg flushed, turned her back on her father as she swung the next sheaf, and put her tongue out; but the rest of the load was thrown off in silence.

Three more days of toil beneath the sun, and the harvest was finally secured. The empty stubble fields looked peaceful, as if enjoying a welcome rest between the harvesting of one crop and preparation for the next. In the rick-yard Ernie's two stacks towered towards the sky. When the last sheaf had been thrown up and Ernie had patted it into place and descended, the whole party stood round to admire.

'They look grand, Ernie, and no mistake,' said the gaffer, voicing everyone's thoughts. 'You've done well, and I'm reight proud of 'em. Leave 'em a couple o' days and you can get 'em thatched. We'll not need to thresh 'em this side Christmas. And as it's the end o' harvest, Ernie, you'd better come and have supper with us, and get Mrs Wagstaff over as well.' He threw his chest out slightly and continued. 'It's been a grand harvest, and I'm grateful to all of you. And that includes you, Arthur. You've loaded this wheat well these last few days. At least, none o' the loads fell off, which is summat.'

'Thank goodness the harvest is over,' said Meg as they wandered in the direction of the farmhouse. 'Perhaps I can stay indoors more now. A day at harvesting now and again . . .'

'Oh, you haven't finished yet, Meg,' interrupted her father with a twinkle in his eye which the girl did not see. 'Ernie'll be thatching in a day or two, and you can draw the straw for him.'

Meg turned and faced her father. Her lower lip protruded and a sullen look spread over her face. Her father recognised the signs and grinned widely. He reached out a powerful right arm and pulled her to him, swung her round, put his arm about her waist and hugged her to his side.

'I was only pulling your leg, girl. 'Course you don't have to help with the thatching if you don't want to. In any case, Ernie'd rather do it on his own. Wouldn't have you as a gift. That's right, isn't it Ernie?'

The other man struggled with his loyalties.

'Ah couldn't never wish for a better mate on the stack, gaffer. 'Er's worked well and 'andy, without any womanish awk'ardness. 'Er'd do well enough at pulling the straw, I daresay, if 'er put 'er mind to it.'

They ate a hearty supper lingering over it until the lamps were lit. The three women cleared away and washed up while Mr Ratcliffe and Ernie, with occasional comments from Sam, ruminated on past harvests, good and bad. To Bob, sitting listening with intense interest, it did not seem possible that harvesting could ever be other than splendid.

The family lingered over breakfast the next morning too, the urgency having temporarily departed.

They sat there chatting until the postman looked in through the open door, a single letter in his hand. His face was red and shining, for the sun was already warm.

'Come in and have a cup of tea, George,' said Mrs Ratcliffe hospitably. 'I'm sure you can do with it. You won't be home for a while yet.'

'No, Mrs Ratcliffe,' said the man thankfully, sitting down at the long table, taking off his cap and mopping his brow. 'I allus reckon Oakleigh's about the half-way mark on my round. Bikin' is 'ard and thirsty work this weather.'

Mr Ratcliffe absently picked up the letter and slit it open with a table knife. He unfolded it and glanced down its typewritten contents. Then his manner changed. His face turned grey, and a look of pain came into his eyes. His uneasiness communicated itself to everyone in the room except the postman, who gulped his tea noisily in between his remarks about the trouble-free harvest.

Mr Ratcliffe drummed his fingers on the table. His wife noticed, and did not offer the postman a second cup. The visitor put his cup down and took his departure. Meg was the first to break the silence.

'Whatever's the matter, dad? You look as though you've seen a ghost. Has the bank gone bust or what?'

'I just can't believe it. To be given notice to quit after twenty-two year!'

'What?' said his wife. 'Notice to quit? There must be some mistake Arnold. The squire would never do a thing like that!' The youngsters just stared in bewilderment at their father.

'Well, here's the letter,' he said wearily, picking it up from the table as if it were an explosive charge. He seemed drained of all energy. 'This is what the squire says . . .

'Dear Mr Ratcliffe,

It is with regret that I find it necessary to give you notice to quit Oakleigh Farm. Because you have farmed it well for more than twenty years you are entitled to know why I have to do this. There are 27 other tenanted farms on the estate, and not all are as well equipped as Oakleigh. Many of them need extensive repairs, and with the cost of wages and materials increasing, I have to look round to find means of raising the necessary cash. I have decided that I must sell at least one farm to provide the money to maintain the others, and since Oakleigh is the most valuable and also, I may add, the best-managed farm on the estate, it is the property most likely to sell at a good price.

From one point of view it is unjust that your own efforts and skill have been the means of making your farm the one to be sacrificed, but I am bound by the econmic facts of estate management.

Of course, this notice will not expire until Ladyday 1913, and I am giving you this extra six months to seek out and lease another farm equally to your liking. I hope that you are speedily successful. You have been an ideal tenant, and I am grateful to you for your unfailing co-operation.

You will receive a formal notice to quit within a day or two.

Yours faithfully,

Charles M. Ratcliffe

P.S. Of course if you wish to buy the farm yourself you would have priority over other prospective purchasers. The upset price will be £6000.

C.M.R.'

There was an uncomfortable silence as Mr Ratcliffe finished reading. He held the letter in his hand and continued to stare at it, as if trying to decipher some hidden message contrary to the printed word.

'Notice to quit!' said his wife bemused. 'Why ever has the squire done that? Only bad farmers are told to leave their farms. This has always been our home, and Sam, Meg and Arthur were all born in the front-room upstairs. To start in another house and another farm at our time of life! How could he do such a thing to us?'

'He's the landlord, Maggie, and can do as he likes. I've always accepted that. But I thought that keeping the place in tip-top condition, doing the land well, keeping religiously to my agreement would ensure that I'd be able to farm here all my life, and that Sam could take it on after me. Seemingly I was wrong.'

'Will you be able to get another farm, dad?' asked Arthur, juvenile anxiety competing with the possibility of a move to an exciting new place.

'I expect so Arthur—somewhere. Farms are allus changing hands. But it might not be where I want, or the size I want, nor the sort of land I like. It might not be a riverside farm for instance.'

'What, leave the dear old Trent behind,' said Meg, 'I shall refuse to go!'

'That's typical of you, Meg,' said her father, smiling in spite of his concern. 'But I'm afraid we have no option but to leave here on Ladyday the year after next, whether we've got another farm or not. We might have to hold a sale and give up altogether, but that doesn't bear thinking about.'

'I should damned well think not,' growled Sam. 'We've allus been farmers, and it's a pity if we can't find another farm in Derbyshire to go to. Not that I like the idea o' moving. We might have to take some run-down farm where it'll take years to get things straight.'

'Hell, Sam, don't make it worse than it is. Whatever farm we take is bound to be different to this, that's certain. There'll be a lot o' traipsing about looking at places, which'll take up a lot o' time. And we mustn't let this place go down either, or we'll be soaked for dilapidations.'

'I reckon nowt to the whole idea,' said Sam disagreeably. 'Since as far back as I can remember, there's been only about two farms change hands on this estate. Why should we be the third? Why the hell should we be pushed out?'

Bob had kept his seat at the table while this conversation was going on. He knew he should not have remained to overhear this discussion, which was for the family only. But he was so concerned for these people that he wished he could soften the effects of this bombshell. So he put his good manners behind him and sat tight.

He had listened carefully to the landlord's letter and taken in the salient points. Leave the farm on March 25th 1913 or buy it for £6000. He was about to speak when the farmer, realising that time was passing and no work being done, brought them all back to earth with a jolt.

'Well, talking about the squire's letter won't earn us our dinner. Carry on getting the muck out on Upper Finches. If we get a drop of rain soon—and I think we're bound to 'fore long—we'll be able to get the plough going. We'll have plenty of time to talk about this.'

Sam and Bob each took a horse and cart to the huge stack of manure which had been moved from the yards in May. To begin with Bob filled the carts while Sam set the muck out in small heaps in the field. Then realising that filling carts was more strenuous than emptying, Sam changed jobs with the younger lad.

'Six rucks to the load and set 'em six by six,' were Sam's gruff instructions. Bob liked the precision of this work. Each heap being six yards from the next in the row and each row being six yards from its neighbour, meant that the rows were straight in every direction. He was careful not to break the symmetry, and to gauge accurately a sixth of his load at each stop, but as he worked his thoughts dwelt from time to time on his employer's new problem.

At dinner-time the atmosphere was subdued, and not as friendly as usual. Bob hoped that the subject of leaving the farm would crop up so that he could produce his own comments, but the meal went on in silence. However, as she was serving pudding, Meg remarked that as the day was so hot she would go down for a bathe later on.

'We shall miss the river when we go,' she added wistfully. Her father grunted, Mrs Ratcliffe sighed, and Sam said morosely, 'We shall miss more things than that. Damn the squire! Now we know why he didn't turn up for the rabbit-shootin' this year. Had this in mind and was ashamed to face us.'

'Maybe,' said his father and fell silent again. But this gave Bob his opportunity, and he said somewhat timidly, 'What about buying the farm outright, Mr Ratcliffe? The squire did suggest it in the last paragraph.'

The farmer was irritated that an employee should presume to comment on such an important matter. 'What on earth are you talking about, Bob. How can a lad like you know about such things. The squire's offer was a formality. He knows perfectly well I can't buy it! A tenant farmer is a tenant farmer.

He doesn't *buy* his farm.'

This was intended to close the subject, but Bob stuck to his guns.

'Why not?'

Mr Ratcliffe's exasperation mounted.

'Just because, that's why.' Then, seeing the hurt look on the lad's face, he realised he was genuinely interested and not asking out of mere curiosity, and went on more evenly. 'Farmers don't own their own land, lad, because their capital is needed for livestock and implements. This way they can farm a bigger place. If a farmer had to buy his farm before he started, he'd only be able to afford a small-holding. So only rich men like the squire own the land they farm. Ordinary working farmers are all tenants.'

Bob's face was a study in concentration, so the farmer continued his explanation, with the shadow of a smile.

'I couldn't possibly afford to buy Oakleigh, Bob. The squire's asking a heck of a price, I must say, but I couldn't buy if he cut it by half. It's not difficult to reckon up my capital; roughly forty cows at say twenty pound, twenty-four last year's calves at ten, fifteen stirk heifers say fifteen apiece, and the rest of the fat beast. Fifty ewes at two or three pound, five hosses at no more than fifty. Then there's the implements, the hay and corn and the tenant-right–that's what you have to pay for the growing crops, the muck and all that. Put all the lot together and I don't suppose it'd come to more than £3000. If I sold everything I'd got I could only buy half the farm, and if I did that, what would I farm it with afterwards? You see, Bob, it's impossible.'

Bob's mind was groping back to his paper-round days, when he had delivered impressive financial journals to some of his father's wealthy customers. They had not interested him, but he had flicked through them from time to time.

'I thought perhaps you could borrow the money–on mortgage. I think it's called.'

'Aye, I've heard of that too.' He was speaking to the whole family now, sensing their renewed interest in the faint encouragement from the other side of the table. 'Such things are possible, I don't doubt. But I've no knowledge of 'em–wouldn't know how to set about it. I s'pose it'd mean crawling to a bank, or asking a local firm of auctioneeers to arrange a loan, or maybe a solicitor. I'm not going to make myself look a fool by asking for a loan I might not be able to get. And the interest these money-lending sharks charge! It's crippling I believe. We couldn't pay it and the rent as well. Do you think we could, Sam?'

Bob replied quickly before Sam's slower thoughts could intrude.

'There wouldn't be any rent, Mr Ratcliffe, would there?'

'Eh?'

'I mean, it'd be your own farm wouldn't it? You'd only pay the interest on the loan and the loan itself a bit at a time.'

'Oh, Ah! Yes, that's right!' The farmer was annoyed with himself for not having seen such an obvious fact. 'But the interest on the loan'd be terrific—much more than the rent and I mightn't be able to raise it. But how come you know so much about these things, young feller?'

'I don't really. But on my paper-round there were some big houses owned by rich men. Stockbrokers in the city or something, and we delivered papers to 'em that dealt with money and investment. I glanced through them now and again in the shop. There was one called *The Investors Chronicle and Money Market Review.*'

'I see. I s'pose if I read a magazine or two like that I'd know more about loans and things. You've certainly set me thinking, Bob, although I doubt if there's much hope of it happening. But how can I get hold of these books? I wouldn't like to order 'em in our local shop and let 'em know what I was up to. Nor would I like to enquire in Derby. It'd look a rum do if a farmer asked for such obscure papers.'

A sudden thought struck Bob, and with it a feeling of guilt.

'I could write home and get dad to send one or two,' he suggested half-heartedly, hoping his employer would veto the idea. But Mr Ratcliffe welcomed it enthusiastically.

'A capital idea! You do that right away, Bob. It's about time you wrote home anyway. You haven't done so since you first came have you? That's a bad do, lad, you ought to keep in touch with your family. Maggie, you should 'a made him! Anyway, write tonight and put in enough stamps to cover the cost and postage.'

'Why not write now?' asked Meg. 'Then it could go by the afternoon post!'

'Write a letter in the day-time?' queried her father. 'Who ever heard of such a thing? You must be daft to suggest it! Bob'll be at muck-carting all afternoon. We don't have to give up the farm for eighteen months you know—missing one post won't matter. Do it right after tea, Bob, and Sam will take the milk while you write it.'

During the afternoon, while he was setting out the heaps of manure under the warm September sun, Bob composed the letter to his father. He felt ashamed when he thought he had been at Oakleigh for more than seven months, and since that harsh letter from his father had not written home. He had been so absorbed with his new job that the cramped little house in Mill Hill had never entered his mind.

He found himself comparing the competent Mrs Ratcliffe with his harassed over-worked mother; the bluff, hearty farmer, with the critical and demanding attitude of Mr Felton; and the noisiness of his younger brothers and sister with the friendly dedication of Sam, the ebullience of Meg and the loquacity of the lovable Arthur.

He pulled himself up. This was disloyalty. But when he compared the sameness of his paper-round with his nightly run to Willington with Bluebell or Diamond, he almost laughed at the difference. He found exhilaration in working with the horses, a quiet satisfaction with the cows, and in the harvesting of crops a supreme fulfilment. He would not change any of it for newsagent's work if his father offered him the whole business with the shop thrown in. The huge farmhouse kitchen where he could walk about without knocking into things was pleasant to live in after the cramped quarters behind the shop. He was so pleased with his farm life that he did not care if he never saw Mill Hill again. He felt a little wistful about his mother, though. She had always done her best for him.

Meg ostentatiously placed writing materials and stamps beside him while he was still drinking his last cup of tea at the evening meal.

'What's the hurry, Meg?'

'You get that letter written right away while Sam's harnessing the mare and loading the churns, and he can post it at Willington. I'd like to think that it's on its way.'

With a sigh Bob took up the pen, dipped it into the ink-bottle and wrote scratchily,

'Dear Father,

I have not heard from you for a long time but I daresay that's because I didn't answer your last letter. But we're always so busy on a farm with the different jobs as they come round. There always seems to be something to do. We work long hours, but as the work is so pleasant I don't notice the time. We have five horses here and I drive all of them, and 40 cows and I can milk most of them. The people I work for are a very nice family and I like it here; I wouldn't want to go back to the old trade-bike. I suppose Billy is getting on well with that now. How is the shop going? Pretty well, I hope. Please give my love to Mum. I often think of her and of you all when I am on my own in the fields.

By the way, will you send me an *Investor's Chronicle* and a *Financial World* as soon as you can? Any date will do, it doesn't have to be this week's. Mr Ratcliffe would like to look through them.

Your affect. son
Robt. Felton.

P.S. I enclose 1/- in stamps.'

Sam came into the kitchen just as Bob licked the envelope.

'Got that letter, Bob? I'm just going.'

'Yes. I've finished it, and as it's ready I might as well take the milk myself. No need for you to go.'

'Please yourself lad. I've plenty to do here.'

Bob carefully placed the letter in his pocket and went out through the cooling shed.

'I'm coming too,' said Meg suddenly. 'It's a fine evening and I want a few things from the shop. I want to make sure that letter's posted.'

Arthur, bent over his homework at the other end of the table, threw down his pen.

'If you're going, Meg, so am I!' and he rushed through into the yard, scrambling into the float just as it moved off.

Mr Ratcliffe recovered from his surprise.

'Hey, come back you two! That mare's got enough to pull without your weight!' As they were now out of earshot, he added resignedly, 'Oh, well let 'em go. They didn't bother to listen anyway. Youngsters! They do as they like these days!'

Mrs Ratcliffe smiled.

'It's nice to see them so friendly among themselves. They've never taken to any of the other lads as they've taken to Bob.'

'Aye, perhaps it's as well Arthur's gone along with 'em. I don't think we want to chuck Meg and Bob together too much.'

'Oh, Arnold. Nothing's going to happen between those two. Meg's too sensible and Bob's too shy. In three or four years' time, perhaps . . .'

'Maybe. I like Bob. He's a bright lad, allus thinking out summat new. Pity he hasn't got a bit more behind him. I hope Meg does a bit better for herself than marry a farm lad, even if he is a good 'un.'

'You're old-fashioned, dad,' Sam put in. 'If Bob goes on as he is, he'll be good enough for any farmer's daughter round here.'

'Perhaps, perhaps! We'll cross that bridge when we come to it. But now the youngsters are out of the way I'd like to unload summat that's been bothering my mind all afternoon. About this notice to quit, now. I'm beginning to think that it's the result o' that Coronation day episode.'

'Arnold! Why ever would the squire behave like that?'

'Well, it must 'a rankled a bit with him. Perhaps I did wrong in going to see him the next morning, taking Sam with me. I'm sure he didn't like the idea of my farm lad fighting with Mortimer. If the circumstances had been different, he'd probably have told me to sack the lad. What a business it all was! If only Meg 'ud flattened Mortimer when he first started getting fresh. And then Bob had to wade in! The gentry don't like getting involved in scrimmages with the likes of us. 'Course, I wouldn't like Bob or Meg to know that I thought this. They might feel themselves to blame, and that'd be unfair. Meg wasn't prepared for what happened, and Bob went in gamely to the rescue.'

'But I don't see what you're getting at, dad,' Sam seemed puzzled. 'What's all this to do wi' our notice to quit?'

'I reckon the squire thinks it's best to get us off the estate and right out o' the village, so he can wipe all this off the slate.'

'I can't believe it, Arnold. If he wanted that, why offer to sell you the place?'

'Ah! That's where he's smart, and he's salving his own conscience at the same time. He knows darn well that tenant farmers don't buy their farms–just as I know it. And I wouldn't ever have thought about it for a second if Bob hadn't kept prodding me, the young monkey! Something might come of it. We'll see what happens in the next few days.'

The Ratcliffes were not kept long in suspense. On the second morning after Bob's letter had been despatched, a rolled package arrived, addressed to him.

'By gum,' said Mr Ratcliffe in surprise. 'Your father's a reight business man to get these back to us so quick.' He took the two journals from Bob's hand and looked with dismay at the solid matter of the text and the tabulated figures. 'Huh! This stuff's going to take some digesting. I'd better leave it until after tea and give the whole evening to it.'

There was also a letter in the wrapper, which Bob opened with some trepidation. It ran,

'Dear Robert,

Thanks for your letter. I am glad to hear that you like the life you have chosen and are living with decent people. Your mother has worried about you in the last months, but now she knows you are happy she won't have to any more. Billy likes the paper round, and is a great help to me in the business, and Betty and Jack are growing up in the way that children do. As I may not see you for some time I offer you some advice as to your conduct which it is the duty of a father to do. Always try to be truthful and honest, and put something by for a rainy day. Succeed in this and you can't be far wrong. If you do ever come down this way we naturally expect you to call and see us.

Your Affect. Father,
John Felton.'

Bob was not disturbed by the tone of finality in the letter. He knew his father meant well, although he had an acid way of putting things. But for a long time now the boy had regarded Oakleigh Farm as his real home.

Mr Ratcliffe settled down to his financial reading after tea, and when Bob returned from the station he was still poring over the journals in the lamplight. At supper-time he announced the result, but not with any sense of achievement.

'I can't make head or tail of the articles or the general information,' he grumbled. 'Might as well try to read bloomin' Latin. But there are adverts of loan companies, and I'm going to write to one of them, setting out the plain facts, and see what happens. It can't do any harm.'

Meg left the table, went to the sideboard and brought out pen, ink and paper which she put in front of her father.

'I didn't say I was going to write it now,' he protested, then looking round at his family, 'I don't know what the deuce you're all grinning at! Oh, all right then, if you're all so set on it.'

As September passed into October the pace of the farm work quickened. Several women came from the village for the potato-picking, at which Meg also turned out to help. Sam spun the tubers out with the digger, drawn by Flower and Violet. As the women picked the potatoes into bags, Ernie and Bob carted them off with Major and built a long tapering 'camp' in the corner of the field, covering it with straw and earth as they went along. It was a pleasant job when the weather was fine, but on damp and gloomy days the work was muddy and depressing. On the final morning of the potato-harvest a typewritten letter arrived for Mr Ratcliffe. He read it twice, then aloud as they all sat, tense with expectation, at the breakfast table.

'Dear Sir, I am in receipt of your letter of 28th Ult. and beg to inform you that this company would be prepared to consider making a loan for the purchase of your farm. On a purchase price of £6000 you would be expected to find a deposit of £1000 and a mortgage of £5000 would be issued to complete the transfer. Our current interest rate is 6% and both capital and interest could be repaid by a set annual sum remitted six-monthly, the first payment falling due three months from the date of completion of the agreement. The annual repayments on a loan of £5000 would be £515 per annum for fifteen years, £437.10 for twenty years and £393.10 per annum for twenty-five years.

If you have a banking account we shall require a reference from your banker, and in any case it is desirable that you should open an account with a reputable bank, as we may require the repayments to be made by Banker's Order.

The farm will of course have to be inspected by a valuer of our choosing, and you will be responsible for paying his fee. We also require you to appoint a solicitor to negotiate on your behalf, as we do not normally deal direct with our clients.

I hope this information is of assistance to you and look forward to hearing from you again in due course.

I am, Sir, your obedient servant, (can't read the signature) Secretary. Oh, yes I can, it's up at the top of the letter, John Hubbard.'

'Well, that's it. What do you all think of it?'

They all tried to speak at once, but produced such a babel of noise that finally Sam and Meg gave way to allow their mother to speak.

'I must say it sounds all right,' she said. 'It's easier to buy a farm than we thought.'

'What beats me,' said Sam, 'is that if we take the longest period the repayments are less than the rent! Sounds ridiculous!'

'Aye, it does look like that at first sight,' said his father. 'I've allus known I was paying a high rent. 'Course, we'd have to pay for all our own repairs and materials, which we get in with the rent now. Even so, I'm a bit shaken myself.'

'We'll be able to do whatever we like with the farm now,' said Meg grandly, 'Improve the house, lay water on, put up new buildings.'

'Hold hard a bit, spendthrift,' her father admonished. 'Don't get such big ideas. I've got to find this £1000 deposit first, and that won't be easy.'

'Any idea of the bank balance, dad,' asked Sam warily.

'No, not really. So long as I know there's enough in to pay the bills and rent and the housekeeping, I don't keep a check on the balance. It should be building up a bit now, 'cos the rent's due this week. Let's see, we sent fourteen beast to the butcher and he paid for all but two which I'll get on Saturday–just under twenty apiece–that's £250. Sixty lambs have gone, that's about £105. Then there's twenty-seven acres of wheat to thresh out and sell which might come to £140.'

'We could sell the twelve bulling heifers,' suggested Sam. 'But it would muck up the milking plan a bit. They'd fetch fifteen or sixteen apiece.'

'And my last year's calves look well,' said Meg bravely. 'All twenty-four of them. They should make nine or ten pounds each.'

'I know all that,' objected their father. 'But if I sell all our young stock, it'll reduce our income for a year or two.'

'Better than losing the farm, dad,' Meg pointed out.

'What about selling Diamond?' said Bob mischievously,

knowing that the others would not dare to mention it.

Mr Ratcliffe stuck his chin out and stared straight ahead.

'No!' he said. 'That hoss stays here until he's learned to stand quiet and work properly, like the others. I've never made a mistake with a hoss yet, and Diamond's not going to be the first. We'll raise the money without selling him. Now how much have we got, if we sell all the young stock?' He made several pencilled calculations on the envelope, producing varying totals. 'About £925 I make it, plus whatever was in the bank before. But £200 is earmarked for the Michaelmas rent.'

There was silence for a few moments, then Mrs Ratcliffe said quietly, 'If you need it, Arnold, there's my Midland Railway shares Uncle John left me. They were worth about £500 last time we checked. He left about £100 worth to each of the kids too, but I s'pose we can't touch that till they come of age.'

'Well, that's next month for me,' Sam reminded his parents. 'And of course you're welcome to that, if it's to help the farm. I should probably have bought summat for the farm anyway. And since I've never drawn any interest it must be worth nearly double by now.'

Mr Ratcliffe seemed vastly relieved.

'That's a load off my mind. Thanks Maggie—and you, Sam. If I've got the railway money to fall back on there should be no problem.'

Bob would dearly have liked to offer a loan to his employer, but his nine or ten pounds in the Post Office seemed too small to mention. Instead he said, 'If it'll help, Mr Ratcliffe, I wouldn't mind working without wages until you're all straightened up. It might help a bit!'

The farmer beamed at Bob and clapped him on the shoulder.

'Good for you, Bob. Thank ye, but I don't think that will be necessary. You've already contributed enough, lad. It was your idea that set the whole thing going. I'll tell you what I'll do Sam,' he went on as they emerged on to the yard. 'I'll drive to Burton tomorrow to see a solicitor—there's one called Tunnicliffe near the station. Then I'll call at the bank and see what my balance is.'

'But your bank's at Derby,' Sam pointed out in some surprise.

'I know, Sam, but I'm sure that branches of the bank are joined up by telephone nowadays. Might find out the amount while I wait. Now we'd better get up to the potato-field, or the women'll be up there wi' nowt to do.'

Chapter Eleven

Mr Ratcliffe returned home from his visit to Burton in high spirits.

'I'm better off than I thought,' he announced with satisfaction as they sat round the tea-table. He had a habit of reserving important statements until all his family were gathered round him, and this usually happened only at meal times. 'There was over £400 in the bank before I sold the fat-stock. There's been a payment for milk sin' then–£60 odd–so my credit's now over £845. 'Course, there's the rent to come off, but even so I'm well on the way to the £1000 deposit.'

'So you won't need to sell any of the young stock,' said Sam with relief.

'Well, no; but I think I will sell about seven of the twelve big heifers. There aren't any cows to throw out, so five'll be enough to maintain the herd. Meg, you know the mothers of 'em. Pick out the five best to keep, and the other seven can go to the autumn sale at Derby in a fortnight. We'll thresh out one bay of wheat as soon as we can get Hibbert to come round–we've got to thresh some oats anyway for the chopping straw–that'll bring in another £50. So Maggie, if you could sell half your Midland shares and lend me the money, we shall get by. Oh, and I've seen Tunnicliffe. He'll be pleased to handle the business for us, so all we need to do is sit back and wait. Bob, hadn't you better get off with that milk? You don't want to cut it fine and upset the porter.'

After the potatoes were safely camped down, the mangolds and swedes occupied their attention. The great globes were pulled from the ground and left in round heaps. As Sam was engaged ploughing for the next year's wheat crop, Bob and Ernie were set to cart the mangolds from the field and camp them in the rickyard. Meg insisted on turning out to help load the carts. Her father was pleased at her willingness.

'I'm not sure that I understand Meg,' he said to his wife. 'There's really no need for her to go out to the mangold field, nor help with the potatoes for that matter. She works more on the farm now than she's ever done, and it's not necessary.'

'Well, if she likes it . . .' Mrs Ratcliffe shrugged her shoulders.

'Yes, but we're well enough off to keep her at home to help you, and make things a bit better for all of us!'

'She's a good girl, Arnold. She gets up early and does the

milk, then digs in at the housework all morning. She doesn't go out until the dinner things are washed up. In the afternoon she could take things a bit easier, but if she prefers to go out in the field why should we interfere? I don't know why she does it.'

'Nor I! But she'll have her own way, Maggie, depend on that. Meg's a charming girl, but by gum, she's stubborn! I don't know where she gets it from.'

Mrs Ratcliffe was seized with a fit of coughing, and put her hand to her mouth. Her husband looked concerned.

'My! That's a sharp cough you've got there. Better take some honey and glycerine. Can't have you barking about the place like that!'

'That's all right, Arnold. Something must've tickled my throat.'

Before the mangold-carting was quite finished, the threshing outfit clanked into the yard. The huge steam engine puffed its lumbering way past the top of the muck-hole, its massive five-foot iron wheels grinding to powder every stone in their track. The train of equipment seemed endless to Bob. First the rectangular threshing drum, which was about eighteen feet long and eight feet high. Behind it was hitched the chopper, then the straw-battener, the water-cart, and finally the sack lifter, which enable the huge four-bushel sacks to be wound up to shoulder height for ease of carrying. The driver was in charge of the outfit, and he and his mate, whose job it was to feed the sheaves into the machine, were easily recognisable by their being blacker and oilier than the others. There were half-a-dozen additional followers of varying age, size and cleanliness. Two of them were tramp-types, who served the machine perpetually, and lived rough on the farms they visited. The rest were men who were temporarily out of regular employment.

With a great deal of shouting and jangling, men rushing hither and thither with chocks and chains, and much manipulation of the low-geared steering mechanism by the driver, the unwieldy machines were manoeuvred into place beside one of the bays of oats in the Dutch barn. As the straw was to be cut into chop for the winter feeding of the cows, the chopper was edged into place across the gaping mouth of the thresher, the unused trusser being left in the cow-yard.

At eight the next morning the long wide belt clapped and bounced, and the wheels all over the machines began to revolve. Sam and Bob had eaten an early breakfast to be present and Sam, being easily the strongest man among the crew, undertook the sacking, tying-up and loading. Bob was directed to help one of the travelling men to carry the bulky sacks of chop up the ladder to the loft above the mixing-place.

After his more leisurely breakfast, the master joined them and took his place on the shrinking corn stack, relieving another man for chop-carrying. This enabled Bob to harness Major, fill the water-cart from the river, and position it where the engine could replenish its tank with its suction pipe. He spent the rest of the day helping with the chop and corn alternately. Meg did not help with the threshing, for with eight extra men to be provided with a mid-day meal she was needed in the kitchen.

A day sufficed to thresh the stack of oats, and the machines were levered back inch by inch to the adjoining bay of wheat, which was also threshed in a day, and the battens of straw built in a neat stack in the bay emptied the previous day.

Everyone at the farm heaved a sigh of relief when the preposterous train jolted and lurched on to the next farm.

'Threshing's all very well,' said Sam, voicing the opinion of them all. 'But it's a damned good job when it's over and we can get back to normal.'

'*When* we get back to normal,' corrected his father. 'But there's a couple o' days' work clearing up after 'em first, and I want Bob to go in to Derby on Friday with those seven heifers. You've noted those we want to keep back, Meg?'

'Yes, dad. I reckon Pansy, Snowflake, Redwing, Granny and Duchess are among our best milkers, so I picked out their heifers.'

'Right! Well you'll have to be up early on Friday morning, 'cause I want 'em sorted out and Bob on his way by seven.'

Bob was aghast.

'Mr Ratcliffe, I'm not sure that I can do that job. I've never been to Derby yet, except when I came here by train, and as for finding where the market is in a big town and driving seven heifers at the same time! I just don't think I can do it!'

'Course you can do it, Bob. It's been done lots of times. Most farm lads driving cattle to market for the first time have never been before. But I'm not going to be too hard on you. Levi, the drover, is taking cattle in for Wainwright and Shaw, and I've arranged for you to meet him at the village, so that you can go in together. I've given him a shilling. You can't come to any harm with Levi, but I daresay you'll have to do most of the running about. And since I'm not buying any cattle, you'll ride back with me and Mrs Ratcliffe in the trap. What could you want better than that?'

Bob sighed with relief. Knowing nothing about cattle droving, he had been frightened at the responsibility thrust on him.

In the event it was easier than he had imagined. On Friday morning the milking was interrupted to drive the heifers in from the paddock, and they were sorted out under Meg's direction. Sam accompanied Bob as far as Shaw's farm, where he joined forces with a limping old man with a grey beard. His heart sank at first, but he soon found that Levi was skilful at his trade.

'Don't hurry 'em, lad. Don't hurry 'em; let 'em graze their way if they want to. They wunt wander far off the road. People keep their gates shut on market days!'

Bob had to do all the running and redirecting at first, but as they progressed, other drovers joined them, and the journey became a pleasant stroll, with occasional sprints to the side or front of the herd. Bob hoped he would be able to identify his own cattle when they arrived at the market, and wondered what would happen if he made a mistake.

They were in the market comfortably by eleven o'clock. The boy was taken aback by the size of the place, and appalled at the never-ending noise. The cattle were sorted out under the expert guidance of Levi, and Bob leaned on the rails of the pen to await his employer.

At the breakfast table at Oakleigh, Meg suddenly announced 'I'm coming with you today!'

Mrs Ratcliffe shrugged her shoulders and smiled faintly, but her husband remarked 'What ever for, girl? You haven't been to Derby with us for six months or more.'

'No, and that's why I want to go today. I want some special wool for my winter knitting.'

'Can't your mother get it for you?'

'Mum's got plenty to do with her own shopping.'

'Oh, all right! You've worked hard lately, so I suppose you'd better come. But there'll be four of us in the trap on the way back! That's quite a load for Bluebell. I think I'll take Diamond. Put him in for me when you go out, Sam, and tie him up by the back door.'

Bob was surprised to see Meg accompanying her father as he walked slowly up the alley appraising the young cattle. They spotted Bob and walked quickly to meet him.

'By gum, our beasts look well, don't they Bob?' Mr Ratcliffe said genially. 'I haven't seen another bunch in here to touch 'em. Now, you'd better be here when they go through the ring, but that won't be for an hour-and-a-half, so you can have a walk round the town if you want. Here's sixpence to buy a snack for your lunch.' He walked contentedly away up the alley, exchanging nods and greetings with everyone he met.

When her father was lost in the throng, Meg pulled Bob's arm.

'Come on, Bob, you're coming round the town with me.'

'Well, I don't know that . . .'

'Of course you are! My dad said so, didn't he?'

'He didn't say that I was to go with you!'

'Of course not! Only I can say that,' she replied, 'You ought to think yourself lucky. I don't walk round the town with anybody.'

Bob felt less at ease here than he would have been at home on the farm attending to the horses or cows. But Meg went on, 'I'll take you to a smart cafe where we can get a tip-top meal.'

'What, for sixpence?'

'Certainly not! But it only costs one-and-three. And if you haven't any money with you, I'll pay!'

'I couldn't allow that.'

But as they walked down the market, he was impressed by the number of young farmers who touched their caps and greeted Meg as 'Miss Ratcliffe'. He noticed that some of them were no better dressed than he and this made him feel less uncomfortable.

Meg's chatter made them linger over lunch, until Bob realised that the time was approaching when the Oakleigh heifers were to be sold. He ended the one-sided conversation, and they hurried in the direction of the market. Bob walked quickly, a few paces in front, his impatience causing him to widen the gap. Meg's anger mounted. He halted reluctantly while she caught up.

'Bob Felton! If you're going along at that pace just to see those heifers sold, you'd better leave me and go on ahead. I'm not used to rushing along at this pace in town.'

'Oh, thanks Meg, I'll do that,' Bob said with relief and broke into a run, leaving the astonished girl standing.

He pushed breathlessly through to the ringside, just in time to see his seven heifers hustled into the ring.

'Here you are, gentlemen, look at this grand lot,' intoned the stout auctioneer. 'From Mr Ratcliffe of Oakleigh. Well-bred, well-reared and well brought-out; and what beautiful colours! Well, they're in front of you, I don't need to describe them! What may I say for these, gentlemen? Fifteen apiece?'

'Yes!' called out several voices eagerly, and the bidding rose quickly by five shilling steps to £17.10., when they were knocked down to Mr Riley of Aston. 'I don't mind selling cattle of this sort,' said the delighted auctioneer, striking his gavel on the round iron rail in front of him with such vigour that tiny fragments flew off in all directions.

Bob moved away from the ring-side and a few minutes later Mr Ratcliffe joined him.

'I'm pleased with the price Bob,' he said gleefully. 'At least a pound a head more than I expected. Now . . .' he consulted his watch. 'It's a quarter to two. I haven't much more to do, but I daresay the women are still on with their shopping. If you see Meg tell her to be at the market entrance at half-past two. I'll bring the trap round about that time.'

Bob hung around the stalls in the general market which occupied the Morledge leading into the stock market. He decided not to look for Meg immediately, thinking that her impetuous ways might land him into another situation he could not deal with. But it was not long before he spotted her among the stalls with her mother. As they were both loaded with parcels, he hurried round and offered to carry part of their load.

'Thanks, Bob,' said Mrs Ratcliffe. 'You might as well take some of it for us. I'm practically done shopping now, so we can go straight back to the hotel and put the stuff in the trap. The rest should have been delivered there by now.'

They made their way slowly through the crowded streets and turned down a side-road by a large inn. Double-doors led into the stable yard, and Bob at once spotted the Ratcliffe trap among more than a dozen others. They deposited their packages, and Bob was sent to collect two more boxes from the covered walk at the back of the inn. 'They'll have our name on them,' Mrs Ratcliffe said. By the time he had collected them, the master had arrived and he fetched Diamond from the long stable. Bob helped to put him in the shafts of the trap.

'Now, mother,' said the farmer, 'I suppose you'd like to travel facing back with Meg while I have Bob to talk to, in front.'

But it was Meg who answered him.

'Nothing of the sort, dad! Let mum travel in front with you. It's her rightful place. Bob won't mind sitting beside me at the back.'

'All right! Have it your own way!'

They all climbed aboard and, sitting back to back, set off at a smart trot. Facing the rear, with his back hard against that of Mrs Ratcliffe, Bob thought this was a splendid way to spend the afternoon, notwithstanding the fact that his foot-room was restricted by the parcels and boxes of provisions. Opportunities for conversation were limited. Mr Ratcliffe occasionally spoke over his shoulder to Bob, and Mrs Ratcliffe in a similar way to her daughter. But as they neared the village, the farmer and his wife became engaged in a deep conversation. Meg moved her head closer to Bob, and said in a stage whisper, 'Bob Felton, don't you ever dare to leave me standing alone in the street like that again.'

'But you told me to,' Bob replied, mystified.

'I didn't mean it, silly. You should have stayed with me, like a gentleman.'

'But I'm not a gentleman; I'm trying to be a farmer!'

She tossed her head and looked the other way until they bowled into the yard. As there was no stock in the drive-side fields, the gates were tied back to give them passage. When Diamond pulled up in front of the kitchen window, Bob jumped down and ran round to hold the horse. Meg called him back.

'Bob, come back here and help me down!'

The lad halted, shrugged his shoulders resignedly, and with an exaggerated flourish took Meg's hand and guided her down the two steps. She looked at him condescendingly then wagged her finger in admonition. He burst out laughing.

Meg flushed, but her father said drily, 'Bob, when you've finished paying court to Queen Ratcliffe, perhaps you'll come round here and hold Diamond. If I let go these reins he'll strike off again for Derby.'

The successful sale of the seven heifers put Mr Ratcliffe in a jovial mood for a day or two. Bob, too, was pleased to think that his aching leg-muscles and tender feet had not been endured for nothing. The younger Ratcliffes, with their strong sense of family loyalty, were delighted that another £100 had been made available to clinch the purchase of the farm, which they now regarded as a certainty. Meg had privately discussed with her mother the possibility of having water brought into the kitchen, and a new stove with a boiler attached. Sam toyed with the idea of building a new fold-yard, so that more young stock could be carried over the winter, and perhaps an extension to the hay-barn as well. Arthur had settled down at the grammar school, and seemed contented to share his time between it and the farm.

Mr Ratcliffe expected news regarding his application for a mortgage, but week succeeded week and he heard nothing. He became worried as the month ended, and feared that his application for a loan had been turned down. But on the last day of the month he received a letter from his solicitor informing him that the loan company's surveyor, Mr John Shakespeare, would inspect the farm on Tuesday December 5th. He would like free access to every field and building on the farm, preferably unaccompanied by the farmer, but for distant fields he might welcome a guide from Mr Ratcliffe's staff.

'Huh,' grunted the farmer, after he had read out at the breakfast table. 'He obviously doesn't want me around! But he'll be glad to have dinner with us nevertheless. Better put on something a bit special, Maggie. We might as well make as good an impression as possible. This chap's opinion is going to mean a lot to us. We can't do much about the farm in three days—

that's probably why they're giving us so little notice. But we'll do what we can. Thank goodness we're so well up wi' the work. We'll do a bit o' tidying up, but on Tuesday, Sam, I want you out ploughing while the surveyor is here. Do a bit o' show ploughing for him!'

'Bit o' window dressin', like?'

'Why not? It can't do any harm and it might do some good. Now we'd best all get back to work. We've had a long breakfast-time.'

'Wait a minute, dad,' Meg said. 'Bob's got something to say. I can tell by the look on his face!'

'Oh, Meg!' said Bob resentfully, flushing. His employer grinned at the lad's confusion, and at Meg's importunity.

'If you've got anything to say, Bob, say it. All suggestions welcomed, lad!'

Bob had the germ of an idea in his head, but had not formulated it into words. Characteristically, Meg had been premature.

'I was thinking of the young stock, Mr Ratcliffe. It looks very untidy where they are now, in the Rickyard Close. There's straw lying about where they've been fed, a bit of hay as well as kale stalks. And there's tons of muck where they've laid about so much in the sheltered part o' the field. If we could get 'em all in the fold-yard just before this man comes, bed 'em up well with plenty o' straw, they'd look contented and comfortable and sort o' fill the eye. Then perhaps we could chain-harrow the ground to level out the muck and straw and that.'

Mr Ratcliffe looked at his young employee for a few seconds without speaking, but Sam reacted at once.

'That's a damn' good idea, Bob. Those young beast'ud look as pretty as a picture in a newly bedded yard, and the racks filled with good hay. If we got 'em in the previous morning I could easily chain-harrow the field.

'You've taken the words out of my mouth, Sam. It's a bit earlier than normal, but it's wuth gettin' 'em in for the effect. Thanks for the idea, Bob. You don't miss much, do you?'

'He wouldn't have said a word if I hadn't prompted him,' Meg said with an air of superiority.

'Of course he would, Meg. He just wanted to organize his ideas before he brought them out, that's all. It might be a good thing if you did that sometimes, young lady,' her father reproved. But he gave her an affectionate pat on the shoulder as he walked away from the table.

Tidying-up operations went ahead as planned. On Monday evening Mr Ratcliffe said to Bob 'Take out a good load o' kale to the cows tomorrow so they can fill themselves up well. But get it done by ten and then go off to Willington with Bluebell and the best cart to meet Mr Shakespeare off the 10.28 train. 'Matter of fact we'd all best start half-an-hour earlier in the morning, so that all the feeding can be done and Sam and Ernie out in the field before this chap arrives.'

Bluebell's coat shone glossily to match the polished harness and the varnished trap as Bob proudly drew up to the station just as the train pulled in. He did not have time to alight. A carriage-door opened opposite the platform gate, and a tall sharp-faced man, wearing smart breeches, brown boots and leggings, a burberry and a bowler hat, came towards him. He took in the mare, the trap and Bob in one sweeping glance and said, 'You're from Oakleigh Farm, I take it?'

'That's right, sir! And you'll be Mr Shakespeare?'

The man nodded and climbed aboard; Bluebell set off at a spanking pace back to Hartnall. The passenger was obviously impressed.

'Mr Ratcliffe certainly keeps a good nag for the station work.'

'Mr Ratcliffe likes all his stock to be good,' Bob replied loyally.

They arrived at the farm, met Mr Ratcliffe outside the kitchen, and Mr Shakespeare made it known that he would like to start his tour of inspection immediately. The farmer said, 'Very good, Mr Shakespeare. Now I suggest you do the riverside fields and the other land across the road first, and then have some dinner with us. In the afternoon you can do the farm this side of the road. I think you'll be able to do that on foot, but the lad can drive you down to the river boundary. Bob, put Bluebell in the float and take Mr Shakespeare all over the bottom ground.'

Bob drove into each of the four river meadows, where Ernie was busy brushing the hedges. Shakespeare had a word with him as they passed by.

'You're well on with your work, my man!'

'Ar!' said the labourer, 'We allus like to do as much 'edgin' as we can afore Christmas, when the wood begins to get 'arder. The gaffer's a rare 'un to push on.'

The surveyor produced an extending auger from his case and bored out a sample of soil in several places. He examined the earth at the tip of the tool with a grunt of satisfaction.

'Seems to me, young fellow, that you've got better soil a foot down than some farmers have on the surface!'

'It's good land down here,' agreed Bob.

'And not much of it liable to flooding,' said Mr Shakespeare, scanning the rise in the ground towards the road. They visited the two arable fields on the higher ground above the river, both of which were now sown with wheat. The pale green shoots showed in clear unbroken rows across the red earth. The visitor made a note or two in his book, and they returned to the farm for a twelve o'clock dinner.

Mrs Ratcliffe and Meg had excelled themselves, and provided a superb meal. Mr Shakespeare became expansive, but pointed out that he could not linger as much as he would like to. Darkness came early in December, and as he would be on foot this afternoon, he would get started again as soon as he had finished his cup of tea.

'I must say, Mr Ratcliffe, I am very pleased with what I have seen of your riverside land. The soil is excellent, the grass has been grazed evenly, and it is free from weeds. The fences are nicely maintained too. As for the two fields of wheat, they are about the best I have seen this autumn.'

Mr Ratcliffe was gratified. 'Glad you think so, Mr Shakespeare,' he said visibly expanding his chest. Then he added, 'I find I can spare Bob to take you round in the float again.'

Having achieved his object, Mr Shakespeare agreed to accept a second cup of tea. Meg having now disappeared, the surveyor thanked Mrs Ratcliffe for an excellent meal, and left the kitchen with Bob, who suggested going round the yard first.

'As you wish.'

They walked down the cowshed into the mixing-place, the visitor taking note of the condition of the buildings. Then into the stable, where he remarked on the cleanliness and the well-maintained harness. Major, Diamond and Bluebell were still in their stalls.

'A little overstocked with horseflesh,' he murmured. 'But that's not a bad thing. Less likely to get behind with the work.'

Bob led him past the new Dutch barn to the two fold-yards, where the young cattle had recently been housed. The gates to the yards were side-by-side, and the surveyor stood where he could look into both yards at once. He drew in his breath in admiration. The yards had been deeply bedded with clean wheat straw a few hours before and the well-fed animals were lying down chewing the cud in contentment. On being disturbed, some got up, stretched, and then sauntered to the gate to investigate.

'What a grand lot of beasts!' Mr Shakespeare said, 'I'd like to have those to sell in Leicester. Beautiful matching colours, well-bred, I've no doubt, and in the pink of condition. Brought into the buildings in good time, too. You are far too liberal with this excellent hay, though,' he indicated the hay-racks still half-full.

Bob sensed that the man suspected the cattle had been fed and bedded for effect, and thought he ought to comment.

Unwittingly, he said exactly the right thing, taking the blame on himself.

'They only came in yesterday, Mr Shakespeare. I'm looking after them, and haven't had time to judge their appetite properly yet. The gaffer might be angry if he saw this. I hope they clean it up before he comes this way.' He looked uneasily over his shoulder. The surveyor glanced at the boy keenly and smiled as they turned away.

'I'll show you the calves now,' said Bob. 'They're Meg's responsibility.'

The girl had left the kitchen immediately after dinner to give them fresh bedding. Mr Shakespeare walked along the alley looking into each box over the doors. The animals blinked their bright eyes as they gazed at the strangers. They looked comfortable in their new straw, each box having its clean water bucket secured just inside the door for easy removal, and a tiny hay-rack filled with the best meadow hay. Meg was in the last box shaking out the straw, and her face was flushed with her exertions. Mr Shakespeare smiled broadly.

'Ah! Now I know why the charming Miss Ratcliffe left us so quickly after lunch. I really do not know which is the more beautiful, the calves or the calf-rearer. I must congratulate you, young lady, on your excellent stock. Now I know why the yearlings are such a splendid bunch. They are so well-reared in the early stages. That makes all the difference. But I must not stay here, lost in admiration though I may be. We'd better move on round the fields, Bob.'

Bluebell was re-harnessed and put in the float and they drove through the herd of forty milkers and then over to Winter Pasture, where the bull kept company with the five retained heifers. The surveyor visited every field on the farm, took samples from most of them, made notes about drains and ditches, and remarked on the good maintenance of the gates. Finally they visited Sam, who was ploughing the last stubble field but one.

Violet and Flower made a superb picture of grace and power as Bob drove the float across the unploughed ground. Their huge strides pulled the plough sweetly through the soil. Mr Shakespeare stepped down from the float and walked along the headland, appraising the furrows. Sam was by then at the distant end of the field, and turned his team easily, skidding his plough along the headland, and setting in smoothly for the return trip with no noticeable pause. He was proud of his skill and cut a dead-straight furrow. He reached the near end, turned, and set in again, before he stopped for a word with the visitor. The mares steamed slightly in the afternoon air.

'A magnificent job of ploughing, young man,' said Mr Shakespeare with admiration. 'You're cutting it clean and deep and setting it up well for the winter frosts. Your team works at a rare pace, too.'

'Aye,' said Sam, speaking more broadly than was usual, 'Mi dad allus said to me "If a job's wuth doin' at all, it's wuth doin' well." And I allus say "It teks no longer to do a good job o' ploughin' than a bad 'un and there's more satisfaction in it".'

'Very profound,' said the surveyor. 'And a precept which you obviously follow. I have seen work at ploughing matches considerably inferior to this. But I must not detain you or your horses will suffer.'

He waved his hand in farewell and climbed back into the float.

'I think you must find Mr Ratcliffe a good employer,' he enquired as Bluebell trotted across the spongy ground.

'Well, I like him as a boss,' replied Bob with obvious sincerity. 'But this is the only farm job I've had.'

'Oh, I see! You came here straight from school?'

'Oh, no! My father has a shop down in Middlesex, and I helped him with the business until this year.'

They arrived at the yard and Bob transferred Bluebell to the market-trap for the journey to the station. Mr Shakespeare went in to the kitchen to say good-bye to the Ratcliffes. He was pressed to stay for a meal, but declined, saying it was important that he should catch the 4.40 train.

'What do you think of the place?' asked Mr Ratcliffe, anxious, but determined not to show it.

'You've a splendid farm here, Mr Ratcliffe, and the place has been farmed well for years, that is quite evident. I cannot recall an occasion when I have received such delightful hospitality, examined a farm in such a high state of husbandry, and admired such stock and such workmanship, all at the same time. I congratulate you, Mr Ratcliffe. If your mortgage depends on my report, you will certainly get it.'

'Nice to hear you say that,' said the farmer.

'I must say,' added Mr Shakespeare, 'That I have taken a liking to the admirable young man who has been my companion all day.'

'Aye, Bob's a good lad, and we're pleased to have him here.'

'Yes, I gathered so much. My experience has been that a good employer never fails to attract good workmen. But I see Bob is waiting for me outside. The train however will not wait so I must depart.'

In spite of her tiring day jogging, Bluebell made good time to the station. The train had not arrived, so there was no hurry. As they stood by the trap, Mr Shakespeare said, 'Good-bye Bob, you've been very helpful. If you ever think of changing your job, get in touch with me at Leicester. I'm sure I can fix you up.' He fumbled in his pocket and brought out half-a-crown, then walked quickly on to the platform as the locomotive clanked in.

Bob was delighted. He had expected only a sixpenny tip, and he drove the mare back to Oakleigh thinking that the day had been one of complete fulfilment.

'Nothing more we can do now but wait,' said Mr Ratcliffe at tea-time. But they were all in a fever of suspense. A week later a letter arrived from Mr Tunnicliffe asking for the £1000 deposit. 'Everything is ready for the transfer of the title,' the letter said, 'and if payment can be made immediately, there is every likelihood that you can take possession on the next quarter day, December 25th.'

Mr Ratcliffe replied at once that he would deliver the cheque personally to Mr Tunnicliffe's office on Saturday December 16th, and he hoped the transfer documents would be ready for signing, so that another journey to Burton would not be necessary. He said to his family, 'Funny day to take a farm over. Still, so long as we get it settled, I don't suppose the day matters much.'

Sam remarked pensively, 'Funny we've seen nowt o' the squire sin' Michaelmas. He seems to be keeping right out of our road.'

On Christmas eve a letter arrived from Mr Tunnicliffe. In it he stated that Mr Ratcliffe could consider himself owner of Oakleigh farm as from December 25th 1911. However, there was a quarter's rent of £100 due to Colonel Ratcliffe, his late landlord, which had been paid by the solicitor and he would like to receive immediate reimbursement. He also enclosed the account for his own professional services.

'Double-sided Christmas box, this,' grumbled the farmer. 'Looks like I'll have to borrow your money after all, Sam, to keep out of debt. But I must say it feels good to own my own farm after a lifetime as tenant. Just a bit overwhelming at first.'

'We can all do as we like, now, I suppose,' said Meg.

'Not a bit of it!' said their father. 'Life'll be just the same as ever, except that everybody'll have to work a bit harder. Remember we won't be able to run to the colonel to get our repairs done.'

The weather had turned colder, and there was a thin covering of snow. All the cattle were now housed and the full routine of winter had begun. The ewes were brought into Front Croft to keep them under close observation over Christmas.

No one at the farm indulged in a lie-in. They were all out of bed sharp in order to get the work finished early and enjoy a rest before Christmas dinner. The women worked hard, bringing out home-fed roast chicken and pork, followed by delicious Christmas pudding, home-made dandelion and blackberry wine, and ending with mugs of strong sweet milky tea. Replete, they dozed in the sitting room until the re-start of work again at three o'clock.

After milking, another huge meal of cold meat, preserved fruit with cream, then pork-pies and bread and butter. Finally, Meg's own effort, a gigantic fruit cake, covered with almond paste, and pink and white icing with the words 'Merry Christmas to all at Oakleigh Farm' across the centre in spidery chocolate letters.

Filled with good things, Farmer Ratcliffe was in a more than usual genial mood and pronounced his verdict on the closing year, standing up in his place like a rural Mr Pickwick.

'1911's been a right good year for us all,' he said expansively, 'A good spring for the sowing, good weather for the hay and corn harvest, the milk's kept up and the stock have sold well. We had notice to quit, which I must admit I didn't expect, but the result of that was I managed to buy the farm, and today it became my property, and that must be a good thing. It feels quite different to be an owner, I can tell you, and I'm not quite used to it yet. But let's all have a drink in some o' this grand home-made wine, and take our hats off to the year that's just going and our jackets off to the year that'll soon be comin' in.'

They were all uncomfortably full, but mellowed by the gaffer's remarks, and murmured agreement. Arthur piped up, 'I reckon it's all Bob's doing. He came early in the year, and since then things have gone right. He's been a sort of mascot.'

'By gum, you've got summat there, lad,' said his elder brother. 'Whenever things looked like stumblin' Bob generally thought o' summat to make things easier.'

'Well,' said the farmer, 'I'll not deny that Bob's been a great help on the farm, and I've been pleased to have him here. I hope he'll stay with us a long time yet. But in the meantime the milk's got to be taken to th' station, so I suggest you get off with it, Bob, and be back to enjoy a quiet Christmas evening.'

The lad got up from the table slowly and reluctantly. Of course he knew that the milk had to go, but somehow he had never felt less like taking it. It was a wrench to leave the Ratcliffe family, sitting happily round the big table. He realised that the sooner he set off, the sooner he would return to the comfort of the evening. He picked up a hurricane lamp from the scullery, and hurried down to the stable to harness Bluebell. As he drove her up to the cooling-shed door, Sam had the cart-lamps ready and the churns rolled out. They were heaved aboard and rolled into place, the backboard pinned up, and Bob climbed in as Bluebell moved off. At the same time there was a scuffle of running feet through the cooling-shed as Arthur and Meg appeared coated and mufflered, the boy still clutching a second helping of Christmas cake.

'Hold on, Bob, we're coming with you,' he called through his mouthful of marzipan. Meg added, 'We're jolly well not going to let you go alone on Christmas Day. It's such a nice night for a run to the station anyway!'

Mr Ratcliffe watched them through the kitchen window.

'Come back, you two,' he said half-heartedly. 'I don't want that mare pulling two extra people to Willington and back!'

'Oh, shut up, Arnold,' said his wife. 'Don't be such a spoil-sport. Come and sit down by the fire in the other room and don't bother about the youngsters. After all, it is Christmas!'

Chapter Twelve

A few days after Christmas, Oakleigh Farm received a visit from its former owner. The squire rode up to the yard gate on his massive chestnut gelding, just as the farmer came round the corner from the stackyard.

'Good morning, Squire. Nice to see you! Anything I can do for you? Perhaps you'd like to come in? Bob here, will hold your horse.'

'No, thank you, Mr Ratcliffe. I will not stay long. First, I wish to congratulate you on the efficiency of your adviser in expediting the transfer of the property. Frankly, I thought it would take several more months—certainly until the spring. And how does it feel to be a land-owner?' he added with a touch of patronage.

'I'm a farmer, Squire, and I hope I'll be as good a farmer whether I own or rent the farm.'

'I'm sure you will,' the squire replied, frowning slightly at the sharp edge in the farmer's tone. 'About the shooting, Mr Ratcliffe. I have arranged two shoots for January, and had expected that Oakleigh would remain part of the estate until after they had taken place.'

'Quite so, Squire. But you're welcome to shoot over my land for the rest of the season. It's only just over a month and one must be neighbourly.'

'But what about future years, Mr Ratcliffe? Oakleigh Farm is almost in the centre of my estate. I would like to think that your land is still available for the birds as formerly.'

The farmer was tempted to say that if the squire had not given him notice to quit, the present situation would never have arisen. But, not wishing to breed acrimony, he said evenly, 'We're not likely to fall out over this, Colonel. Think over what you would like to do and send me a letter with your proposition. Whatever happens, I'll not be shooting your game, and nor will Sam, as I hope you know.'

'I certainly should know after twenty years,' the squire said shortly. 'Thank you for your co-operation, Mr Ratcliffe. But my horse is getting restive. I must move him on to get the itch out of his feet.' He turned his mount with a flurry of snow and trotted smoothly out of the open gate.

'The squire wasn't very affable this morning,' grumbled the farmer at the dinner-table. 'Not a very good attitude for a man asking a favour. Can't understand it!'

'Seems to me the squire's beginning to realise what a mistake he's made,' said Mrs Ratcliffe, in one of her flashes of shrewdness. 'It's my belief he never wanted to sell the farm at all. Just wanted to get rid of us, and offered to sell us the place to make it sound genuine. Now he's wishing he hadn't!'

'Well, he can keep wishing,' growled her husband. 'I've got the farm, and I'm going to keep it–by hook or by crook. It's a grand feeling to be the owner of the land you farm. My feet seem lighter every time I step out o' the back door.'

'I'd forgotten that it 'ud affect the shootin',' admitted Sam. 'And there's the hunt. Will it make any difference to that, dad?'

'That's a point, Sam. But as far as I'm concerned, the only difference it makes is that now they've got to ask my permission instead of riding over the land on the squire's say-so.'

'Will it make any difference to the Hunt Ball, dad?' asked Meg anxiously.

'The only difference it'll make is that they'll welcome us with open arms instead of just tolerating us,' said her mother drily.

'Oh come, Maggie, it's never been quite like that! Over the years we've had some pleasant Hunt Balls. I've never noticed any condescension. It's allus seemed to me that huntin' is a sport that links up all the classes–the land-owners, the farmers, the tradesmen, labourers and the like. And though I've never been an out-and-out keen follower myself, I'm not going to put obstacles in their way; and we'll be going to the Ball as usual.'

'Don't know that I'll go,' said Sam.

'You ought to, Sam,' said his father. 'There'll be quite a few suitable girls there, and it's about time you started to sort 'em out.'

'Whenever I go into a dance-hall it seems to me that most of the girls are sorting me out, with their whispering and giggling. Just like a bunch o' bulling heifers!'

'Sam, don't be so disrespectful,' said his mother sharply. 'And remember that your young sister is in the room. That's no way to talk! Of course the girls get a bit excited when they see you coming. You're the biggest and smartest young chap in these parts!'

Sam grunted, not without satisfaction at this flattery, and to change the subject, said, 'How's the dress going, Meg?'

'Nearly finished. Just got the sleeves to tack in. I'll fetch it and show you,' and she rushed out of the kitchen.

'I only asked how it was comin'. I don't want to see the bloomin' thing,' grumbled Sam after her. But Meg was not to be denied showing off her needle-work, and soon came back with the gown over her arm.

'Look at this,' she said proudly, extending the unfinished

cream dress in front of her. 'Isn't it lovely? I got the pattern from mum's *Everywoman's Encyclopaedia*. I've only the sleeves to put in now. They are elbow length, and will have white swansdown round the edge, the same as the neck and the tunic.'

'That stuff's velvet, I reckon,' said Sam.

'That's right. The overdress is panne velvet—at least, that's what Mrs Rawlings called it when she ordered it for me.'

'Pan velvet?' queried Sam. 'Frying-pan or sauce-pan? Fat lot old Rawlings knows about it! She's having you on, I reckon.'

'Oh, shut up, Sam and don't be so silly. *Panne*—P, a, double n, e, not p,a,n. Mrs Rawlings 's been a dressmaker all her life. What do you think of it Bob?'

Bob swallowed hard and racked his brain for the right thing to say. 'I'm sure it'll look grand when it's finished,' he ventured. 'But why do you need two? What is that longer one underneath?'

'Well, I don't know! It's called a two-tier dress, silly! They're all the rage now. The underskirt is satin, and it's meant to be like that. Oh! You men! I wish I hadn't brought it out now.' She tossed her fair hair, and returned to the sitting room with her precious burden.

'You shouldn't tease her, Sam,' said his mother. 'Or you, Bob. It isn't fair. She's worked hard at that dress, and been clever with it, too. When it's finished it'll be as well-made a dress as any at the Ball. And she's only had a little bit of help from me and Emily Rawlings.'

For the next two or three weeks Meg could talk of nothing else. Bob was heartily sick of hearing about the ball, but a little envious too. Admission was by ticket only, and as a farm-worker and newcomer he did not qualify.

Sam reluctantly agreed to go, and Bob was to stay at home to keep Arthur company. But on the day preceding the ball, Mr Ratcliffe was the victim of a very heavy cold, and declared that he would not attend with eyes and nose running. 'Embarrassing for me and unpleasant for everybody else!'

'Then that settles it,' said Sam. 'I'll not go either. I'll stay here with you and Arthur, and Bob can drive mum and Meg.'

Bob was not averse to the long ride, but did not like the idea of waiting about at the nearby inn for five or six hours. They set off at seven o'clock. The layer of snow which had been hanging about since Christmas was now thawing in the milder air, and the wheels threw up a spray of dirty water. Mr Ratcliffe's best trap looked smart at home, but less so among the gigs, dog-carts, broughams and carriages of the gentry. There were also a few motor-cars, at which both horses and drivers gazed warily. Anxious to get away from the press of vehicles,

Bob drove Bluebell to the stabling, and Meg and her mother made their way into the ballroom.

Meg kept close to her mother. She was slightly over-awed by the occasion, and knew she would be one of the youngest girls present. It was her seventeenth birthday and this outing would be the most delightful of her presents. She knew only a few of the other girls, but her mother was able to renew many old acquaintances. Colonel Ratcliffe was there, smart and military looking, and Mortimer, slim and elegant in his evening dress. Meg flushed slightly when the Squire approached them.

'Ah, Mrs Ratcliffe! So pleased to see you here—and you too, Miss Ratcliffe. My word! What a beautiful flower Oakleigh Farm has produced! At all events you will not lack partners, although it appears you have not brought your menfolk with you. A great pity—but no doubt more pressing things keep them at home.'

'More oppressive than pressing, I would say, Squire,' Mrs Ratcliffe said shortly. 'My husband's got a very bad cold and wouldn't enjoy the crowd. My son didn't need any such excuse to keep him at home. He regards social occasions as rather tiresome.'

The squire raised his hands in mock horror and moved easily away to acknowledge other guests. Meg watched him making his way round the room as the music and dancing began. He paused for a few words with Mortimer, who was chatting animatedly with a group of women from the county families. The girl was surprised to see him take Mortimer a few paces to one side and speak to him earnestly for half a minute or so. Mortimer nodded and rejoined his friends.

Sitting close beside her mother Meg began to think of herself as a wall-flower. The self-assertive daughter of Oakleigh farmhouse had been left behind, and in this company she felt shy and ill-at-ease. There were plenty of young farmers whom she knew slightly, and one or two from Hartnall whom she knew well; but they were all of Sam's age or older, and probably still thought of her as a schoolgirl. The band played a valeta and then a polka. Her feet were itching to dance, and she tapped the floor with her new shoes. They were of white satin with silver straps and heels, and for the first time in her life she knew the delight of pure silk stockings. It had seemed a waste to conceal the elegant clocks, but now all her efforts were going to be wasted, she thought bitterly. But she knew she looked attractive in her new dress. Even Sam had said so before she left home! The simplicity of the gown gave it an elegance for which she had hardly dared hope. The satin underskirt fell in graceful folds to her instep, and extended at the back into a hint of a train. She had told herself that she must remember not to trip over it when she turned. No need to worry about that now, either!

A lump was rising in her throat as she thought of the care with which she had worked the bead embroidery on the ends of the silver-fringed satin sash—the only touch of colour in the outfit. She had thrilled when she put on her long white kid gloves, and she was especially proud of her dorothy bag, which she had made from the remnants. She had worried about the tortoiseshell pins staying in her newly put-up hair, and touched them with her hand to find that they were still perfect. But it didn't seem to matter now. Coming over in the trap she had bitten her lips to make them glow more red. Now she bit them out of sheer disappointment and to keep back the rising tears.

Meg looked at her mother sitting beside her, but Mrs Ratcliffe was long past the intense emotions of youth, and was gazing benignly round the packed room. Mortimer Ratcliffe was standing exactly opposite them, talking easily to Lady Gwendoline, a relative of the Master. Meg's glance passed over him, and she tried desperately to will someone to ask her for the next dance. She realised how utterly futile it was.

The M.C. announced a waltz and immediately the band struck up the first few bars of 'The Chocolate Soldier'. One of her favourite tunes! How she loved the waltz. She felt herself about to cry, and knew she would soon have to hide in the cloak-room. But Mortimer, inclining his head slightly as he excused himself to his companion, turned and walked across the floor with deliberate and assured strides. She realised in panic that he was going to ask her to dance! Her face paled and then blushed crimson. She had decided earlier to ignore him. He bowed slightly, smiled and said, 'May I have the pleasure of this first waltz, Miss Ratcliffe?' looking straight into her eyes and taking her arm as if by right.

Her mind refused to function. Should she decline? Instead, she got up mechanically and melted into his stance, picked up the music with him and glided away into the centre of the floor. For a full minute they danced alone. There was surprised admiration in the room. Guests commented on the handsome spectacle, the athletic aristocrat and the beautiful girl dancing together as if they were one.

But Meg was not conscious of the admiration. She was intoxicated with delight. She knew that she danced well, and was a fitting partner for this young gentleman. She contrasted the perfection of his rhythm with Bob Felton's stumbling efforts. But this gave her such a feeling of disloyalty that she put such thoughts out of her mind. At least Bob was sincere in everything he did, but there was nothing sincere about the young squire. His conversation was an empty formality. Easily, and without a trace of embarrassment, he referred to the episode on Coronation night.

'Oh, Margaret—I may call you Margaret, mayn't I? I have never apologised to you for the affair in Vestry Field last June. Absolutely caddish of me, you know, but I must plead that I didn't know what I was doing. Too much wine and all that, you know. I am forgiven, aren't I?'

He looked straight into her eyes forcing Meg to blush and turn her head away.

'That's over and done with,' she said shortly, and added, quite untruthfully, 'I'd forgotten all about it until you reminded me.'

She wanted to forget it and think only of her present pleasure in the ball. The band played out the piece, but they were the last pair to leave the floor. As he led her back to her seat, he murmured, 'Thanks for a delightful dance Margaret. I insist you have the final waltz with me. May I see you enter it on your programme? I shall ask them to play "Destiny".'

Meg pencilled the little card and blushed self-consciously. She was not used to the formality of ball-room procedure. For the rest of the evening a succession of young men partnered her, and she did not miss a single dance. Polka, schottische, valeta, lancers and quadrilles; young farmers and some of the younger gentry followed the lead set by Mortimer and begged for her favour. Her toes suffered at times, but she thought that being the belle of the ball—as she undoubtedly was—compensated for the discomfort. Maggie Ratcliffe, delighted at the popularity of her daughter, was amused to overhear the comments of two older farming girls.

'Just look at that Meg Ratcliffe queening it. Who does she think she is?'

'Cinderella, I should think. Getting in as many dances as she can before she goes back to her rags at twelve o'clock!' she nudged her companion as she realised they were standing within earshot of Cinderella's mother.

At two o'clock the master of ceremonies announced the last waltz. Meg smiled as the band struck up the well-known air. Mortimer had been as good as his word. He was now walking towards her from half the length of the ball-room away. But Meg felt proud when he claimed his privilege and put everything she had into those last few minutes. The squire's son and the farmer's daughter waltzed round the room with an energy and grace which belied the hour. Mrs Ratcliffe, who had spent some time on the floor with her neighbours earlier in the evening, now sat back contentedly in her chair and basked in satisfaction. Her eyes searched the room for the squire and found him just when Meg and Mortimer were gliding past. Colonel Ratcliffe wore a smile of relief as if a load had been lifted from his mind.

There followed the National Anthem, and the Hunt Ball of 1912 was over. In the bustle of departure, Mortimer ushered Meg and her mother out through the main door. Bob was waiting there with Bluebell, who was looking smart and fresh. He helped Mrs Ratcliffe to climb in on the off-side and Mortimer with a flourish helped Meg to her seat on the near-side. He clapped Bob comradely on the shoulder and said, 'You've got a valuable load there, young fellow. Take great care on the way home.'

This was intended as the final thrust of the olive branch. Bob, disliking the patronising tone, did not answer, but jumped up, sat beside Meg, and took the rein. He guided Bluebell skilfully through the untidy assembly of vehicles. The night was very dark and a faint drizzle was falling, which became heavier as they left the village. Mrs Ratcliffe produced an umbrella from under the seat, and she and Meg shared it, huddling together. Bob was without a top-coat. The only one he had was the ex-railway garment he wore on all sorts of farm-work. Flecked with milk-splashes, heavy with ploughfield dust and with hayseed lodged in its deep nap, he had shrunk from wearing it while sitting close to the two women in their ballroom finery. He pulled the lapels of his jacket across his throat to keep his shirt dry.

A mile or so further on Bluebell faltered in her stride and reduced her speed. A clinking noise interrupted the firm clop-clop of her hooves. Bob was wondering what it could be when Mrs Ratcliffe spoke.

'Sounds as though the mare's losing a shoe, Bob. You'll have to stop and have a look.'

Bob wondered how he was going to do that in the pitch darkness, and Meg must have read his thoughts.

'I'll come down and hold a lamp for you, Bob!'

'No Meg, you stay where you are,' said her mother. 'You'll ruin your new dress climbing down in this puddly road. I'll get down and hold the light.'

Bob pushed up one of the lamps out of its socket and gave it to Mrs Ratcliffe, who grasped it by the long metal sleeve. Bob seized the tuft of hair on Bluebell's left fetlock and lifted her foot. Sure enough the shoe was coming away and would have been cast in a few more yards.

'Tear it right off, Bob,' ordered the mistress. 'See if you can pull the nails out. We'll take the shoe with us. It's good enough to be put on again.'

They returned to their seats, which were now wet with the persistent rain. Bluebell set off willingly enough at a slower pace. She kept it up for a mile or so, but then her gait became unbalanced, and she nodded her head every time she put the unshod foot to the ground. Finally she stopped of her own accord, and Bob sensed that she was sweating hard.

'What are we going to do now?' he asked miserably. Mrs Ratcliffe sighed.

'I'm afraid you'll have to get down and lead her, Bob. She's gone right lame in that foot, so she won't drive. If you lead a lame horse, it gives a bit of encouragement, like. It means walking all the way back to Oakleigh, and not a very fast walk at that. Drat the rain! I don't know what our clothes'll be like when we get there. I'm sorry for your new dress, Meg.'

The girl did not answer. Her evening had been so enjoyable, she was lost in delight still. Nothing could spoil it now, not even the ruin of her dress. She huddled closer to her mother under the inadequate shelter of the old umbrella as Bob led Bluebell on, hobbling on her three sound legs. The rain fell harder, the increasing wind lashing it into his face as he urged Bluebell on by hand and voice.

He was soaked to the skin when they arrived at the farm, over an hour later. His right arm ached from his efforts to prevent the mare from drooping her head every time she put her tender foot to the ground. But he helped Meg down, she holding her precious gown high to prevent its being fouled by the muddy wheels, then rushed round to help her mother. But that resourceful lady was already on the ground and hurrying in to the kitchen. Bob quickly put Bluebell into her stall, where a feed was waiting in the manger. He dried her off as well as he could with a clean sack, and strapped her rug on so that she should not cool off too soon. Then he returned in his sodden clothes to the kitchen, where Mrs Ratcliffe had ready a steaming cup of cocoa.

'Drink this up, and get off to bed, Bob. You must be wet right through. Take this clean shirt and socks with you, and leave your others on the floor. We'll sort them out tomorrow, or rather, later today. By gum, it's half-past four! Another hour or so and it'll be milking time for you.'

But for once the master was easy on his young employee and left him to sleep. Bob awakened with a start to the clang of buckets on the concrete yard, and looking at his pocket watch in the greyness of the approaching dawn found that it was after seven o'clock. He dressed quickly and hurried out to the cowshed, sleepy-eyed and tousled-headed. The gaffer smiled.

'You managed to wake up, then Bob. You had a rough night, seemingly, and I didn't feel like calling you out when you'd only just gone to bed. It's going to be a wet day, anyway, so there's not much lost.'

The remainder of February brought mild damp weather which continued well into March. The sowing of the spring corn became difficult and frustrating, for the soil clung to the boots, and to the wheels and coulters of the drill. The lambing paddock was so muddy and cold that the ewes had to be moved twice on to a fresh field; and even then the weaker lambs, seldom having a dry coat, chilled and died.

The rain of 1912 was certainly counterbalancing the drought of 1911. The potato-planting, which Bob enjoyed so much the previous year, took place in sticky conditions, and there were frequent showers when they sheltered under the oak trees in the hedgerow. Sam would join them there, complaining bitterly about the waste of time.

On any morning that the sky looked dull and cloudy, even if it were not raining, Ernie would say gloomily, 'Ah'm afraid it's gooin' to be a wet time all through the summer.'

Mr Ratcliffe took this pessimism with pained resignation, Sam gritted his teeth, while Bob's heart sank in despair. When Meg was present she always reacted spiritedly.

'Oh, shut up, Ernie! Don't be so miserable! Always looking on the black side! It'll be bad enough if and when it happens, without having it in advance as well.' Ernie would turn away shaking his head with the air of a man who is never wrong.

This year he was not wrong. Every week brought its quota of damp days. The Trent was as high as its banks most of the time, and occasionally flooded the lower parts of the meadows. The grass grew in abundance, but so did the weeds. Hoeing became a dirty unrewarding job. In the absence of the sun, the weeds did not wither, and a shower would cause them to take fresh root. Every attempt at horse-hoeing meant frequent stops to clear the blocked tines, for the ground was covered with long weeds which refused to die.

The hay crop grew luxuriantly, but the perpetual dampness in the bottom of the sward made mowing a slow operation. During the rare spells of sunshine, Sam went out to mow as much as he could. But the conditions slowed down the work and in an effort to increase the amount done Bob was sent out with the old machine behind Major and Diamond. He was proud to be entrusted with this task, and spent much time the previous evening bent over the machine with spanner and oil-can, and sharpened the knives until they felt like razor blades.

In the field he tried hard, but the thick wet grass wedged itself in the points of the cutter-bar, locking the wheels so that they skidded on the wet turf. He had to dismount and free the knife by hand, and sometimes Sam would come up behind him, which meant that both machines were halted.

After the hay was cut, the thick rows were slow to dry and needed much turning and shaking out with hand-forks to make hay. Mrs Ratcliffe, Meg and Mrs Wagstaff as well as two women from the village spent every sunny hour trying to get it fit for carrying. In an effort to speed things up, Mr Ratcliffe bought a new Bamford side-delivery rake, and this proved a valuable asset for rowing up the hay ready for the pitchers, instead of the eternal hand-raking round and round the field.

The weathered hay developed a dark mould, and when it was dry enough to carry, this came off as a clinging black dust; so by the end of one of the rare hot days, the haymakers looked more like coal-miners. The young men went down to the Trent to rid themselves of their black looks, but bathing this year was a chilly affair compared with the heat-wave of 1911. The young people sometimes lost heart trying to secure the hay in usable condition. But Mr Ratcliffe never flagged in his efforts. As soon as the sun appeared he would order everyone down to the hay-field to shake out an area of the crop.

'If we can get one load dry and on the waggon, it will be something achieved,' he said regularly. 'And it'll be one load less to get.'

By unrelenting perseverance, the hay-fields were finally cleared and the bays in the barn were filled with what Ernie described as, 'Some good 'ay, some bad, and some good for nowt.'

But if the haymaking had been sometimes infuriating and sometimes depressing, the corn harvest was worse. The corn having been lashed by countless storms had collapsed on itself, and was now a tangled mass of damp straw interlaced with thistles, cleavers, swine-grass, fat hen, twitch and other weeds. The interlopers stood defiant among the pitiful remains of the wheat and oat crops. The binder which had run so sweetly the previous harvest could not cope with such damp entanglements. The shapeless sheaves refused to be stooked properly and easily collapsed, necessitating daily visits to set them up again.

Immediately before the sheaves were to be carried and stacked, Mr Ratcliffe insisted on having them thrown down and the butts exposed to the sun and wind, for the frequent rains had penetrated to the very centre of some of them. He was determined that the oats should be absolutely dry before being put into the stack.

'The slightest bit of dampness will cause mould in the stack,' he explained to Bob. 'And we depend on the oats to feed the hosses. They might eat mouldy or heated oats, but it'd play havoc with their wind, and give 'em belly-ache as well, no doubt. I don't aim to ruin any of 'em.'

So the oats were dried painstakingly, a load or two at a time, and if even a light shower came up, the work was stopped until the sheaves could be dried again. But with the wheat it was different. These sheaves too were thrown down so that they could dry out thoroughly, but if it rained subsequently, the loading went on until conditions became impossible. Bob queried the wisdom of this at supper one evening.

'It's like this, Bob,' explained his employer. 'Wheat straw's hard and coarse, and it doesn't settle down so tightly in the stack as oat straw—there's always plenty of air. So a bit of dampness on the surface of the sheaf doesn't matter much—it can dry out in the stack if left long enough. That's why we're building more stacks this year, so the damp sheaves can be kept separate and threshed much later. But small stack is going to dry out more certainly than a large one. We've got to do some threshing early, because we need the straw, so we're keeping the best dry corn in separate stacks.'

Towards the end of September the dismal summer tried to make amends for its earlier abominable behaviour. The last few days of harvesting were warm and free from rain. The potatoes were lifted and stored in the pleasant conditions of an Indian summer. The mangolds and swedes were carted off in the warmth of autumn sun. Meg insisted on going out to help, although her parents assured her that it was not necessary.

'I can get two or three women from the village to do that job,' her father told her.

But as in most things, Meg had her own way, and went out every afternoon to help Bob fill the carts. Because of the distance from the farm, Bob operated two carts, Major in front and Diamond hitched to the rear of Major's cart. He had some difficulty in manoeuvring his two carts through the narrow field gateway at first, and on his first day hit the gatepost with his rear cart, fracturing it at ground level. Unfortunately Mr Ratcliffe had just arrived at the field.

'Be more careful, Bob,' he said testily. 'Isn't a nine-foot gate wide enough for you to drive a six-foot cart through?. Come to the gate straight in line and not on the curve. And keep going straight until you're well through. Can't afford to buy gateposts this winter!'

Bob went about his work red-faced and hurt, until Meg

cheered him up.

'Don't take it so much to heart, Bob. Twasn't all your fault. That wretched Diamond doesn't follow properly. He wanders about all over the place. Next time I'll lead him through.'

While Bob and Meg carted off the mangolds, Sam and the two big mares were fully occupied in ploughing the stubble for the autumn sowing. By the end of October the roots were all harvested, and the wheat and winter oats sown.

Mr Ratcliffe reviewed the situation as they sat at tea on the day Sam drilled the last field.

'It's been a difficult year, but it could 'a been wuss. Funny thing, the last year I was a tenant was one o' the best years I've ever had. The first year I'm on my own land is about the wust. But we'll pull through. The lambs and fat beast have sold reasonably well, the seed corn's gone in well, and we've got plenty of hay to see us through, even if some of it's not so good. And there's plenty of autumn grass about for the young cattle. So we've no cause to grumble.'

'Who's grumbling?' Meg asked under her breath, and answered herself. 'Only you, as far as I can see!'

Chapter Thirteen

Meg was excited when it became known that a dance was to be held every alternate Saturday in the Commemoration Hall in Hartnall village.

'What's it all in aid of?' asked Mr Ratcliffe. 'It's to build up a grand fund which will be shared by the W.I., the church, the Boy Scouts and the Girl Guides,' explained his wife. 'The vicar and his wife are doing the organising. The music will be provided by local people.'

'Well, all I can say is, I hope they harmonise well otherwise there'll be some comical dancing.'

'Don't be unkind, Arnold! They'll do their best, you can be sure. The W.I. are going to do the refreshments, so I'll be there some nights when it's my turn.'

'I shall go to every one,' said Meg. 'And so will you, Bob! Then I can teach you to dance properly.'

'How much is it to go in?' asked Bob, not noticing the slightly disapproving look which passed between the farmer and his wife.

'Only sixpence, you miser! I know you can afford that much!'

'Now then, Meg,' said her father shortly. 'Bob will decide for himself whether he wants to go. But if it's for the benefit of the village, we'd all better show up from time to time. And you might as well teach Arthur to dance as well. As it's a Saturday night affair, it will have to be finished and cleaned up by midnight, so none of us will be too late home. What about you, Sam?'

'I don't know that I want to learn to dance,' interrupted Arthur. 'It's a silly way of going on!'

'If I can dance, so can you my lad,' said Sam firmly. 'Yes dad, I'll probably go myself most times.' He had a strong sense of loyalty to the village, but he also knew that his parents were concerned that Meg and Bob should not make a habit of walking home together after midnight.

Bob had no intention of avoiding the fortnightly dances. He would enjoy being taught dancing by Meg, and by now he knew enough of the villagers not to feel shy. He had bought only working clothes since he came to Oakleigh, and he had outgrown the suit he had worn from Mill Hill. But he had spent money on nothing else, and his savings had grown. He felt that he could afford a new suit for the village dances. He could hardly afford to have one made to measure by the village tailor, and he never had occasion to visit either Burton or Derby where one would expect to find a good choice of ready-made clothes. He mentioned his problem to Mrs Ratcliffe, who solved it at once.

'I'll take your measurements, Bob, and bring you a good suit off-the-peg. I don't mind at all, lad. I did it for Sam until a couple of years ago, so I'm sure I can do it for you. You must tell me how much you want to pay.'

'I'll leave that to you, Mrs Ratcliffe. I'm eighteen now, and don't suppose I'll grow much more, so I might as well have a good one. Hadn't I better have some lighter shoes and another shirt as well?'

On the following Friday he became the proud possessor of a smart and serviceable grey tweed suit, which cost forty shillings, and town-style black shoes costing ten. Mrs Ratcliffe also bought him a white cotton shirt with collars.

'That's a present from me, Bob,' she said. 'You've been helpful to me as well as the farm!'

The village dances helped the winter pass pleasantly and quickly. Bob found it something to look forward to, and Meg's enthusiasm was boundless. She and Bob went to every dance, but always some other member of the family went too, Mrs Ratcliffe most frequently as she was involved with refreshments. Sometimes Arthur accompanied them, and Sam quite often. Sometimes Mr Ratcliffe himself would turn out while his two sons stayed at home.

They walked home from the village hall just after midnight, in the moonlight, in rain, in frost and in snow, but there were always three or more in the party. Not that there was any suggestion of courtship between Bob and Meg. There was no opportunity; Meg's parents thought it better that such a situation should not be allowed to develop.

The winter passed smoothly. Vigorous chores round the cow yard or equally strenuous field work by day followed by comfortable, if sleepy, evenings in the warm kitchen. Bob cherished the two hours leisure after returning with the milk-float at eight o'clock until bed-time about ten. Sam relieved him more frequently these days, as Bob was no longer regarded as simply 'the milk lad'.

The Hunt Ball came round again—a little later this year. The village dances had reawakened the interest of all the Ratcliffe household, and tickets were bought for Bob and Arthur. As the whole family were going, two vehicles were needed. Bob went with Meg and her parents in the trap with Bluebell, while Sam and Arthur rode in the milk-float (newly painted for the occasion) behind Diamond.

Meg was more confident of herself this year. She was certain she would not be a wallflower. This time she had her own trio of partners, and could be independent of the other guests if she chose. Mortimer, she knew, would not be present to give her the lead this year. News had come from the Hall that he could not get away from Sandhurst.

Loyally, she reserved the last waltz for Bob, and left several other dances open. Bob surpassed her expectations. Although not naturally graceful, he was thorough in everything, and he danced with a careful precision that was faultless.

Soon after one o'clock Mr and Mrs Ratcliffe felt they had had enough and left for home, taking with them a rather bored Arthur. He had declined to test his skill on the ball-room floor, even with his mother as partner. Meg decided to stay until the end, and the two lads naturally could not leave without her.

Soon after three o'clock they set off for Oakleigh behind the energetic Diamond, who evidently had his mind set on his comfortable stall at home, and determined to get there as quickly as possible. They bowled along at a rare pace in the bright moonlight, the iron-tyred wheels of the float making a robust cracking noise as they crumpled the thin ice of the pot-holes. Meg, sitting tightly wedged between Sam and Bob was as happy as a queen. The warmth of her body thrilled Bob, and he felt satisfied that his first incursion into the social world had not been unsuccessful. Sam's driving was as skilful as his dancing, and he felt that there were few things more fulfilling than driving home after an enjoyable evening a spirited horse, with two likeable people beside him. Perhaps he should go out more often. After all, his father was a land-owner now, not a mere tenant farmer.

'Isn't it wonderful?' said Meg, clasping her hands in front of her knees. 'To think that we're all young, and life in front of us, with dozens more Hunt Balls to come!'

'Don't count your chickens, Meg,' said Bob with caution.

'And don't you be a spoil-sport, Bob,' she reproved. 'You've had a good time tonight, haven't you?'

'Yes, I jolly well have. So good that I can't believe it can go on.'

'You're an old wet-blanket, Bob!'

'Well, I don't know, Meg,' said Sam. 'We've had a good life so far, without any of the worries some people get. Everything seems set fair for 1913. The state of farming's not bad at all. I don't see what can go wrong. Dad owns the farm now, so we can't be turned out. We can cope with everything else. Yes, I'd say we've got a good life ahead!'

The spring work went forward smoothly in what Sam and his

father described as 'average conditions'—quite free from the delaying wet periods of 1912. The lambing was comfortable and prolific, the spring oats drilled well, and the potatoes were planted well. The grass grew sufficiently strong, and the weather was warm enough for the cows to be turned out at the end of April.

'Grass day's allus a day to look forward to,' Ernie said contentedly. 'It's like bein' let out o' prison, not only for th' cows but for us as well. Now we can get away from the yard for a bit everyday.' They all agreed with him.

The mangolds were sown in a good deep tilth and germinated quickly. The cabbages were planted and few failed. The heavy crop of lambs throve well, and at the end of May the ewes sheared quickly and easily. Bob now took his turn at shearing with Sam, and found great pleasure in it. He had learned to grip the ewe with his knees easily and confidently, secure in the knowledge that she could not escape; and the sight of a fleece taken off in one piece and rolled into a tidy bundle like a lady's muff was gratifying.

The wool was quickly despatched, and Mr Ratcliffe soon received the cheque.

'Everything going fine this year, so far,' he said with cautious satisfaction. 'The weather's been just right, with about enough rain to keep things growing well. It's not going to be a drought year like 1911, but I'm sure the haymaking'll be a big improvement on 1912!'

The roots grew so fast under the ideal conditions that the hoers fell behind and achieved less work each day as the plants grew bigger. Meg came out for an hour or two in the afternoon, although she did not like hoeing. Arthur was ordered out to the field on Wednesday and Saturday afternoons by his father.

'If you're so keen on farming, Arthur, you'd better start learning some o' the hard jobs. We're getting behind wi' th' singling, so you can start and do some. Every little helps!'

'I don't like hoeing,' grumbled the boy. 'It makes my back ache. I'd rather do some horse-work.'

'It makes everybody's back ache, more or less,' replied his father. 'As for horse-work—well, I don't know! Perhaps you can do a bit o' hoss-raking later on. But I'm not promising it mind! You might not be available when it has to be done, and I'll not put it off for you. Don't try to grow up too soon lad! Your childhood's the best time of your life, if you did but know it.'

Arthur was not convinced, but did his best with the hoe, not only on his half-holidays from school but on a few evenings as well. This enabled Sam and Bob to leave the mangolds and to mow the hay seeds on Top Long furrow, a twelve-acre hilly field on the extremity of the farm. A new Bamford mowing machine had been purchased for this season, and Sam proudly harnessed Flower and Violet to this brightly-painted acquisition. Bob was equally proud when he hitched Major and Diamond to Sam's old machine.

After the singling, haymaking followed its normal course. Sam would mow early in the morning and sometimes Bob would take out his team after breakfast to finish the field in a single day. But as the work progressed the younger lad was more often turning or rowing-in with Major or Diamond. The clover hay from Top Long-furrow was carried in good condition and stacked in the Dutch barn. The crop was heavy and the field took three days to clear, starting after dinner each day. On the fourth day, Bob, after an early dinner, was sent with Diamond to horse-rake Top Long-furrow. The day was Wednesday, and Arthur arrived home from school just as Bob was leaving the kitchen. The boy enquired at once what everyone was doing, and when he learned that Bob was horse-raking the first cleared field, protested loudly that he had been promised the job.

'I said you could do some,' said his father sharply. 'I didn't say you could do it all. I want Bob to go and get on with it so we can pick up the rakings this evening. In any case, it isn't safe for you to drive Diamond. That hoss is too self-willed and needs firm handling. You'd better get off Bob, or you'll never get it finished.'

Bob hastily left the kitchen, harnessed Diamond, and put him in the horse-rake, which he man-handled out of the depths of the back cart-hovel. He drove through the front-yard, and as he clanked past the kitchen window caught a glimpse of Arthur at his dinner, looking dejected. As always, Diamond was in a hurry, and frequently broke into a half-trot, causing the curved metal tines of the rake to bounce in their sockets and rattle alarmingly. The horse was never happy with noise behind him, and the bumpy drive increased the racket. Bob was glad that he did not have to stop and open the gates. Both of the drive-side fields were to be mown this year, so the gates were tied open to allow free passage. He turned left past the First River Field, where Sam was mowing, and then followed the headland of the mangold field to get to the hayfield at the far end. The rake was quieter on the softer ground, and Diamond less agitated.

Bob drove backwards and forwards across the field, emptying his rake in four places to make straight rows across the field. It was surprising to see how much of the crop had been left. Although hardly noticeable as it lay, when raked up the rows were quite bulky. Diamond walked at a good pace, determined to get this light task done as quickly as possible. Although he had done it other years, the extra loud clang every time Bob operated his levers to empty the rake still caused the horse to jump slightly.

Bob had a good view of the lower part of the farm from the centre of the field. In the distance he could see that Sam had now returned to his mowing. A field further away, the Trent shone silver in the afternoon sun, and in the adjoining field the ewes and lambs grazed contentedly. When he looked again a few minutes later, they were all moving intently to the near upper corner of the pasture, which at this point adjoined a field of blue-green oats. The ears were just emerging from the broad leaves, adding a few white-green splashes to the rippling sea of grain. A tight knot of ewes was crowding close to the hedge, and he could just hear some excited bleating. Then he saw a single sheep squeeze through a gap in the hedge into the oats. A few seconds later another sheep struggled through, and the head of a third appeared.

This will never do, thought Bob. If they all break through, they will trample and spoil a sizeable area in no time. He had better go down and hustle them out. But Diamond could not be left alone untethered. Bob thanked his lucky stars that he had left the rope-halter on the horse, underneath his bridle. He drove Diamond to the entrance-gate and tied him securely to the top bar; then, hurriedly breaking off a thickly-branched hazel stick from the hedge, ran down the mangold field, along the road, and into the oat field where the ewes and lambs were now spreading out with relish.

Bob ran backwards and forwards across the corner to contain them, whistling, shouting, waving his arms, and beating the air and the corn with his leafy stick, creating as much disturbance as he could. The sheep were alarmed at such noisy antics, and quickly stampeded back to the hole through which they had come. But the hole was small, and its surrounds were thick branches, so the aperture could not be enlarged. The recalcitrant sheep could only squeeze back one at a time, and Bob was afraid that the rearmost, becoming impatient, would attempt to double back past him. But the follow-my-leader sheep all filed back.

When they had all returned to their field, he cut some long sticks from the hedge with his pocket knife and threaded them through the hole and into the thick bushes on each side, and then laced them with a few short lengths of binder twine. Sweating with his exertions, he returned slowly across the mangold field, walking diagonally over the rows, thinking how well they had grown since singling. He was suddenly shocked to hear a scream and jangling sound. He pelted across the mangold rows in the direction of Diamond. He ran through the open gate, but saw nothing. Diamond and the horse-rake had vanished, but there was a commotion over the brow. He tore up the field over the short grass, hearing more shouting, and his heart nearly stopped as he came within view of his outfit.

Diamond was pulling the rake round and round in a short circle, the near-side rein being so tight as to lock the horse's head round short, as if the rope were entangled in the rake. On the ground under the wheel, and draped in such a way that his drooping head protruded through the tines of the rake, was Arthur. His legs and arms were twisted at unnatural angles, as the wheel screwed round in one place, dragging the boy with it. The maddened horse continued its plunging side-step.

'Oh God,' Bob gasped as he sped forward. 'What can I do? What can I do?' But he saw at once that he must approach the horse from the inner side to prevent his frenzied circling. If he approached from the other side, he would only goad the horse to more violent movement. Jumping forward, he seized Diamond's bridle, speaking gruffly to the horse at the same time. But the horse was maddened by the unaccustomed restraint of the tight rein, and jumped nervously, bringing his left forefoot down hard to scrape Bob's shin and bruise his instep. The struggling youth scarcely felt it as he grasped the bridle with both hands. Diamond was champing his jaws, and Bob inadvertently let his left hand slip into the horse's mouth. The teeth lacerated his finger and jarred the bone. He removed his bleeding hand and snatched loose the slipknot which secured the rope reins to the bit. Freed from the restraint of the locked rein, and soothed by Bob's voice, Diamond came to an uneasy standstill.

Bob considered his next step. He knew he must free Arthur. but if he released Diamond, the horse would move off at speed with tragic consequences to the injured boy. He could not hold Diamond *and* release Arthur at the same time. Diamond must be unhitched and turned loose. The well-being of Arthur was more important than a wandering horse. Painfully, Bob held Diamond's bridle with his left hand and freed first the breeching-chain, and then the shoulder-chain, with his other hand. Then, edging round the horse's head, he changed his grip on the bridle, unhooked the chains that side, and threw off the back-band. He let go the horse's head, and said, 'Go on, Diamond!' The sweating horse surged forward, broke into a hard trot, and thudded out of sight, collar bouncing and harness jingling.

Arthur was moaning slightly and attempted to move. Bob ran round the back of the rake and gently lifted up the pair of tines which trapped the boy's neck. Arthur's eyelids flickered and he murmured, 'I can see you, Bob!'

Working quickly, but with the utmost care, Bob manoeuvred Arthur's head and shoulders forwards towards the front of the rake until they were clear of the tines. Then he hurried round to the front of the machine, and pulled the lever which lifted the tines off the ground. Arthur's left leg protruded through the spokes of the iron wheel. It was bent at a horrifying angle, and the flesh was chafed and bleeding. Bob shuddered as he pictured the boy being dragged round and round by the crazy horse, one leg trapped in the wheel, and his head imprisoned between the tines of the rake. The end of the tight rein, which had caused Diamond to circle so madly, had got tightly wrapped round the boy's other ankle, quite out of reach of his hands.

Not wishing to move Arthur unnecessarily, Bob lifted the shafts of the horse-rake and wheeled it slowly backwards, clear of the twisted body. Then he knelt beside the lad, placing his folded jacket beneath Arthur's head, and he endeavoured to comfort the youngster.

'You're all right, Arthur, now I'm here. Just take it easy until we can get you home.'

To his relief Arthur seemed to gain strength, and spoke more clearly.

'Yes, I can see you, Bob. I'm glad you came. Don't go away will you? It was awful. I thought I was going to die. I feel a bit better. But my legs—I can't move 'em. Why's that, Bob?'

'Just the circulation, Arthur,' said Bob. 'The rein wound itself round your ankle, and the other leg was through the wheel so the blood was cut off, you know.'

Arthur fell silent and closed his eyes, as if reassured. Bob shuddered as he gazed down at the broken body and twisted limbs. If only help would come! But he would not leave the boy alone with his agony in the hayfield.

Arthur opened his eyes again and started to speak, fast and clear at first, but then dwindling to a slow mumble as if he found the effort beyond him.

'I'm sorry I took Diamond, Bob. I knew I shouldn't but I saw you busy with the sheep and I thought I'd better get on with it while you were away. I knew dad would be wild if it rained before we got the field cleared. Diamond went faster than I thought, and before I'd time to get used to the rake. When we got to the first row, I went to tip it, but the foot lever went down further than I thought, and I slipped off the seat and went down with it. Diamond jumped forward as I fell, and then I was dragged round and round.'

His voice faded away, and Bob bent closer over him.

'Hush, Arthur. Don't fret yourself. Just rest. You can explain when you're better.'

A minute later the injured lad spoke again.

'I don't feel right, Bob. I wish mum would come. She would know what to do. I'd be all right if mum were here. I know I would! D'you think she's coming Bob?'

'She's on her way, Arthur, you can be sure! Diamond would go straight home. But it's a long way to the farm.'

Desperately he looked round towards the gate, hoping to see someone approaching. But there was no one. Only the pitiless sun shining from a cloudless heaven. There was no shade within a hundred yards, and he dared not move the boy.

Arthur spoke again, but in a lower tone and disjointed, as if he were becoming delirious. With agony in his heart, Bob bent low over the boy's greying face to catch the words.

'Bob, hadn't you better get on with the raking so we can get the hay up? Dad'll be wild if we miss it. There's a storm coming up, I'm sure. It's getting so dark. I can only just see you, now, Bob. It's going to rain hard. I felt such a big spot on my face, such a big splash. And there's another. It must be raining but I can't see. I wish mum . . .'

His voice failed, there was a slight jerk of his chest, and throat and his head slumped to one side, the eyes still open.

Automatically, and through his own tears, Bob put out his hand and pulled down the eyelids. He heard metallic creaking behind him, and turned to see Meg bouncing over the field towards him on her bicycle, face flushed and her hair streaming.

'What's the matter, Bob? Are you all right? Diamond charged in and we knew something must have happened. You're not hurt?' Then she saw the form on the ground. 'Arthur!' she screamed, jumping off her bicycle and allowing it to fall. 'Arthur! What happened? Are you badly hurt?'

She dropped down beside her brother, lifted his head and kissed his face several times.

Bob touched her on the shoulder. 'Meg, I think he's . . .' But she realised it herself at the same moment.

'Oh, no,' she sobbed, 'It can't be! It can't be!' She bent over Arthur's body again, fondling his face and weeping. Bob stood by, not knowing what to do. Shaken by his grief, he was in no condition to comfort another. But he could not leave them alone. So he remained until Meg recovered self-control.

The girl stood up, and returned her handkerchief to the pocket of her apron.

'Take my bike, Bob, and go direct to the doctor's. Ask him to come up here to the field. I'll stay here with Arthur. He is my brother, you know. . .' as Bob seemed to demur. 'If you meet dad on the way, you'd better tell him. When you've seen the doctor, call at home and bring back Bluebell and the float.

And you'd better break it to mum—as gently as you can.'

Bob set off at once, glad to be doing something. His own injured limbs were aching now. He met his employer coming out of the field where Sam was mowing. Mr Ratcliffe looked surprised to see Bob on Meg's bicycle and his bloody hand and wrist. He was about to give utterance to his amazement when Bob said hurriedly, 'Arthur's had a bad accident, Mr Ratcliffe. Up in the seed-field. Meg's there! I'm just going for the doctor.' He remounted the machine, and pedalled off quickly. He could not bring himself to tell his employer that his child was lying dead.

The doctor was at home, his motor-car outside the front door. He listened to Bob's story, glanced at the youth's arm and leg and said, 'It looks as though you want some attention too, young fellow; but I'll see to you later. Get cleaned up as soon as you can. I can drive straight to the field, you say? Good! Wilson!' He called for his white-coated chauffeur, and they chugged away.

Bob cycled back to the farm. He dreaded meeting the mistress, so he cycled straight to the stable. Diamond was standing in his stall, unsecured and still wearing all his harness. Bob put on his headstall and harnessed Bluebell. Then Mrs Ratcliffe appeared in the stable doorway.

'What's going on, Bob?' she asked sharply. 'Something terrible has happened. Good Lord, boy, just look at your arm and leg. Leave that mare where she is and come into the house at once and wash that blood off. No messing about, now!'

Bob turned his head away from her as he put Bluebell's bridle on.

'It's not me, Mrs Ratcliffe. It's Arthur. He's, he's . . . Meg and the gaffer's up there and I'm to take the float up for him.'

Her face went white. Her Arthur! Her baby! The finality of it struck her as she read Bob's haggard face. Then, with an effort, she partly recovered herself.

'I'll go up with you, Bob. Bring the float round to the kitchen door. Mustn't go out o' the yard without a clean apron and a hat!'

A sudden sense of affection caused Bob to throw three battens of straw into the float as well as a horse-blanket. Then he and Mrs Ratcliffe rode in silence as Bluebell trotted quickly up to Top Long-furrow, arriving just as the doctor was about to depart. He paused to say a few words of condolence to Mrs Ratcliffe, genuine sympathy, for he had brought all three children into the world, and attended them through their childhood illnesses. When the motor had bumped away the stricken mother kissed her son's cold lips and looked across at her husband.

'His back was broken, Maggie,' said the farmer quietly. 'And probably internal injuries as well. He couldn't have lived.'

Bob spread the straw in the bottom of the float. Arthur's body was laid on the horse blanket and transferred to the vehicle. So in a deep bed of clean straw, Arthur Ratcliffe made his last journey to the farmhouse where he had lived the whole of his young life. No one rode with him. It seemed disrespectful. Bob led the mare, and the dead boy's father, mother and sister walked behind, a poignant trio. As they neared the farm, Bob looked out over the hedge, and saw Sam still mowing in the lower River Field. He was shocked at first, then thought, 'Sam doesn't even know! We're taking his brother home dead, and he's still mowing because he doesn't even know it's happened!'

Arthur was borne into the sitting room and laid on the big settee. Then his mother attended to the last requirements of his body—no one else needed to touch Arthur, she said. The next morning the undertaker arrived from the village—the same man who had built the float, the trap and the farm carts. For another twenty-four hours the youngest Ratcliffe lay in his polished oak coffin, visited from time to time by his mother and sister.

During these three days Mr Ratcliffe hardly spoke about the tragedy. On the evening prior to the funeral he announced sombrely, 'I've arranged for Arthur to be buried right beside the stile in the churchyard wall. That's as close to our land as he can be. He'll be facing this way, looking towards the farm, so perhaps we can think that we haven't lost him altogether!'

As the weather kept fine, the haymaking had to go on, but in a half-hearted, silent fashion. Meg and Ernie worked on the stack, speaking only in monosyllables. The same applied to Mr Ratcliffe and Bob in the field, so great was the shadow cast by the loss of the brightest member of the family. Mr Ratcliffe had said nothing to Bob about the cause of the tragedy. He could not bring himself to catechise the young fellow on the details. There was no point now in apportioning blame. It did not occur to Bob to defend himself, as he had overlooked the fact that only he and the dead boy had known about the escaping sheep.

On the Saturday afternoon in the hot July sunshine Arthur's body was lowered to rest a few feet away from the boundary of his father's land. The graveside was thick with villagers, and there was a contingent from the grammar school. Back at Oakleigh, a meal had to be provided for relatives from distant farms. On such a melancholy occasion, Bob could not stand the sight of so much company in the farmhouse kitchen, and changed hurriedly to help Ernie with the milking. The visitors did not prolong their stay, however.

Bob left early with the milk, and on his return found that the gaffer, Sam and Ernie had picked up two more loads of hay, and after these were unloaded, two more were secured to clear the field. However crushing their personal grief, hay still had to be made while the sun shone.

At eleven o'clock on Monday morning the inquest was held in the Commemoration Hall, where they had spent so many pleasant evenings the previous winter. Bob dreaded the ordeal of being the chief witness. To repeat baldly the grisly and heart-rending details was more than he wanted. But the County Coroner from Derby was a kind man. He took the medical evidence quickly, and as Dr Warnaby was a friend of the family, he had also been able to identify the body.

Then the clerk called 'Robert Felton' and Bob, sick at heart, stepped reluctantly forward and took his seat in the chair provided, in front of the coroner's desk facing the jury of villagers, some of whom regarded him with accusation.

The coroner said, 'This is an unhappy duty we have to perform, young man. But I must ask you to tell us briefly and clearly the circumstances which caused the unfortunate death of your comrade. You were the only one present at the time of the accident, I understand?'

'I wasn't there at the time of the accident, sir. If I had been, it wouldn't have happened!'

There was a stir of surprise among the people in the hall, especially the Ratcliffe family. The coroner raised his eyebrows.

'Oh, Indeed? Then I have been misinformed. But were you not there with your horse? You did not leave him unattended, surely? Perhaps you had better tell me what happened.'

'Well, sir, I was raking this field, which is high up and in places gives a good view. As I came over the top I could see down towards the river and Sam—that's Arthur's brother, sir—mowing in one field, and the ewes and lambs grazing in the other. Suddenly I saw the sheep pushing through the hedge into the next field, which was oats. I knew that wouldn't do, so I thought I'd better go down and drive them back. I knew Diamond wouldn't stand on his own, so I tied him to the gate with a halter, and ran down to hustle the sheep back into their own field. I was there ten minutes or so, and as I was coming back, I heard the sound of the rake moving and a shout. When I got to the middle of the field, I saw Diamond dragging the rake round in circles, and Arthur on the ground, jammed in the tines and wheel.'

'Why was the horse behaving in such an extraordinary fashion?'

'The near-side rein was tight, sir, and looped in a tangle round Arthur's right ankle.'

'Could the horse have escaped on his own and run over the boy?'

'No, sir. The halter had been untied from the gate and properly looped up on the horse's hames.'

'Then Arthur must have untied it himself. You did not give him instructions to carry on raking?'

'No sir. Diamond is not a safe horse for a young lad to handle. And I didn't see Arthur. He wasn't in sight when I left the hayfield.'

'I see. Then we can only surmise what happened. But what did you do next?'

'Arthur told me what happened just before he—before he died, sir,' Bob's voice broke and he paused before he went on. 'He told me he came to the field to watch and keep me company, like, and seeing Diamond there doing nothing decided to push on with the job, as he knew his father was anxious to get the field cleared that night. But with a horse-rake, sir, when you tip it, you have to work a hand-lever and a foot-lever at the same time. The foot-lever goes down a long way, and Arthur wasn't prepared for it, and he lost his balance and went down with it. He tumbled in front of the rake, and the rein twisted round his leg as he fell.'

'I see. Describe what you did next!'

'By the time I got there, sir, Diamond was excited and plunging a bit. I had to fight him to a standstill. Then I untied the tight rein from his bridle, unhooked the chains that held him in the shafts, and let him go free. I lifted the tines and freed Arthur's head, and moved his foot from between the spokes of the wheel. Then I rolled the rake right back so it was clear of him. I put my jacket under his head, and we talked—at least, he talked as long as he was able to.'

'Did it not occur to you to go for help?'

'I didn't like to leave him, sir, especially after he asked me to stay with him. I knew the horse would go straight home, and somebody would come out to see what'd happened. The—the end came in about a quarter of an hour, just before his sister came on her bicycle.'

'Thank you, young man. What a very moving story. I am bound to say you acted with resource beyond your years, and no blame can be attached to you for this tragic end to a young life.'

White and shaken, Bob returned to his seat beside Mr Ratcliffe. The mistress reàched across her husband and gripped Bob's hand. The farmer put his left arm behind the lad's shoulder and squeezed vigorously.

'Ah Bob, lad,' he murmured. 'You've nowt to reproach yourself with. You did everything you possibly could, more than anyone could expect. I'm right proud and grateful.'

Chapter Fourteen

The haymaking dragged on into early August, but it seemed longer. The help which Arthur had given, sometimes enthusiastically, sometimes reluctantly, was sadly missed. In the corn-harvest, his absence was even more noticeable, as he would have been on holiday from school. There was no bantering conversation. A pall seemed to lie over Oakleigh Farm.

The harvest was finished early in September, and on the following Monday morning at breakfast Mr Ratcliffe said abruptly, 'Sam, I want you to take Diamond in to Burton Smithfield and get him sold. I can't bear to see that hoss about the place any more. I know that what happened was not entirely his fault, but he keeps reminding me. I can't stand any more of it.'

Bob was disturbed to hear this, for he had grown fond of Diamond and his self-willed ways. But then he remembered his remarks about the horse being suitable for a funeral, and felt guilty. He hoped everyone else had forgotten.

Sam returned in the late afternoon, having walked from Willington station. He joined the other three on their stools in the cowshed.

'There'll be a cheque for seventy pound in the post,' he told his father without enthusiasm. 'So we made a profit on him after all. I told 'em everything, and that he was a good fast hoss but wouldn't stand. But it didn't stop 'em bidding. Went up to seventy guineas in no time at all. Foster of Etwall got him. Smartest hoss in the county, he said afterwards.'

'Handsome is as handsome-does,' replied his father without a trace of feeling.

The following winter was quiet and joyless. Meg had lost some of her vivacity, her mother became greyer, while Sam and his father were silent to the point of taciturnity. Bob's heart was sad as he drove Bluebell to the station, thinking of the occasions when Arthur had been his cheerful companion. The return to the kitchen fireside was uncomfortable. It seemed impossible that Arthur and his constant library book would never be seen again in that family circle. And when he went up to his top-floor bedroom, the thought of Arthur's empty room next door increased the depression.

The dreary atmosphere weighed heavily. For the first time since he came to Oakleigh three years before, Bob toyed with the idea of changing his job. He was now nineteen, a fully experienced workman, and would have had no difficulty in finding another place. Mr Shakespeare the surveyor had practically invited him to try, and had promised help. But the youth dismissed the idea as being disloyal. His departure would only increase the despondency in the Ratcliffe household. Besides, there was Meg. Bob's fondness for her had not lessened since Arthur's death, in spite of the change in her. It showed she had a depth of feeling which he had not previously suspected, and it somehow made her more lovable, if temporarily less companionable.

For the most part the winter had been damp and mild. There had been ample fodder; the cows had milked well and the ewes were in good condition and looked set for a prolific lambing. The first lambs were dropped at the end of February. There was more than a hint of spring in the air; the landscape was drying nicely in the brisk wind. Fragments of straw swirled round the walls of the manure pit, and dust eddied on the concrete yard. The sun shone for a good span each day. The scene was bracing, and Bob was exhilarated by the prospect of new life which spring never fails to produce.

On the first day of March, Sam said at breakfast, 'Well dad, the time's come round again. I might as well start working the ground for the oats. It's fit enough, and the weather's set fair.'

'Aye, lad,' said his father. 'Time enough, as you say. The spring's come round to put new heart into everything, including us. When we buried Arthur yonder, I think a part of each of us went to the grave with him. But we've mourned long enough. We can't bring him back, but we can think back, past his death, and think of the bits of cheerfulness he brought into the house. Arthur was a sprightly lad, and wouldn't want us to be miserable the rest of our lives. He's not far away, and we can still think of him as here in spirit.

'But we've got corn and taters to put in, and lambing to attend to, and we'd better concentrate on it. Start harrowing the oat ground with the heavy harrows today, Sam, and tomorrow when it's dried out a bit, Bob can start putting on the fertiliser behind you. I shall want you to help a bit with the lambs, Meg, but I don't want to take you away from your mother too much.'

Mrs Ratcliffe said evenly, 'I'm a farmer's wife, Arnold, and I was a farmer's daughter. I know just what's important and what isn't. Meg's free to go out on the farm as much as ever she did.'

'What about another hoss, and another lad?' asked Sam, voicing a proposal which had been in his mind for some time, but which he had been unwilling to raise until he was sure that his parents had come to terms with their grief.

'Yes, Sam, I think we could do with both. But I'm not going to drag myself over to Crewe as I did three years ago. You can go and pick one out yourself, and I only hope your choice is better than mine turned out to be! As to another lad, I think we want a youngster to help Ernie with the yard-work now that Bob spends most of his time on the land. What about it, Maggie? Will you put up with another lad?'

'If it's necessary, Arnold. It'll be strange having an ordinary working lad in the house again. Bob's always been like one o' the family,' she added hastily so that her meaning could not be misunderstood. 'He won't have Arthur's room, though. No need for that when there's two other empty rooms on the top floor.'

In reply to Mr Ratcliffe's advertisement in the *Derbyshire Advertiser*, a burly workman cycled into the yard on Saturday afternoon, accompanied by his small son riding a lady's bicycle. The man introduced himself without formality.

'Mah name's Kent, Mr Ratcliffe. Ah'm a blacksmith at th' Rolls-Royce works. Albert 'ere bin odd-job lad theer sin' 'e left skule last year. 'E's fowerteen now, and as he don't like the foundry, we tho't we'd like to put 'im on a farm wheer 'e could fill out a bit.'

'There's certainly plenty o' room for that,' said Mr Ratcliffe good-naturedly, but looking with misgiving at the sickly-looking Albert. 'He doesn't look very strong, does he? Anyway, if he's keen that counts for summat, and he's bound to grow. I'll take him on for the summer and pay him half-a-crown a week. If he doesn't take to it, he can go in October and I'll hire a lad at the Statutes. When can Albert start?'

'He can stay now, if you like,' said the blacksmith, anxious not to lose the opportunity to get his son into what was obviously a well-fed home. 'E's got his working clothes on. Ah'll bike over tomorrow with his others.'

So little Albert Kent was installed at Oakleigh as cowman's lad. His presence enabled Bob to put in full-time with the horses at field work, after breakfast each day. Sam, brimming with importance, went to Crewe later in the month, and brought home a six-year-old chestnut mare, which was by common consent christened Ginger. She was teamed with Major to make a handy pair for Bob's use.

Gradually the atmosphere recovered from the gloom which had filled it since Arthur's death. Bob found himself integrated with the family even more closely than before, Mr and Mrs Ratcliffe treating him the same as Sam and Meg. Albert Kent was a shy, silent boy who did not speak until spoken to. He ate his food quickly and with relish, leaving the kitchen immediately after each meal to mope about the buildings until someone else arrived to set him to work.

Sam was still regarded as senior waggoner, but Bob was now sufficiently skilled to take an equal share in the two-horse jobs, including early-morning mowing. So long as somebody called him, he was quite prepared to get up before four o'clock, harness his horses by lamplight, hitch them to the mowing machine, and clank away to the field in the darkness. But he soon declined to collect his horses from their grazing field in the early morning darkness.

'It's not good enough,' he said forcefully. 'Waste half-an-hour trying to find 'em, and then wait another half-an-hour while they have a bit o' feed. When I know I'm mowing the next morning, I'm going to keep 'em in the stable all night. They'll rest better, they'll have chance to eat more, and they'll be handy to make an early start.'

Neither Mr Ratcliffe nor Sam objected. They were quite willing to allow Bob to bring in another of his innovations. But Bob was amused to notice that on the next occasion Sam was assigned to early-morning mowing he too kept in Flower and Violet overnight.

The first field, which was clover hay for the horses, was finally cleared on the last day of June, and two other hay-meadows were in the final stages of making. They all sat down thankfully at nine o'clock to a hearty supper.

'Well, we've got one field in as June hay, lads,' said the farmer with satisfaction as he left the table and sat down in his fireside chair. 'We don't do that every year. If this weather keeps on, and I think it will do for a few days yet, we'll get two more fields cleared this week. But to do that, we'll have to slacken off a bit on the mowin'.'

He sighed contentedly and picked up the *Daily Mail*, which Bob collected at the newsagents in Repton on his return with the milk float. 'I think Albert can start taking the milk,' went on the farmer as he scanned the front page of the paper. 'We can spare him from the hay making easier than we can spare you, Bob. It's only a lad's job anyway, and you're well out o' that class now. Better take him with you tomorrow night and show him the ropes.'

'He's grown a lot these last three months,' replied Bob, eyeing the red-faced Albert and winking at him. 'Must 'a put on a stone in weight!'

'That's because of the muck he puts in his boots,' began Sam mischievously. 'I've seen him at it . . .' His father interrupted.

'Well, I'm danged, listen to this. The Crown Prince of Austria, Franz Ferdinand, was murdered at Sarajevo on Saturday afternoon. Shot by an assassin. And his wife as well! What terrible things they get up to out there.'

'Thank goodness, it's nothing to do with us,' said Mrs Ratcliffe from the sink.

'That Emperor of Austria's family's been unlucky,' pursued her husband, laying the paper on his knee.

'Don't you remember, Maggie, the month we were married, this emperor's son got shot in a hunting accident or summat. I remember thinking to myself how lucky we were–just married and taken on our first farm, and as happy as bumble-bees in a clover field. There was this young prince, everything in the world he could possibly wish for, and he had to blow his brains out.'

'What a memory you've got, Arnold. I do remember it vaguely. But those things allus happen a long way away, so they can't affect us.'

'This poor old king does seem to have had more than his share of sorrow,' said Meg. 'I suppose they'll have a war over this. They seem to squabble among themselves every two or three years.'

'Well it can't affect us,' said her father returning to his paper.

The bumper crops of hay were secured in fine condition and in good time. After a long day at hay-making, Sam and Bob frequently bathed in the Trent together, as they had done in the scorching summer of 1911. As July moved to its close, Mr Ratcliffe became more and more pleased with progress.

'It's been one o' the best growing seasons in my experience. Long hot spells, but with a couple o' wet days now and again to keep things growing. We've finished the hay in record time, and we'll start harvest this month. We'll get half of it cut before July's out, I do believe!'

The ripe corn crackled under the baking sun as the binder rattled round the dusty fields. The weather was perfect, and on August Bank Holiday the first field of wheat was stacked in the Dutch barn. The day had been exhaustingly hot, and after feeding the horses Sam and Bob hurried down to the river for a quick bathe before supper. Mr Ratcliffe had already scanned the paper before he sat down to the meal, and expressed his misgivings at the news. But the family were too tired and hungry to care. In harvest time, foreign news makes little impact. But the following evening, while they were still unloading the last load of sheaves, Albert returned from the station with the paper, which carried the dread announcement of war, declared the previous midnight. The boy said everybody in Willington and Repton seemed to be talking about it.

The work of harvesting went on without pause, but after supper the paper was taken apart and distributed, so that everyone could read some of the news.

The shrewd Meg was puzzled. While the paper carried uplifting stories of gallant victories by Belgian, French and British troops, yet on the published maps the German armies were shown as progressively further forward in their advance on Paris.

It was Bob who answered her.

'The papers don't tell us everything, Meg. You can depend on that. And what they do tell us is written in the way most likely to cheer us up!'

'I'm sure you're right, Bob,' said the master, who had been similarly mystified. 'These little battles that we read about, successful though they may be, don't seem to have any effect on the position as a whole. It's all very well for the papers to talk about the war being over by Christmas, but that doesn't tally with Kitchener calling for 250,000 volunteers. That's about twice as many men as the whole peace-time army!'

'I'm thinking of joining up, dad!' announced Sam suddenly. Mr Ratcliffe spluttered into the mug of hot tea he had lifted to his lips.

'What? Sam, what are you talking about? This is a soldier's war, not a farmer's. If it goes on, farming's going to be more important, and perhaps more difficult. They'll get plenty of men for the army. What makes you think you'd make a good soldier?'

'I'm big and strong, aren't I? There's not a man for miles round can beat me for strength and fitness. My God, I'd like to get among these bloody Germans! I'd beat hell out of 'em. These atrocities in Belgium make my blood boil!'

'No doubt! Everybody feels that way more or less. But Sam, wars are not fought by strong men swinging battle-axes against each other. Modern fighting seems to be shooting from behind sheltered positions with rifle and machine-guns!'

'I know that as well as you do,' retorted Sam, reddening. 'But strength and endurance must still count when you're marching long distances. Besides, I'm a fair shot with a gun, as you well know.'

'I know that it's plain daft to hear you talk about joining the army on the spur of the moment. Your place is here on the farm, which'll be yours one day. The farm needs you, and I need you; and what about your mother and sister?'

'Bob's here, and he's about as good a chap as I am now. You can get other men or lads, and Bob can teach 'em the work. He's good at that. Look at the way he's brought on young Albert, here. 'Course, I wouldn't think of going if you were hard-pressed, but that's just not the case. As long as Bob's here, I reckon I'm free to go.'

Mrs Ratcliffe's lip trembled, but her husband put a hand on her arm, and spoke to his son in a more conciliatory tone.

'Look, Sam, leave it for the time being, until the situation stabilises a bit. They'll get their two hundred and fifty thousand men all right without drawing on farmers. There are plenty of men straining to get at the Germans, but there'll be out-of-work men among 'em, threshing-gang types, and others doing jobs of no importance. Let them be taken in first, and when they've been trained, if they want another batch, then you can think about it again. I want both you and Bob here, Sam. But you're four years older, been born on the farm, and you're my own flesh and blood. Bob's a grand chap–I'll say that in front of him–the best I've had working for me. The longer he stops here the better I'll like it, but he's too good to stay here as under-waggoner for ever. He's worth a better job than this. I'm getting old. I'd soon like to take things a bit easier, and leave more to you!'

Bob flushed at this fulsome praise, but could think of nothing to say. He looked across at Meg, who was also flushed and her breast was heaving as though she had something important to say and could not get it out.

'All right, dad! As you say, there's no need to rush off at the first sign of panic. I'll leave it awhile and let things settle down. If it's over by Christmas, as some of 'em say it might, then it won't be necessary to go at all. But if it keeps on then I'll have to join up. In wartime this farm shouldn't need two fit young men. The family must do its share, and farming must give up its share of men too.'

Mr Ratcliffe sighed with relief and his wife brightened. But Bob was thinking furiously. He had no particular wish to join the army–he loved the farm life too much for that. He had grown attached to the Ratcliffe family and was grateful to them for accepting him into their intimate circle. But he realised he had a duty to his country, although he was detached from the patriotic fervour which obsessed most people he met these days. He thought his duty to the Ratcliffes over-rode his national obligation, but if he could combine the two, what better solution could there be? If he enlisted, Sam could stay at home with his parents; but Oakleigh Farm would still be contributing its share of youth to serve the country.

He went to bed thinking how best he could achieve this. The nearest recruiting-centres were at Burton and Derby, but how could he go to either in the day-time? True, the harvest was nearly over, but work was still pressing, and there were the potatoes and mangolds to lift. In any case, he had never asked for time off since arriving at the farm, three-and-a-half years before, and while he had no doubt that he could get away, such a request would be bound to invite enquiries. Secretiveness was not part of his nature. To avoid a scene similar to that which had just occurred, he thought it essential to enlist surreptitiously, and present his employer with the accomplished fact. He was still searching his mind for a way when he fell asleep.

At breakfast-time the next morning, Saturday, the post-man arrived while they were still at the table. Meg went to the door and returned with a postcard, which she handed to her father.

'Well, I'm dashed. They don't give us much time do they? This is from Wilkinson's. As you know, I sold 'em that wheat from Squarelands for seed, and they want a ton of it today! Today, mind you! I like that! Anyway, the customer's allus right, even in farming; so you'd better take it in, Sam.'

'I don't want to go, dad. Let Bob do it. That drop o' rain in the night makes it certain that we shan't carry the rest o' the sheaves today, but it'll just have been enough to make the clover field soft enough for ploughing, and I'd like to make a start.'

'All right. You go then, Bob. Take Major, he's a bit faster than either of the mares. You'd better push along and get there early, as in some o' these town businesses they knock off at one o'clock. Use th' dray—the load'll ride easier than on a cart. And bring back half-a-ton of bran and half-a-ton of linseed cake—no need for the hoss to walk back empty. From the same firm, of course. It's at the far end of the town from here.' He gave detailed directions.

Bob was not displeased at the prospect of an easy eight-mile journey, and saw to it that the corn was loaded quickly. Major stepped out well, trotting on the downhill gradients, and they approached the Trent bridge just after half-past eleven. As he drew level with 'The Swan', a soldier stepped out and called to him to stop.

'Pull your 'orse in 'ere, lad,' he ordered, motioning to the entrance to the hotel yard.

'What's the matter with you? I've no business in there! Come on Major!' and Bob flapped the reins indignantly.

But the soldier seized the horse's bridle.

'This is the Army givin' orders, and you'll be in trouble if you don't comply. We want this 'orse in that yard!'

Bob jumped down from the dray and approached the soldier. But at the same time a burly sergeant came out of the yard.

'What's the trouble, Shipton?'

'The lad doesn't want to stop, Sergeant.'

'I've got this grain to deliver,' expostulated Bob.

'That's a pity, but the Army can't take account of private

arrangements. We're from the Remount Department, and can take any horse we choose. Lead him into the yard, Shipton.'

Bob followed, feeling sick at heart. What would Mr Ratcliffe think of this? A smart-looking officer was in the yard awaiting them. Bob noticed that he had three brass buttons on the top of each shoulder, and a crown.

'Have you got the authority to do this?' Bob asked boldly.

'Yes, lad, I certainly have. But I'm not going to show it to you. The army needs horses, and if we can't buy sufficient we requisition them. And if you don't co-operate, you might find yourself in trouble.'

'What am I to do with this load if you take my horse?'

'You'll just have to walk home and get another one! Now, set the dray over by the wall, take the horse out, and remove his saddle.'

'My boss needs this horse.'

'The army needs him more, young fellow. We want every horse that's fit, and will take them unless they're entires or mares-in-foal. I suggest you tell your employer to get his mares breeding if he has any, or he might lose them.'

'You can't put mares in foal at this time of the year,' Bob said, rather contemptuously.

'There's another year, boy, and perhaps several years after that. Before this war is over we might be requisitioning horses which are not yet foaled.'

The officer, who obviously had veterinary experience, was examining Major thoroughly. Bob had a brain-wave.

'Why not let the horse go and take me instead?' he suggested.

The officer permitted himself to smile.

'By Jove! You never give up, do you? But we're after horses, not men. I'm not saying that we couldn't make use of you. But if you want to enlist, there's a recruiting centre not far away—the Bell Hotel in the main street. Now trot that horse up and down the yard a few times.'

Bob did so, and the man listened carefully at Major's head and neck. But the horse had been pulling a ton of wheat on a heavy dray at speed for over two hours, and such sustained effort caused him to breathe rather noisily. He had done this all the time Bob had been at Oakleigh, but it had not affected his speed or performance.

The officer drew back and conferred with his sergeant. Bob overheard the words 'roaring' and 'forging'. They talked for a few minutes. Finally the officer returned to Bob.

'You can put your horse in again and get off, young fellow. Fine, energetic horse you've got there, but I don't like that noise in the windpipe, and I'm not altogether pleased with the way he trots. He sometimes clips his front feet with his hind shoes, and that wouldn't do for the artillery.'

Bob replaced the saddle, hitched Major into the shafts, and jumped on the front of the dray to drive away before they changed their minds. He set the horse at a trot over the bridge, down the long street, past the Bell, which he eyed thoughtfully, and then over the railway bridge to the corn merchant's premises on the other side. The foreman complained of the lad's late arrival, but produced plenty of assistance to unload the wheat and load up for the return journey.

Major broke into a trot down the long railway bridge and kept it up through Horniglow Street, until Bob eased him to a stop outside 'The Bell'. Recruiting posters adorned the outside of the building, and Bob sat a few minutes staring at Kitchener's pointing finger. Then his mind was made up. He jumped down, hung the reins on the hames, gave Major a friendly pat on the shoulder, and walked round to the Drill Hall at the rear of the hotel. Entering, he faced a sergeant seated at a table.

'I've come to join up,' he said firmly, but felt his heart sink into his boots.

'Have you, now? Then you've come at a good time—Saturday dinner time when everybody's at home or in the pub. You can have all our attention! I'll take your particulars.'

Bob gave the information without enthusiasm.

'I won't ask you to sign before you've had your medical. Go into that room there and give this card to the M.O.'

The doctor was a grey-haired man with a weather-beaten face, wearing a white coat over his army uniform.

'Come in, lad, and strip off. I shan't keep you long.'

He whistled with admiration as he appraised Bob's stocky form, and made a quick formal examination.

'By God, lad, you're nearly a perfect specimen. Tough as wire and as healthy as a badger! Read me a paragraph from that newspaper. Thank you! If all our recruits were as fit as you, this war wouldn't last long, I'm certain. Now, you go back to the sergeant and he will issue you with your kit and pay you the King's shilling. Then you'll be in the army!'

Just like that! thought Bob, but said, as he struggled into his breeches and socks, 'I don't know about the uniform. I'm not quite ready for that yet.'

The doctor looked at him with surprise, but Bob walked out of his office still pulling his shirt over his head.

'Ah! There you are, lad,' said the sergeant. 'I don't know what you're putting that on for! Sign here, put on your uniform, and I'll tell you where to go.'

'Thank you, I know where to go,' said Bob coolly. 'I've got a horse outside with a load of cattle food, and that's got to go back to Oakleigh Farm before I become a proper soldier.'

'Well, I'll be . . . I'll have to see the captain about this.'

He disappeared through a door and Bob heard him expostulating. In a few seconds he returned, following an officer.

'What's all this, young man? You can't hold the army to ransom, you know!'

'Don't want to sir,' said Bob steadily. 'I dropped in to enlist while I was in town on my employer's business because it's the only chance I have. But I must finish the job I'm on! I can't leave his horse and dray standing in the middle of Burton. I'll come back straight away, if I must.'

'Hmm! That won't be necessary. You're obviously a conscientious chap. Take your horse back to the farm, and your kit with you. But report here in uniform at nine a.m. on Monday. If you're not here, you will be regarded as being absent without leave!'

'I'll be here, sir. Thank you,' said Bob, much relieved. The sergeant doled out the items of uniform one by one. 'Get 'em inside that kitbag, Felton, and get out of 'ere before we change our mind. You're unique, you are! In fact, you're just about the uniquest recruit I've had in ten years. Now get out, and I 'ope you're late on Monday!'

Bob wasted no time, pocketed his shilling, and hurried out to the patient Major. He threw his kitbag on the dray and sat on it for his last journey back to Hartnall, wondering all the way if he had done the right thing.

Mr Ratcliffe, Sam and Ernie had already started milking when he entered the yard, and he was able to hide his kitbag in a corner while he unloaded and put Major away in the stable. But he postponed his announcement until he judged a suitable time had arrived.

He joined the milkers, and afterwards they went in to tea as usual. Bob ate the meal in silence, his mind full of sombre thoughts of his strange new future.

'Bob's quiet tonight,' said Mrs Ratcliffe. 'Hand your cup up, if you want more tea. That's the second time I've asked you!'

'Bob, I was thinking that we ought to press on with the ploughing a bit faster. On Monday, if we can't pick up the rest of the sheaves, perhaps you'd better get out the old balance plough and get cracking in the Lower Nine-Acre. The draught won't be too much for your pair, if you don't set it too deep.'

'Sorry, Mr Ratcliffe. I shan't be here. I enlisted today and I'm in the army now!'

There was dead silence for a few seconds until Meg broke it. She clenched her fists.

'Bob, how could you!—and without asking, or even telling *me*!' The reproach in her voice disturbed him.

'I—I made up my mind on the spur of the moment. Anyway, one of us had to go. It'd look bad, otherwise, and it's better if I go. So I'm in the army, and I have to report at the Bell at nine o'clock Monday morning. 180211 Private Robert Felton, 1st North Staffs, that's me,' he concluded with a hint of pride.

Mrs Ratcliffe recovered herself. She was the first to realise the real reason for his action, and walked round the table to where he sat. Much to his embarrassment, she kissed him on the cheek.

'Bob, lad, that was right brave of you. But don't go away and forget us. As far as we're concerned, this is still your home. There'll always be a room in this house for you as long as I'm alive!'

'Yes, yes, that goes without saying. Bob, you came here on a sudden impulse, and you're leaving us just as suddenly, but in the years between you've been a great help to us, lad. For a long time I've looked on you as one o' the family, and allus shall.'

'That's all very well,' grumbled Sam. 'But if Bob's going, it means I'll have to stay here. Can't leave you quite on your own! The galling part of it is, I *want* to go, while he doesn't seem to want to at all!'

'Don't be so dalled awkward, Sam,' said his father. 'If it's as you say, then he's making all the bigger sacrifice. Why, you'd pine to death if you had to leave your beloved hosses and the farm where you were born! Nine o'clock Monday, Bob? I'll get Albert to run you to Willington in the float, and tomorrow night we'll all go to church and pray for your safety.'

'Talking of hosses,' said Bob. 'You nearly lost Major today,' and he told the story of his encounter with the remount department.

'By gum, that's a nice state of affairs,' said the astonished farmer. 'I never thought they'd go on like that. Thought they'd buy their hosses properly, like gentlemen.'

'Looks like we'll have to buy plenty o' mares and go in for a reg'lar breeding programme,' commented Sam, already beginning to recover his enthusiasm. 'Or else use old crocks which they won't take.'

'I don't think that would suit you—or me,' said Mr Ratcliffe with grim irony. 'Thank God we put Bluebell in foal last spring. It'd break my heart to think of her sprottling about trying to pull an o'er heavy load under a hail o' bullets!'

'Aye, some o' the poor devils'll be getting shot to pieces all the time,' Sam said. 'And there wunt be many hospital cases among the hosses, you can bet. A quick bullet'll be the end for most of 'em.'

'It doesn't do to think of it too closely. It's too dreadful for words,' said Meg, finding her voice at last after the consternation Bob's announcement had caused her. 'But what about hay? If the army's taking all those horses, they'll want hay for them; and what's to prevent them seizing that, too?'

'Oh, give over Meg, do,' said her father. 'Don't make things wuss than they are! But you're probably right. If they can't buy all the hay they want easily, they'll commandeer it from the farms. It means we'll have to make every hundredweight of hay we can, grow as many oats as we can, breed as many foals as we can, otherwise we'll have no hosses left to work the place! It seems as though this war-time farming's going to be more difficult than I thought. We shall need all your strength and experience before this is over, Sam!'

The next day Bob helped with milking as usual. Nor did he forego the usual Sunday after-lunch repose in the sitting-room. He could not help thinking that he was doing everything for the last time. He looked at Meg hard, wondering if he dared tell her what was in his mind. Tonight would be his last opportunity.

After an early tea, Mr and Mrs Ratcliffe, Meg and Bob went to church together. They sauntered slowly along, taking the long way round. The familiar service uplifted the young man, as it rarely failed to do, and he sang with gusto.

After the service, the parents moved to the main door where they got involved in endless conversation. Bob and Meg left by the side-door—the Ratcliffe entrance—and sauntered down the little path to the stile, Meg leading the way. She paused at the stile and looked down at Arthur's grave. The jar of flowers—red roses today—which Mrs Ratcliffe never failed to bring every Sunday morning still made a brave show in spite of the heat of the day. Bob read the inscription to himself again.

In Loving Memory
of
Arthur James Ratcliffe
Died 3rd July 1913
Aged 13 years
'The Lord Gave, and The Lord Hath Taken Away'

Meg gave a sob. Bob took her by the arm and led her gently away. On this his last night at the farm he did not want her to give way to the melancholy of last year. There were things he wanted to say, but he did not know how to begin. They walked silently side by side across Church Meadow and into Front Croft. The friendly cows scarcely bothered to move out of their way until commanded by the familiar voices. The couple reached the farm gate and leaned over. The buildings were silent and empty as if enjoying a Sunday evening rest. No one was around, for Sam had taken the milk and Albert had gone home. Bob thoughtfully scanned the yard he knew so well, and wondered if he would ever see it again.

Meg read his thoughts, and pulled his arm.

'Oh, come on, Bob, don't look so sad. Buck up! You'll see it all again. When the war's over you can come back here for good. Dad and mum told you it was your home, didn't they? You will come Bob? To see us on leave, and that, I mean?'

She tightened her grip on his arm, and, he smiled at her concern.

'Let's walk down to the river,' he said. 'It's peaceful down there—a good place to talk.'

They turned their back on the farm and walked up the main drive, where Bob had driven the milk so many times, in complete silence. Bob was touched by Meg's subdued manner. This was a Meg he did not know. During the whole of his time at Oakleigh she had adopted a bossy attitude, a sort of ownership which he now realised had delighted him. They crossed the road leading to the village and entered the First River Field, automatically securing the gate behind them. Daringly, Bob put his arm round Meg's shoulders, and she instantly moved closer to him, her head leaning on his breast. It seemed to him that they were communicating without words. In this fashion they walked through the open gate into the lower meadow, and made for the shingled drinking-place. The broad Trent swirled round the bend, friendly and comforting. From its surface the evening sun reflected in sheets of dazzling brightness. The current murmured cheerfully as it hurried over the pebbles, and gave a hoarser chuckle where its flow was impeded by a larger stone.

'It always makes me glad to see the old river,' mused Bob with affection.

Meg responded to his mood at once.

'I know what you mean, Bob. When I was at school I read that Americans call the Mississippi "Old Man River" because it affects their lives so much. The Trent is a bit like that for us. We played here as children, picnicked here, fished here—at least, Sam did—bathed here, and once or twice skated here. And we never run out of grass at this part of the farm, as you know.'

They walked along the bank away from the shallows, swinging their clasped hands, until they came to the clump of willows. This was where Bob's first bathing expedition three years before had ended with the bullocks trampling on the clothes he had foolishly left on the ground, and one of them had dragged away his shirt. Sam had said later, 'We won't have any more of that,' and on their first free evening he and Bob had come down together with a cartload of rails and fenced the cattle out. Since then they had been able to undress in clean and untrodden seclusion.

Bob and Meg clambered over the fence, the girl raising her pale blue dress with an uncharacteristic lack of modesty which surprised and embarassed him. The grass, untouched by livestock, was withered, broken and quite dry. The air was still hot and they settled down in a small open space a few feet from the bank of the river which at this point ran silently and deeper.

'It seems terrible to be leaving all this,' Bob said at last, 'And perhaps never to come back.'

'Aren't you afraid, Bob?'

'No, Meg, not afraid; I just feel strange and unhappy at the thought of living in an army camp instead of on the farm, where I'm so fond of everybody. Especially you, Meg. My God, how I'll miss you!'

'I'll miss you, too, Bob.' She moved closer to him. 'You've been part of our family for so long, and you've never been away for a single day since you first came to us. I can't imagine home now without you being there, reliable and predictable and always on the spot at the right time, like on Coronation night.'

'Don't bring that up, Meg. It's best forgotten,' he said, uncomfortable. This was the very spot where he had tried to wash away from his bruised features the traces of his fight with the squire's son.

'Mind you, I'm sure I could have handled Mortimer. I was just beginning to get my temper up. I think I would have throttled him–I'm strong enough, you know. But then I saw you and knew it wouldn't be necessary. But when Mortimer kept hitting you in the face, and drew blood all over, I thought you'd have to give up after all.'

'I never give up.'

He turned and looked her full in the face.

'I've never given up loving you since I first saw you that night in the kitchen when I stood in front of your father like a tramp before a magistrate.'

His deep passion showed in his eyes. But it was like the slow heat of a charcoal-burner's fire, unquenchable but controlled. Meg answered it with eyes that flashed. They pierced his brain with a frank invitation. But he was too shy or too startled or afraid to recognise the message for what it was. After all, she was the gaffer's daughter. He retreated a few inches.

'I felt a bit like that, too, Bob. When I saw you standing there, you looked like a stray puppy, nervous and miserable. I wanted to take you in my arms and make a fuss of you. To think that we've lived in the same house all these years, felt this way, and never told each other!'

At last the key turned in the lock. He reached over and kissed her on the lips. The contact with her flesh was exquisite, and he prolonged it. She did not object. He found that his hands were doing incredible things, fondling her body, probing into secret places which before had existed only in his fantasies. To his astonishment, she did not resist him. Instead, she turned towards him with a sigh of delight. Throwing out her strong brown arms she clasped him round the shoulders and then rolled back swinging Bob on top of her own body. Three-and-a-half years of fond companionship funnelled itself into this explosion of passion.

This was the end of their old familiar world of contented restraint. Yet it was also the start of a new world, ecstatic in its revelations, but somehow terrifying in its forebodings.

The guns in Picardy could not be heard, nor any other dissonance. The silence seemed to sanctify the copse. Above the deep pools of the river, in the shade of the bushes on the opposite bank, clouds of insects faintly hummed. The occasional plop of a hunting perch or carp accentuated the tranquility. Overhead, the brilliant sunshine seemed reluctant to fade. It enveloped the trembling leaves of the willows and filtered through to the lovers on the tangled grass below.

With the thrill of abandon, Bob took his farewell of the woman he loved in the age-old way of the departing warrior.